YESTERTIME

A Novel of Time Travel

Andrew Cunningham

Books by Andrew Cunningham

Thrillers
Wisdom Spring
Deadly Shore
Yestertime

"Lies" Mystery Series
All Lies
Fatal Lies
Vegas Lies
Secrets & Lies
Blood Lies

Eden Rising Trilogy
Eden Rising
Eden Lost
Eden's Legacy

Children's Mysteries
(as A.R. Cunningham)
The Mysterious Stranger
The Ghost Car
The Creeping Sludge
The Sky Prisoner
The Ride of Doom

To the real Jim Lawrence, everybody's Uncle Jim ... East Boston Royalty!

To Charlotte ... my light, always!

PART ONE

Chapter 1

NEAR FLAGSTAFF, ARIZONA—2021

I tripped for the third time in the last five minutes. The rocks and roots seemed to jump out at me. This time, I almost ended up meeting a cactus face to face. I think it was time to call it quits. What had begun as an adventure had become a waste of time.

I climbed up onto a large flat rock. On a sunny day, it would have felt like I was crawling onto a frying pan, but the clouds had moved in earlier, cooling everything off a few degrees. I laid down looking up at the darkening sky. This sight was much more interesting than my mission.

I had come to Flagstaff a week earlier to be with a childhood friend who was dying of cancer. I hadn't talked to him on FaceTime for a few weeks and was shocked to see what the ravages of cancer had done to him in such a short time. He was still conscious and coherent when I arrived and seemed genuinely happy to see me. He had never married and was somewhat of a hermit, so he had no one who cared about him. We had been close since grade school and it was only the physical distance that had kept us from getting together in recent years. I lived in Florida and he in Flagstaff. Of course, I was now feeling guilty that I hadn't come out to visit him. Then again, he hadn't visited *me* in Florida.

However, he was the one who was dying, not me, so I was the one stuck with the guilt.

He died three days ago, and I had taken care of his cremation. He had wanted his ashes spread out in the desert. That seemed simple enough. Then I read about a ghost town within an hour's drive of Flagstaff and figured I could spread his ashes and then visit the town. I'd always had an interest in the old west and ghost towns. Not one of those theme park style ghost towns with the simulated gun battles and the over-priced gift shops—a *real* ghost town. Hollow Rock seemed to fit the bill. Set in the mountains outside Flagstaff, Hollow Rock was named for the abundance of caves in the surrounding hills.

The information I found online said that Hollow Rock wasn't in the best of shape, but that it was still worth seeing. Large parts of the blacksmith shop and the jail were still there, and the remains of other buildings could be seen. I wasn't expecting a full-blown town. I just wanted to be able to imagine myself walking down the main street.

Well, the online site needed a little updating. I could tell that a town had once been there, but not much else beyond that. There were some foundations of buildings and a lot of rotted wood, but I couldn't tell what they had once been. Good thing I hadn't paid money to see it. Despite my disappointment in the town, I thought Harry would've gotten a kick out of having his ashes spread along Main Street, so that's what I did, letting some fall to the ground, then throwing the rest in the air to let the wind take them.

Afterward, I spent an hour walking through the town, trying to find something of interest, before finally giving up. I was now on the rock resting up for the trek back to my car. The closest I'd been able to park was a half-mile away.

The clouds were darker now. Much darker. I'd waited too long. I would never make it back to the car before the heavens opened up. I had seen some overhanging rocks near the cliff face close by. Hopefully, it would just be a brief downpour and I could return to my car soon afterward. I sat up, my muscles suddenly sore. I shouldn't have rested. I could feel my joints creaking as I crawled off the rock. I had done too much walking without drinking enough water. My fifty-year-old joints felt like seventy.

I felt a drop of rain. And another. Suddenly it was pouring. I ran up a hill toward the cliff face. A flash of lightning came dangerously close, followed by one of the loudest claps of thunder I had ever heard. I covered my head—for whatever good that would do against lightning. I reached the cliff, and water was gushing down the side of the rock wall. Suddenly I thought about flash floods. Could one reach me up here?

I could barely see the town of Hollow Rock a hundred feet below me. Already there was a foot of water covering the crumbling foundations of the buildings. Floods were probably the reason the blacksmith shop and jail had disappeared.

I felt my way along the rock wall looking for one of the many overhangs I thought I'd seen. I still had the container in my hand that once held Harry's ashes. Maybe the rocks didn't overhang that much after all. I had already walked about fifty yards along the wall. I should have just tried to make it back to the car. Too late now.

I ran across a barrier of bushes blocking my way. I couldn't go around them, as a sluice of water had already formed on the outside of the bushes. If I stepped in it, I would be swept down the hill. I pulled on the bushes and the branches moved easily. I pushed my way through and found myself at the opening of a small cave. The cave entrance was about three feet tall. If I ducked down, I would be able to make it inside.

I hesitated. Desert. Cave. Rattlesnakes. Mountain Lions. I could crawl in and find myself set upon by a family of rattlesnakes or lunch for some big cats. Not a happy thought. On the other hand, I was getting worried that the loose rocks on the hill I was on would be washed away … along with me.

I grabbed a handful of rocks and threw them into the cave entrance. I didn't hear any hissing or rattles. But then, the noise from the rain and thunder out here was loud. I threw more rocks and then repeated it twice more. I still couldn't hear anything, and nothing crawled out of the cave entrance. I pulled out the little flashlight on my keyring and went down on my knees. I pointed it in the cave. It was a decent size—about 20 by 20—with smooth walls. There weren't a lot of places a rattlesnake could hide, and I didn't see any big furry things. It seemed safe to go in. Nonetheless, as I entered, I kept the flashlight on, with its weak beam bouncing off the walls and ceiling. I was pretty sure it was empty now, so I moved a little faster. Once inside, I did a final check for snakes. Nothing.

There was one spot I hadn't been able to check. A smooth stone wall extended part of the way into the center of the cave and I couldn't see what was on the other side of it. I huddled against the far wall and shone my light into the space behind the extension.

A surge of excitement shot up my spine.

In the corner of the cave was a box. And it looked very old.

Chapter 2

The storm outside was at its peak. The lightning and thunder were almost continuous, and I hoped my car hadn't washed away. We often had severe storms in Florida, but I don't think I had ever seen one as bad as this. But I couldn't think about that now. I had something else to occupy my attention.

I crawled over to the box, still searching the cave with the flashlight as I went, and wishing I had something more powerful than a keychain light. I didn't want to be surprised by a snake, a spider, or a scorpion that I might have missed.

The box was half-covered by a yellow rain slicker. That could've come in handy a few minutes earlier. The slicker had seen a lot of use. It was ragged around the edges and had numerous rips in it. I moved the rain slicker off the box, and the slicker broke apart in pieces. It had been there for a very long time.

I could tell now that it wasn't so much a box as a small trunk. It once had leather straps that went through buckles, but the leather had long since disintegrated. The few pieces that were left were hard and broken. I let the beam of my flashlight circle the box. I was looking for holes in the box. I didn't want to open it and have a family of rattlesnakes pop out.

Despite my nervousness, I really had nothing against snakes. I liked snakes. I also knew that a chance encounter with a rattlesnake in the middle of nowhere could end very badly for me. So I was just being extra cautious. To the left of the trunk was another small alcove. I wasn't going to press my luck by investigating it. I gave it a cursory look with the penlight from where I was crouching, but the beam was too weak to see much.

I put my attention back onto the trunk. It seemed to be well-built, with no holes or cracks. There were no distinguishing marks, such as initials or a name.

There was no lock, so I carefully lifted the lid and was met with a smell. Not musty, just old. Lying on top was a hat—a Stetson cowboy hat. It was medium brown with old sweat stains. Under the hat was a leather vest. There was nothing fancy about it, but it looked like it had once been comfortable. I tried it on. It fit, but age had made the leather hard and uncomfortable. I put on the hat. It also fit me. Was I trying on some dead guy's clothes? A little weird. I took them off and folded the vest.

I was trying to get a feel for the age of the contents. "Old West" was all I could think. That was just a guess. Until I saw the newspaper.

Under the vest was a faded blue shirt, and under that, a copy of the *Hollow Rock Gazette*, dated September 7th, 1870. Now I knew the age of the trunk. I carefully removed the newspaper and gently laid it atop the vest. I didn't want to take the chance of opening it and having it fall apart. I could check on that later.

As I picked up the newspaper, a piece of paper fluttered to the ground. It was small—about 5x8 maybe—and had a jagged edge. It had been ripped from a larger page—the rest of which was missing. There was a single sentence:

Funny that I'm going to die a hundred years before I was born...

Huh?

What did that mean?

I put the note aside and looked through the rest of the trunk. A pair of jeans, another shirt, and some cloth bags that had company names imprinted on them. The names were faded, but I could barely make them out. One bag had contained flour, another coffee, and another once had sugar. There was also an unopened bottle of whiskey. They were all very old. I could easily believe that they were about the same age as the newspaper.

The bags no longer contained what was advertised on them, but they weren't empty. I picked up the flour bag and emptied it onto one of the shirts. Some coins fell out. They were old, like everything else in the trunk. I picked up a three-dollar gold piece in beautiful condition, imprinted with the date 1870—the same year as the newspaper. There were a dozen other coins, all well-used, and all with dates in the 1860s.

The coffee bag held something bulky. I emptied it onto the shirt. It was a revolver—a very old revolver. I had seen one of these before. I think it was from the Civil War. I'd have to look it up. At some point, I'd take it to a gun store and have them clean it up. They could also date it and tell me the manufacturer and the caliber.

Why would someone pack a trunk back in 1870 and leave it in a cave? For whatever reason though, it was an exciting find. The trunk was kind of heavy, but I figured I could carry it back to my car.

There was one bag left: the sugar bag. I dumped it onto the shirt.

And then my heart sank. I suddenly felt duped. Was this someone's idea of fun? A practical joke? They knew the person opening the trunk would think they had found something of significance from the 1800s. I certainly had.

Not anymore.

The bag contained a small digital camera, two memory cards,

and a driver's license.

The disappointment hit me hard.

I picked up the camera. It was in terrible condition. I tried turning it on, but the button stuck. After a little work, I was able to pry open the battery compartment and was met with two batteries that had long since leaked out their innards. I picked up one of the memory cards. It seemed to still be in decent condition. I'd have to check it out when I got back to the hotel.

Then I saw the corner of a piece of paper still in the bag. I opened the bag and carefully pulled out the paper, which had become brittle. It was another handwritten note. I compared the two notes. The first piece of paper was probably ripped from this one. They seemed to go together. The note read:

To the finder of this trunk, please don't be confused. I packed it on September 8th, 1870. Herb Wells stole my notebooks. They had everything in them. Damn him! I'm hoping that whoever finds this trunk will know what to do with the memory cards. The pictures tell part of the story. The notebooks tell the rest. Look for them. If you don't know what memory cards are, please put everything away until the 21st century. It'll make more sense then. And if all goes well, maybe I'll be the one to find the trunk.

What in the world did I just find?

Chapter 3

A strange note, for sure. I looked at the driver's license. It was a Massachusetts license of recent vintage. The expiration date was 2015—six years ago. The name on it was Stan Hooper. The picture was of an average-looking guy with graying hair and a short beard. His date of birth read 1970. So, he was my age. It meant that whoever packed the trunk lived in the 21st century. And yet, the writer of the note—Stan, maybe?—thought that someone might find the trunk earlier than the 21st century. That made absolutely no sense. Then my spine tingled again. *"Funny that I'm going to die a hundred years before I was born."* Stan was born in 1970. The newspaper was from 1870. And what the hell did he mean by *"If all goes well, maybe I'll be the one to find the trunk?"*

It was a joke. It had to be. This Stan guy was staging an elaborate hoax.

And yet … something was fascinating about it. Somehow, it didn't feel like a joke. The newspaper looked legitimate. The hat and vest looked appropriately old. The coins, the gun, and even the whiskey were authentic. But the camera and memory cards? They were so out of place in the trunk, they made the whole thing ridiculous.

I looked outside the cave entrance. It was still raining, but the thunder and lightning had ended, and it seemed a bit brighter.

Maybe the storm was coming to an end.

I carefully placed everything back in the trunk and lifted it. It wasn't too bad. It was well-made, but there wasn't anything that heavy in it. Could I carry it the half-mile to my car? Probably. All of a sudden, I was happy that I had driven from Florida to Arizona and not flown. It would be easier to transport the trunk. The note wasn't believable, but the trunk held some interesting stuff.

I carried the trunk over to the cave entrance and waited for the rain to stop. My mind was racing. I was hooked more than I wanted to admit. Was it because, as a freelance writer of magazine articles, I *really wanted* there to be a fascinating story attached to this? No. There was more to it than that. It wasn't because I wanted to write about it. It was a personal interest. Who else finds a trunk full of questions in a small cave in the middle of nowhere? There had to be something more to it than just a hoax. Crafting an article about it would just be a bonus.

Step One was going to be a stop at the local library. I would check online. I had a feeling though that copies of the *Hollow Rock Gazette* were only available—if at all—on microfiche, and the local library would probably have it. It would enable me to see if the newspaper I had in my possession was the real thing. If it was available on microfiche, it might be worth printing out a few issues before and after this one—as well as another copy of this one, considering the age of the paper.

The rain had become a mild drizzle. It was time to go. I ducked out of the cave and pulled the trunk out after me. I looked down at the town of Hollow Rock. There was no water to be seen. The desert had already soaked up the rain. That meant the walk back to my car shouldn't be hard. I lifted the trunk. Well, not heavy, but not exactly light either. Over the half-mile, I was going to be setting it down a few times.

Then I had another thought. What if someone saw me? I'd

just have to take a chance. I didn't see anyone earlier when I was out here. The chances of someone being here now, right after a rainstorm, were even less likely.

I picked up the trunk and started on my way. I slid down the hill and managed to stay upright. It took me almost an hour to go the half-mile to my vehicle. I found myself setting the trunk down more and more the closer I got to the car. Luckily, I was the only one out there, so I wasn't seen. I lifted the trunk into the back of my SUV and breathed a sigh of relief when I got behind the wheel.

When I arrived back at my hotel, I covered the trunk with some beach towels I kept in the back of the SUV and carried it to my room. I looked for the *Hollow Rock Gazette* online and found nothing, other than a Wikipedia article saying the newspaper folded in 1878. I looked at my watch and called the local library. They were open for another two hours and yes, they had the *Gazette* on microfiche.

I rushed over there and had a librarian show me how to use the microfiche. I hadn't used one since grade school. As someone who was pretty adept at a computer, I felt a little embarrassed to be getting help with something so old-fashioned.

The newspaper was only six pages in length, so I printed out a half dozen issues in addition to the one I found—three on either side of the September 7th date. By the time I was done, the library was about to close, so I headed back to the hotel, stopping for some take-out along the way.

I was tired. A day mostly in the sun had wiped me out, but I wanted to at least get a cursory look at it all, so I took a shower to wake up and then went to work.

I opened my laptop and inserted one of the two memory cards. I was greeted with scenes from an old western town. The re-creation was good—almost as good as a movie scene. Almost all of the pictures were taken from low on the body and sometimes there was a piece of cloth half covering the lens.

Whoever was taking the pictures was doing it discreetly.

There was one picture—a selfie—of a man who looked familiar. Was it Hooper? I picked up his license and compared the pictures. It was definitely Hooper. His beard was longer and his hair bushier, but it was him all right. He didn't look particularly happy in the picture.

When I moved on to the next picture, I froze. It was another one of Hooper. This time he was standing next to a sign. The sign read: *Welcome to Hollow Rock. Population 228.*

Chapter 4

What?

There had to be a rational explanation. Did they have some sort of "Hollow Rock" celebration, where they built a replica of the town and held a party? If that were the case, wouldn't they have left the replica town intact as a tourist destination?

I went online and typed in "Hollow Rock Celebration." Nothing. I tried different variations and still came up empty. I abandoned that and went back to the pictures, this time concentrating more on the buildings than the people. The main street looked authentic. It had the stereotypical hitching posts and water troughs. They were chipped and worn as if a lot of horses had used them. Most of the horses had well-worn saddles. The buildings, while apparently constructed quickly, looked lived in. The sidewalks were wooden and set above the road by about a foot. Judging by the amount of rain I saw in the town during the storm, raised sidewalks made sense.

I wanted to look at these in order, so I put the second memory card in the computer to see which comprised the earliest pictures. The first couple of shots looked like Stan was more familiar with Hollow Rock, so I took out that card and reinserted the first one. I labeled the second one, so I'd know which was which.

Pulling up the pictures on the screen, I looked at the people.

The women appeared tired—even those who were smiling. Modern women playing a part would look like … well, modern women playing a part. The men, too, looked worn out. These people—the men and the women—worked hard. It showed in how they walked, how they stood—many of them sort of stooped over, dealing with pain of some kind—and how they dressed. They had a no-nonsense quality about them. These weren't actors from central casting wearing carefully designed costumes. They were real people.

In western movies, the men all wore Levi jeans and had tied-down gun belts. While there were a few in these pictures who fit that description, most wore baggy pants with old-looking pistols stuffed in their belts—belts that were often just pieces of rope. They didn't wear Stetsons like the one I tried on from the trunk. They wore shapeless ragged hats. Some of the nicely dressed men wore bowlers. The first were probably farmers and the second, townspeople—storekeepers, lawyers, undertakers, and such. The cowboys of myth and legend still existed though, and were sprinkled throughout the town. I chuckled. Some of them even looked bow-legged.

I was looking at the thumbnails and picking and choosing which pictures to look at. But there were a few hundred just on this card. Way too many to look at right now, especially as tired as I was. When I arrived home, I would go through them one by one.

I exchanged the first card for the second. I just wanted to see what some of the last pictures looked like. I scrolled down the thumbnails and near the end, one of them caught my attention. I wasn't sure why, there was just something different about it. I opened it up and felt the blood drain from my face.

It was a dead man. He was lying on the street. Again, the picture was taken secretly, from down around the photographer's pants pocket. There were a half dozen pairs of feet around the dead man—probably people looking down at him. There was no doubt that this was a real person and not an actor. But he was a real dead person. Half his cheekbone was shot away, and he had a bullet wound in his chest. There was a lot of blood next to the body. What would make this a Pulitzer-winning photo nowadays was the hand holding the gun. Along with the feet next to the dead man, the camera caught a wrist and the hand with the gun. The shooter must have been standing right next to Hooper— assuming he was the photographer—and the picture showed a wisp of smoke coming from the barrel. It was an artful picture of an ugly scene. I'm sure it wasn't meant to be artful, but it was, nonetheless.

Something else about the picture though. I caught what looked like the edge of some lace on the wrist of the shooter. The picture cut out all but a tiny edge. It sure looked like lace. And the hand holding the gun looked feminine. I enlarged the photo. It was a small, delicate hand.

The dead man had been shot by a woman.

These pictures were real. But real of what … and where? Certainly not of the dead town below the cave. I thought back to the note. Born in 1970 and died in 1870? Baloney. There was an explanation. I just had to figure out what it was.

I felt a little dizzy. I went over to the bed and laid down. This was all too much to deal with. My chest felt heavy. I knew the signs. I was stressed. I closed my eyes and took some deep breaths.

I must have fallen asleep. When I woke up, it was morning. My laptop was still sitting open on the desk. It was now in sleep mode. I took out the memory card, and shut the computer down. It was time to head home. There was nothing more I needed to do for Harry. They had found some relative somewhere who could take care of cleaning out his belongings and selling his house. I didn't want to do anything else with the pictures, Stan Hooper, and the trunk until I got home. I wanted to be in my own house. I could organize my notes better at home. On the trip back I would start planning out the next steps to take.

One thing was for sure: I would tell NO ONE about this until I could make some sense of it because frankly, none of it made sense. The pictures could have been staged. My gut told me they weren't though. Everyone looked too real. And the picture of the dead guy was certainly not staged. He was most definitely the victim of violent death—and I had seen a lot of violent death in my life.

The other items in the trunk were old, but it didn't mean they had been sitting in the trunk for 150 years. They could have been put there yesterday.

So where did it leave me?

With lots of questions and no answers.

Chapter 5

I packed my car, being ever vigilant. I was going to be super-protective of my find until I figured out what was going on. So, to anyone watching, I probably looked guilty of something. It was still early, but I wanted to get going. I stopped by a McDonalds and picked up breakfast at the drive-thru counter. I didn't want to leave the trunk alone in the car, so most of my meals on the road would be drive-thru. My bowels would be a mess by the time I got home from all the fast food. Maybe I could get a decent meal at night when the box was safely in my hotel room. Bathroom breaks on the road would have to be fast. I just didn't want to leave my car alone for more than a couple of minutes.

Was I paranoid? Most definitely. There were just too many unknowns and I didn't want to have the trunk stolen before I could figure out some of those unknowns. Who was Stan Hooper? And how did his Massachusetts driver's license end up in Arizona, in a trunk that was supposed to be 150 years old? Who took the pictures, and when did they take them? What was the cryptic note all about? An explanation existed ... somewhere.

According to my GPS, Flagstaff to my home in West Palm Beach would take about 33 hours. Two nights in a hotel and three long days of driving. Ugh. At least it would give me a lot of time to think.

And then I felt guilty. I had come to Flagstaff to be with Harry during his last days. I should be thinking about him, right? The truth was, I hadn't thought about him once since finding the trunk. That was sad. Like Harry, I didn't have many close friends, and our weekly calls—until he started to get sick—were high points for both of us. Harry's cancer was discovered too late for any treatment to help. He hadn't been feeling well for a while but hadn't bothered to get checked out. From the time he was diagnosed to the day he died was less than two months. Maybe that was a blessing. It was a painful final few weeks for him. While I was with him, he was alert for parts of the visit until the pain became unbearable and they had to increase his pain medication, making him pretty out of it. He was doing his best to keep the meds to a minimum though, despite the pain. He wanted his last hours to be conscious ones.

I had a few other friends, but no one could replace Harry. I'd never married—just never found the right woman—and had become somewhat reclusive in recent years. When I wasn't out interviewing people for stories, I pretty much stayed home.

I let the sadness consume me for a few hours that first day of my drive. By lunchtime, I was ready to move on. I'd said my goodbyes to Harry at the hospital and I said a final silent goodbye as I pulled into a rest area on I-40.

I also had a second mission in mind for coming to Flagstaff, but finding the old trunk had pushed it from my mind. I was now kicking myself for not taking the extra time to research it a little more. Over the years, I had done a lot of research online, but having the opportunity to visit Flagstaff was going to make it a little more personal, because, although I had never been there before, Flagstaff had an indirect influence on my life.

My parents died when I was eleven. To this day, I had trouble thinking of them without choking up. We were living in Rochester, New York, and I was spending the day at a friend's house when the police showed up. I heard them ask my friend's mother if they could talk to me and I knew immediately that something bad had happened. There were two officers—a male and a female—along with another woman who I soon found out was a social worker.

It was a gas explosion. It had leveled the entire house. They told me that my parents were killed instantly and didn't suffer. Was that supposed to make me feel better? My whole life changed in that instant. The worst part? I didn't even have any keepsakes to remind me of them. No family photos, no "Best Father" and "Best Mother" tacky trophies that I had given them on their birthdays. Even my collection of stuffed animals was gone. Everything had been destroyed in the explosion and corresponding fire.

I went to live with my aunt and uncle in New Jersey. They were good people who tried to give me the childhood that had been cut short, but I was never quite the same. They had a son about my age who I got along well with. I wouldn't say that we became as close as brothers, but we had a good relationship. He went into the Marines and was killed in the Gulf War in 1990. After leaving home, I stayed in touch with my aunt and uncle, until their deaths a few months apart a couple of years ago.

One of the few keepsakes that I had thought about over the years was a photo that was on the wall of our den. It was a picture of my great-great-great (I was never sure how many "greats") grandfather on my mother's side, Charles Martin. It was taken during the Civil War by none other than the famous Civil War photographer, Mathew Brady. It was an original photo—probably worth a fortune, not that it mattered. We never would have sold it. Charles wasn't a kid when he enlisted. He was probably near thirty. The photo was classic Brady—Charles in full uniform, his rifle at his side, his cap slightly off-kilter, and a big smile on his face. Over the years, I had memorized every bit of the photo.

The reason it meant so much to me was that Charles was one of my inspirations for becoming a writer. After the war, he started writing dime novels. They were all the rage. They were really just pamphlets—usually about a hundred pages in length—printed on cheap pulp paper. Most of them took place in the west with hero cowboys fighting off savage Indians and dangerous outlaws. They always ended with the hero saving a helpless female. Kids—and adults—ate them up and the publisher couldn't pump them out fast enough.

Charles Martin became one of the most famous of the dime novelists, along with Prentiss Ingraham, Ned Buntline, and others, writing over 300 stories. Although he made good money from his novels, he traveled the west, working odd jobs for inspiration, often making the jobs central parts of his stories. I had never found any of his novels—most had disintegrated after a few years because of the cheap paper—but I had always held him in high regard.

Charles retired to Flagstaff and died in 1901. During one of my moments not visiting Harry in the hospital, I went in search of Charles's home. It was now a shopping mall. Sadly, that was as much research as I was able to do. Harry died the next day, and then I discovered the trunk. The chances were I'd never make it back to Flagstaff.

*****

After lunch, I put my attention on Stan Hooper. I know I had told myself that I would do most of my research when I arrived home, but I could do a little looking into him from the hotel.

However, my investigation was postponed a day. I arrived at the hotel that night around suppertime. The hotel had a decent restaurant. I had a quick meal, then went back to my room and fell asleep. I think the combination of my sadness about Harry and the questions I had about the trunk just exhausted me and I didn't want to deal with anything.

The second night, I was in a different frame of mind altogether. After a much more leisurely meal at a nearby restaurant, I returned to the hotel anxious to get started on my research. I opened my laptop and got to work.

I typed "Stan Hooper" and "Boston" into Google and got a lot of hits immediately. There were a lot of Stan Hoopers listed in Boston. It didn't matter. There was only one who dominated the headlines. He'd had many articles written about him. In fact, there was one from the Boston Globe from only a couple of months ago. The headline read: *"Police Still Have No Clues to Whereabouts of Man Who Went Missing in 2011."*

He vanished four years before his license expired and had now been gone ten years. The article condensed the story nicely for me. A girlfriend had reported Stan missing after numerous attempts by friends and coworkers to contact him. She said he had been secretive and nervous lately. However, coworkers at the small publishing company where he worked saw no change in his behavior.

That immediately sent up a red flag for me. Someone was lying—either his coworkers or his girlfriend. If he was nervous, coworkers in a small company would notice it. And if they hadn't noticed anything wrong it meant his girlfriend was making it up. The police must have picked up on it too, as it was reported that they'd had many conversations with the girlfriend. Neighbors had reported shouting matches between the two several times in the weeks before he went missing.

There was little else of importance in the article. The man had just vanished into thin air. A picture accompanying the article confirmed that my Stan Hooper was the same as the missing Stan Hooper.

I was faced with a dilemma. I had information about a

missing person. Wasn't I obligated to go to the authorities? I had his license, which would be a major clue in any investigation. I also had memory cards with pictures of him. But who knows when and where those pictures were taken? There was no timestamp connected with them. The date hadn't been set on the camera.

So yes, normally I would be obligated to report what I had found. This wasn't normal. This was just weird. I spent another couple of hours reading articles written at the time of his disappearance and Googling the heck out of his name and the investigation, but they didn't provide anything more than the recent four-paragraph recap article did.

I was getting tired but decided to look at a few more of the pictures on one of the memory cards. Altogether, between the two cards, there were over a thousand pictures. It would take quite a while to go through them all. However, I could view a few more tonight.

Most of the pictures I looked at were just more of the same: townspeople going about their business. I'm sure that when I looked at them all, there would be more of a variety, but for right now I was stuck in the town of Hollow Rock.

And then I saw it. In a town of 228 people, there were bound to be some who showed up in several pictures, but there was one man who seemed to be occupying Stan's attention.

There was something familiar about him.

And then it hit me. He was the dead man in the picture with his face half shot off.

There was another story going on here—a deadly one.

*****

I arrived home late the next night. It had been a long, strange trip, and I didn't see it getting any less strange in the coming days.

I lived in a townhouse in one of the newer communities in West Palm Beach—courtesy of a small inheritance from my aunt and uncle—and I luckily had a garage. It allowed me to unpack my SUV in private.

I hid the trunk in a closet and put the memory cards and Stan's two notes in my gun safe. I was still feeling paranoid, but at least the items were secure.

Good thing, because I was awakened early the next morning by a loud rapping on my front door. I crawled out of bed, putting on a pair of shorts and a t-shirt. The knocking continued.

"I'm coming!" I yelled. I glanced at the clock. Nine o'clock. Okay, so maybe it wasn't early.

I opened the door to find two men with serious expressions. The men had sort of an official look about them, but they were dressed in jeans and sneakers, with flowered shirts—one green and one orange. One of them waved some sort of credentials at me and said, "Ray Burton?"

"Yes."

"Can we talk?"

"About what?" I asked.

"Stan Hooper."

Chapter 6

How the hell did they know about my research into Stan Hooper? I hadn't told a soul about it.

"I'm sorry," I said. "Who are you with?"

"NSA," replied the one with the green flowered shirt. He showed me his credentials, slower this time. They looked real, but what would I know?

I looked the men over. Green shirt looked somewhat hippie-ish, with blonde-gray hair down past his ears, a graying mustache, and John Lennon-type wired-rimmed glasses. The one in the orange shirt was completely bald and clean-shaven and had bulging biceps. Both looked to be a little younger than me.

"Don't you people usually wear matching blue suits with shiny shoes?" I asked.

"You're thinking of the FBI," said green shirt, with a hint of a smile. He added, "I guess some of our counterparts do as well, but we're in kind of a unique division."

"And what is that?" I still hadn't let them in.

"We can't tell you," said green shirt. He reached into his pocket and produced a card, which he handed me. "You can call this number to verify who we are. We can wait."

"Okay, I'll do that." I closed and locked the door.

The name on the card was Mitchell Webster. Before calling

the number, I cross-referenced it online to make sure it really was the NSA. The number matched. I called it and got the switchboard. I explained the situation and she asked me for a code number listed at the bottom of the card and then transferred me. The male voice at the other end confirmed the identity of Mitch Webster, then asked if I was Ray Burton.

"Uh, yes."

"I can assure you that they are legitimate."

I hung up. This was all so weird. They knew me and knew of my interest in Stan Hooper. All I could think of was that they had his name flagged and that my internet searches had set off an alarm.

I hesitated before going back to the door. It meant that they knew something about Stan's disappearance and that it probably wasn't something simple like murder or abduction. I wasn't ready to give them any information yet. These were the situations where people who knew too much disappeared. Okay, I was ready now.

I returned to the door and invited them in.

"I'm Mitch Webster and this is Charles Smith," said Mitch. "Thank you for talking to us."

"I'm not sure how I can help," I said. "How did you know I was researching Stan Hooper?" Of course, I already knew the answer to that.

"Your internet searches," answered Mitch, giving no more information than that.

"I'm sure a lot of people have searched his name over the years," I said. "Why me?"

"Other circumstances. Why are you researching him?"

"As I'm sure you know," I said sarcastically, letting them know that I knew they were going through my life, "I am a freelance writer. I came across the story of Stan Hooper's disappearance and thought it might make a good story."

"Will it?"

"I don't know. I was researching it on the road. Once I got settled back in, I was going to make the decision. If so, I would do what I usually do, contact one of the magazines I write for and see if they would be interested in it. Or I would just write it and try to sell it to one of the magazines. I do it both ways. But I haven't decided on anything yet. I just got home."

They were quiet for a moment, so I asked, "What is your interest in Stan Hooper?"

Instead of letting me answer, the bald one, Charles Smith, asked, "Why were you in Flagstaff?"

"How do you know I was in Flagstaff?" I pretty much knew the answer. I just wanted to hear it from them. After all, I hadn't done any of my Stan Hooper research in Flagstaff, so it wasn't my internet searches.

"We just know," answered Smith.

"Are you ... like God?" I asked, wide-eyed.

That got a chuckle from Mitch.

"You know," I said, "if you expect me to be cooperative, I'd like a little transparency in return."

"That's fair," said Mitch. I almost liked the guy. Almost. Not so much the other guy. "After we noticed your interest in Hooper, we checked your phone records and saw that you'd been in Flagstaff."

"What you are really saying is that you didn't check phone records. You accessed my phone's GPS and could tell exactly where I was at any moment of my trip."

"We *did* check your phone records."

"There's a non-answer that confirms my theory," I said. "Just to let you know, my hour-long stop on my way home at a rest area outside Albuquerque was to use the bathroom. I figured you'd be wondering that."

They both chuckled this time.

"So, can I ask why you were in Flagstaff?" asked Mitch.

"You're the NSA. You don't know?" Getting no answer, I said, "I was there to say goodbye to a lifelong friend." A sadness came over me as I explained. "His name was Harry Lang. You can look it up. He was diagnosed with cancer two months ago. He died while I was there."

"I'm sorry," said Mitch. I think he might've meant it. Maybe. "We also saw that you went to Hollow Rock. Can you tell us why?"

"Well, that obliterates your explanation of using my phone records, considering I didn't call anyone from there."

Silence.

I sighed. "I went for two reasons: One, I needed a break. Being with Harry those last few days was tough. I've always wanted to see a real ghost town and I saw that there was one around there. If you check my internet searches, you'll see that I looked up ghost towns…"

"We didn't check your internet searches," interrupted Smith. "We just had a flag on Hooper."

"Uh-huh," I deadpanned. "And on Hollow Rock, as well. Anyway, Harry wanted his ashes scattered across the desert. I thought he'd get a kick out of having them scattered at the site of a ghost town."

"Did you find anything?" asked Mitch.

I got a little nervous with that question. Did they have a satellite watching me? I doubted it.

"Rain. I found rain," I said. "Hollow Rock was a washout in more ways than one. Despite what it said online, there was nothing left of the town—just a few building foundations visible under the dirt and sand, and a lot of rotten wood. I scattered Harry on what was probably the main street of the town. Then it started raining hard. I saw some overhangs of rock against the cliff wall. Since my car was parked a half-mile away—which I'm sure you know—I headed for the little bit of shelter I could find until the rain stopped. So that's what I found. Rain."

I looked at them with a pissed-off sort of expression. "Anything else?"

"No, I guess not," said Mitch. "We appreciate your cooperation."

"One question," I said. "The obvious question. Why the NSA? You don't get involved in missing person cases. And everything I read about Stan Hooper leads me to believe that he was a pretty vanilla kind of guy. So where does national security enter into this picture?"

"I'm afraid that's classified."

"Gee, how surprising."

They stood up. The meeting was over.

"If you do follow up the story and find anything … um…unusual, could you call me?"

"Unusual like what?" I asked. "Besides generally pissing me off, you're not giving me much to go on."

"If you run across the names Herb Wells or Alan Garland, we'd appreciate a call."

Shit. I think my expression flickered. Did they catch it? If so, they didn't say anything.

"I will do that," I said. "If I decide to write the article, you might see some calls to Boston when you're looking at my phone records. If I feel that it is worthy of a book, I might even go up there—in case you're checking my 'other' phone records." I made some air quotation marks around the word "other."

I wanted to be able to research this without them becoming too much of a nuisance.

We said goodbye and when I closed the door, I leaned against it and sighed deeply. Other than the flicker at Herb Wells's name, which they might not have caught, I thought I handled myself pretty well. And now I knew that there was another person involved in this. Someone named Alan Garland.

Two things came from their visit: One: I knew that I had to research this more deeply. It might turn out to be fodder for a book after all. And two: I was going to have to make copies of the pictures and hide them in several places.

This was getting interesting. And just a little scary.

Chapter 7

I waited a couple of hours, then took a trip to my local electronics store. On the way, I stopped at the ATM and took out a lot of cash. The NSA was watching me. It probably meant they were watching my credit card purchases, so anything related to Stan Hooper that I didn't want them to see was going to have to be paid for in cash.

Hopefully, though, I had sufficiently convinced them that I was considering an article about Stan's disappearance. That would give me a lot more leeway when I wanted to ask questions and do research. I also had a feeling that they didn't totally believe me and would be watching me carefully.

I bought an external hard drive with a lot of storage, as well as a half dozen memory cards. I spent the afternoon making copies of all the pictures, then took a drive to my bank and put one set in my safe deposit box.

I had a choice. Look at the pictures or research Hollow Rock? I decided to research the town. I reasoned that the pictures might mean more once I had the history of the town.

And the NSA guys? If they asked, I would just tell them that they got me curious about Hollow Rock. I'd put the ball back in their court.

I went online and looked up Hollow Rock. There was a small Wikipedia entry and a couple of articles in the Flagstaff newspaper that mentioned it. There wasn't much though. I don't think the town had a whole lot going for it. Just one of those forgotten towns that had no impact on history.

The town was established in 1866 when a small deposit of silver was discovered in the surrounding hills. A mining company swooped in with close to a hundred workers, and the town of Hollow Rock was born. Town construction began immediately and by 1867, Hollow Rock was a full-fledged town. While the town's culture was centered around the mine, there were also some ranches in the area.

By 1869, the town hit its peak of 228 residents. The town had its own newspaper—which I was well aware of—two saloons, two restaurants, a hotel, a school, a church, a general store, and several other stores, numerous boarding houses for the miners, a blacksmith, a lawyer, and a doctor who doubled as a dentist. Rumor had it that Billy the Kid came through Hollow Rock in 1877, but no incidents resulted from his appearance.

Later in 1877, the mine played out and the mining company left town almost overnight. With no work, most of the miners followed suit, and in a week, the town's population dipped below a hundred. One of the saloons and one of the two restaurants closed and things weren't looking good for Hollow Rock. The newspaper shut its doors in early 1878 due to a lack of readership—and a definite lack of news. When the hotel closed in the summer of 1878, the town's fate was sealed. The population rapidly decreased and by 1881, the few remaining residents fled to the new town of Flagstaff. And with the rumor of the railroad coming to Flagstaff, the ranchers switched their allegiance to the new growing town.

So my question now was: what happened to Stan Hooper, and who were Herb Wells and Alan Garland?

It was time to look at the pictures.

I decided that since I now knew the history—short as it was—

of Hollow Rock, it made sense to look at the pictures before reading the issues of the newspaper. Now I wanted to get a feel for the people of the town.

I grabbed a beer from the fridge and pulled my old, second laptop out from its storage space under my desk. I disabled the Wi-Fi and the Bluetooth on the machine and inserted the first memory card. I had considered copying all of the pictures to my main computer, then realized that the NSA probably could sneak into my computer whenever they wanted and steal the pictures. If I used a computer not connected to the internet in any way, there was no possibility of them accessing it.

I started from the beginning: the selfie of Stan, the picture of the town sign, and secret pictures of various townspeople. There were a lot of selfies of Stan. I wouldn't say that he looked overly happy in the pictures, but he also didn't look like he was suffering. He had numerous pictures of the entrance to the cave where I found the trunk, without all the bushes I'd had to push through. Hmm, that was interesting.

Then the pictures switched to the town. These would be a lot more interesting. I saw some of the same pictures I had seen when I first looked at them briefly. Now I studied each one in a lot more detail.

This Stan guy was good. It was elaborately staged. So much so that I looked for anything that would prove it all to be false—a plane in the sky or the contrail of a jet, a car, a powerline— anything that would expose it for the hoax it might be. That should be easy enough. But no. There was nothing.

While a part of me was still looking for inaccuracies, I was finding myself examining the people closely—their expressions, how they seemed to be interacting with others, and how they dressed.

The hats that a lot of the men wore bore little resemblance to the kind worn in the western movies—or that Stan had left in the trunk. Instead of being shaped, many of the hats just had a round shapeless brim. Some of the cowboy hats were almost pointy on top. Those who worked with cattle wore leather chaps. Most of the real cowboys had holsters, although I noticed that some were turned around, so the butt of the gun faced forward.

The townies often wore suits. Some carried guns, but not all. I had seen the farmers in earlier pictures, but not the miners. Stan had many shots of the miners coming home from a day's work. They looked like every other picture of miners I had ever seen— dirty and exhausted men trudging back to their bunkhouse. I imagined them eating something, then collapsing on their bunks, only to start over early the next morning.

The women wore what looked like heavy dresses. Most were blue, gray, or black. Occasionally there would be a colorful outfit.

It was strange to be seeing pictures like these. I was used to seeing grainy black and white archived pictures from the 1800s, and here were the same kinds of pictures in crystal clear color. They felt real somehow, like I was observing a day in the life of the old west. I didn't know what to think anymore. There had to be an explanation.

To stage something like this would require a lot of money and a lot of time. And what happened to the town? This wasn't just some guy's attempt at a joke. This was something more.

I went through more of the pictures of the town and its people.

What also made it seem real was that the sight of a camera from the 21st century would scare anyone from that time, so all of the pictures to this point had been taken secretly. A nice touch to the hoax—or whatever this was.

They were all taken secretly. All except one.

It was a picture of two women with their arms around each other. Neither looked particularly happy, but they were smiling for the camera.

If he was trying to make this seem real, why would Stan make the mistake of showing the camera this one time?

And then I looked more closely at the women. There was something familiar about them. I had seen each of them somewhere else.

And then it hit me. I suddenly felt dizzy and I had to close my eyes.

No way!

This couldn't be true.

I quickly set the laptop on the floor and moved over to my main computer. I went online and typed in a name. A picture came up and I moved it to my second monitor. I typed in another name and when the picture came up, I moved it to my third monitor. I now had two women staring at me from 32" monitors.

There was no doubt about it. Those two women and the two women in Stan's photo were the same.

I jumped up from my chair and walked around the room.

"Oh shit!"

If this was real—and, God help me, I was starting to wonder if it was possible—I had just landed in the middle of two of the biggest mysteries of all time.

Chapter 8

History is full of stories of famous people who disappeared off the face of the earth: writer Ambrose Bierce, aviator Amelia Earhart, robber/hijacker D.B. Cooper, and countless others.

In 2009, actress Natalie O'Brien and her boyfriend, Randy Brown, disappeared while on vacation. I remembered that story well. Natalie had been in some of my favorite movies and I had a little bit of a crush on her. She became a hero to women everywhere when she declared that she would never have any "enhancement" work done. Of course, many women countered that it was easy to say that when you were as beautiful as she was. No matter what, she was a great actress with a promising career ahead of her.

And then she was gone.

Natalie and Randy had kept their vacation secret, but as always happens, they were seen. There were reports of sightings in Colorado and New Mexico. And then their car was found in Sedona, Arizona. For weeks, canyons in the area were searched. Had they fallen to their deaths? Natalie was known as an outdoorswoman, so that theory was doubted by most who knew her.

And then it was discovered that their car had been stolen. They caught the thief, who said he found the car abandoned in Flagstaff, but that he had nothing to do with the couple's disappearance. The authorities believed him, and eventually, the search ended.

The rumors, however, lived on. As with every disappearance, the tabloids had a field day—many field days in fact—and every possible angle was examined. One story was that their relationship was on the rocks. Had Randy murdered her and fled the country? Had she tired of the famous life and was now living a quiet life in Mexico? In Switzerland? In Belize? Name a country and she was seen there.

When it all sifted out, we were left with the fact that Natalie O'Brien had just plain disappeared.

Now, here she was on my computer as clear as day, in a picture supposedly taken 150 years ago. There was no doubt in my mind that I was looking at Natalie O'Brien. Maybe her presence could somehow be explained away if it was just a picture of her. But it wasn't just her, and that's where it all became more than a little perplexing.

The woman standing next to Natalie was Beryl Dixon.

Beryl Dixon was long before my time, but everyone knew the story. A mystery author in the 1920s and '30s, she was nearly as prolific as Arthur Conan Doyle and of her contemporary, Agatha Christie—and was becoming nearly as popular as Christie. And then, like Natalie, she just disappeared.

The rumors this time had a hint of truth to them. She lived a lavish lifestyle and was suspected to be in serious money trouble. Creditors—some legal and some not-so-legal—were after her. It was thought that she was in so much debt, she could write for the rest of her life and never pay it all back.

Short in stature and long in personality, the 40-year-old author just up and left one night from her twenty-seven room Los Angeles mansion. She left envelopes stuffed with cash for all the staff and gave her chauffeur some cash to anonymously buy her a cheap car. It wasn't until many months later that a car discovered broken down on a stretch of road outside Flagstaff was matched to the one Dixon's chauffeur bought for her. The most prevalent rumor had her being murdered by one of the loan sharks, and her body left for the animals to dine on.

Her face had become as recognizable as Amelia Earhart's, so it was no bit of luck that I knew who she was. The woman in the photo was definitely Beryl Dixon.

And now I had a photo of two of the most famous missing persons standing arm in arm—Natalie still looking the 30ish she was when she disappeared, and Beryl still looking 40. How could that be?

Photoshop?

That was certainly an explanation—and the most likely explanation. Maybe, but there was something very real about this picture, and the fact that it was mixed in with hundreds of other pictures told me it wasn't fabricated. Then again, maybe that's exactly why it was mixed in with the others, to take the focus off Photoshop.

My head spinning, I continued looking at the pictures on the laptop—a little faster this time, as my mind was still on Natalie and Beryl.

There she was again. Natalie. This time she was walking down the wooden sidewalk in front of the hotel. She was alone and had a lonely look about her. What had happened to her boyfriend, Randy?

I saw a few more pictures of Natalie over the next few minutes. Sometimes she was walking alone and sometimes she was conversing with the other women in town.

Then I saw a picture of Beryl walking with a man toward the camera. They were arm in arm in a loving way, but the man was looking right at Stan—at the spot by his leg where he was holding the hidden camera—and he was scowling. He knew the camera was there.

The man looked familiar. And then it hit me. He was the dead man near the end of the second memory card.

I took a break. It was time for supper. I wasn't starving, but I knew I needed to eat something. I needed nourishment to get through all this.

*****

It was almost nine o'clock by the time I got back to it. I ate my supper and then ran to the bathroom soon after and threw up. My stomach was a mess. I was wishing I had never found the trunk. The thoughts of it being a hoax were diminishing by the hour.

What was the alternative? That someone had mastered time travel? Seriously?

I had never read much about time travel. I knew nothing about the science of it. The only book I'd read was the classic *Time and Again*, by Jack Finney. If I remembered right, the hero in that book was able to go back and forth in time whenever he wanted. That didn't seem to be the case here, at least, if I could use Natalie's facial expressions as a guide.

And in a Star Trek movie, I seem to remember them circling the earth numerous times at warp speed to get back to the 20th century.

In the movie *The Time Machine*, Rod Taylor used a red velvet chair to go through time.

That was the extent of my time travel knowledge.

I returned to the photos, although there was a part of me that didn't want to. And then I thought: *What if I just bundled everything up and handed it over to Mitch Webster? Wouldn't it be safer in the hands of the NSA?*

Ha. They'd find some way to turn it into a weapon.

No. For now, I just had to keep quiet about it. Down the line, I might find it necessary to relinquish control of it. Not yet.

Lots of pictures were similar, and I found myself flipping through them a little quicker. And then I slowed down again. Another man was suddenly showing up regularly. He was a middle-aged man wearing a suit and tie, with a bowler hat perched on his head at a slight angle. One picture was of him with his hat off, wiping his brow. He was nearly bald. What hair was left was black. In another picture, his coat was open, revealing a star attached to his vest. The sheriff, or maybe town marshal.

What caught my attention was the fact that Stan was catching his attention. He was almost always looking at Stan with a thoughtful expression. He was trying to figure out something. Stan had probably done or said something that didn't fit the times, and now the marshal was suspicious of him.

I finished the first memory card and decided to look at the town newspapers before continuing.

I had a total of five issues—two before and two after the one that Stan left in the trunk. I picked up the first one. The first thing I noticed was that a "Beryl Christie" was listed as an editor and reporter—the only reporter the newspaper had. That had to be Beryl Dixon. With her writing skills, it made sense that she'd be working at the newspaper. The "Christie" last name had to be her paying homage to Agatha Christie.

The town marshal's name was Max Hawkins. There were a few stories of him throwing drunks in jail. He seemed to be a capable guy who didn't take guff from anyone.

There was a story about roving bands of Apaches. A farmer had been killed and some of his stock stolen. Natalie was mentioned in that first issue. She was going by the name of Natalie Fox. Natalie was performing nightly at one of the saloons, singing and acting out scenes from various plays.

There was no mention of Stan.

Each issue of the newspaper contained one chapter of a mystery by local author and reporter Beryl Christie. She was still writing her mysteries. I don't know why, but it made me happy. I was going to have to go back to the Flagstaff library and print out copies of all the *Hollow Rock Gazettes*. Maybe there would be a complete book. I wondered if I could do something with it. Advertise it as a long-lost Beryl Dixon novel?

And then I had my answer to the identity of the dead man with his face shot off. The man walking with Beryl in an earlier picture. In the edition that Stan had saved, was a story of a shooting—the shooting. The victim was Herb Wells!

There was very little to the story, written by the owner of the newspaper. Maybe he purposely kept it short, as the shooter was none other than his employee, Beryl Christie. It was reported as a lover's quarrel, with Beryl just defending herself. She wasn't charged. End of story. No way was that the end of the story. There had to be something else that precipitated the shooting. I'd probably never know what it was.

I sat back and closed my eyes. I had to think.

I returned to Stan's *"died a hundred years before I was born"* comment. I knew what he was trying to say. I just refused to believe it. It was all part of the hoax. It had to be, right? Then there were the pictures of Natalie and Beryl, two women from different times who absolutely should not be together in a picture. And then there were the other pictures of them. They weren't Photoshopped—of that, I had no doubt. Then there was the picture of a live Herb Wells, followed by a picture of a very dead Herb Wells.

I fell asleep that night with Herb's mangled face stuck in my brain.

Chapter 9

The next morning, after a sleepless night, I was back at the pictures. I was hooked now. I had to see them all.

I started with the first one again and went through them slowly. I had looked at many of them already, but I wanted to see them again, this time with a more critical eye. I wanted to look at backgrounds—was there something out of place with the buildings? Was a person in the background making a face or doing something that didn't fit? I flipped through most of the desert scenes fairly quickly, as I had already looked at them for planes and powerlines. It was the town I was most interested in.

About an hour in, I reached the collection of photos of the miners. I remembered seeing the remains of a mine when I was walking through Hollow Rock. It looked eerily similar to this mine. Maybe they all looked the same. The miners were real. I thought about movies and documentaries I had seen about mining life. This certainly fit. But if they all looked the same, who was to say the pictures were taken in Hollow Rock?

I was doing everything possible to disbelieve what I was seeing. I couldn't allow myself to believe it. Then I kept going over in my mind the picture of Beryl and Natalie together. There had to be an explanation, right? Suddenly, that same picture popped up on the screen. I stared at it for almost fifteen minutes.

I threw my hands up in the air and went to find some food in my fridge. When I came back, the picture was still there, haunting me. I had to move on.

I clicked through them, a little faster this time, until a few minutes later when my world would be rocked as never before.

Stan was taking photos of the saloon. It was a slow day, which is why he probably felt safe taking the pictures. The place was almost empty of customers, so he was taking shots of the walls, the piano, the bar area, the bartender…

Oh. My. God.

My chest tightened. Suddenly I couldn't breathe. I started to hyperventilate. I pushed off the chair and landed on the floor with a thud. I put my head in between my knees and closed my eyes. I tried to take deep breaths. They wouldn't come, so I breathed through my nose. It lasted forever. I didn't think I was crying, and yet, I had tears running down my cheeks. I was having flashbacks to my childhood and my parents.

When it finally subsided, I climbed back into my chair and looked at the screen again. There was no doubt about it. The bartender was none other than Charles Martin, my great-great-great-grandfather! I had spent my first eleven years looking at that face on our den wall. It was imprinted in my brain. There was no doubt at all who it was in Stan's picture.

Was this where Charles Martin lived before later moving to the new town of Flagstaff? Or was it just one of his stops to take a job while he wrote more of his dime novels?

More importantly, the feelings I'd had when I saw the picture of Natalie and Beryl were now confirmed. As much as I wanted to, I could no longer deny it. The proof was there.

Stan Hooper was really in Hollow Rock in 1870.

There was now no doubt in my mind.

Time travel was a reality.

*****

I left the computer and took a shower. I was soaking wet from sweat. I stayed in the shower for well over a half-hour, just standing there and letting the water run over me. If anyone had asked me afterward what I was thinking in there, I wouldn't have been able to answer.

I finally got out, dressed, and went back to the computer. Maybe I was hoping that the picture wouldn't be there anymore. It was still there. And there were three others after it, all featuring Charles Martin. He had no idea he was being photographed. He looked content wiping down newly washed glasses.

And now the big question: I had the pictures. I had Stan's note. I had his driver's license. I had proof about time travel. What was I going to do about it? I couldn't walk away from it. I was in way too deep now. The NSA was involved, but my gut feeling was that they knew very little. They had run across something and were now fishing. There was no way I was going to share any of this with them. I had to investigate this on my own. Where to start?

I knew that Stan came from 2011, but was Herb from the 21st-century too? If so, how did Herb and Stan know each other?

I had a feeling that I'd find the answers in Boston.

Chapter 10

I was about to die and there was nothing I could do about it.

"I'm a journalist!" I yelled. "I'm a journalist!"

I glanced over at the dead man lying beside me. I had already wet myself and now I could feel the bile rising in my throat. The hut I was in smelled of death … of urine … of feces. The walls were splattered red, with bits of skin and bones stuck to the dried blood.

The other men in the room laughed as the one standing in front of me raised his pistol.

"We especially hate journalists," he said in a quiet voice.

He pulled the trigger, and the explosion was deafening.

I was jolted awake in my seat with a hand touching me.

"Sir. Sir. Are you okay?"

I opened my eyes. Everyone was staring at me. The man beside me was the one who had touched me, but two flight attendants were also standing there, looking very worried. Even the woman in the seat in front of me had turned around and was staring at me from over the seatback. I knew that I had probably grabbed the attention of just about everyone on the plane.

It took me a moment to get my bearings and slow down my breathing. I was on the flight to Boston. I had fallen asleep and had *that* dream, the nightmare I'd had regularly for the last ten years.

"I...I'm sorry," I said to everyone crowded around me. "I had a bad dream. I apologize for the commotion." I glanced down to make sure I hadn't wet myself. It wouldn't be the first time after that dream. Luckily, all was dry.

A flight attendant asked me if I wanted some water. I politely declined. I thanked the concerned people around me and decided that it would be best for me to stay awake for the rest of the trip.

Once things had calmed down, the guy next to me—an older gentleman who looked like a college professor—said, "Wow, that was a doozy of a dream."

"It's not the first time," I responded. Usually, I refrained from discussing it, but this guy seemed almost fatherly.

"You're a journalist?" he asked.

"I always wonder what part of the dream is going to come out aloud," I said. "I guess I know which part of it came out this time. I used to be a journalist. Now I'm just a writer."

"And it was this experience that ended the journalism career?"

"Let me guess. You're a shrink. Sorry. Psychiatrist."

"No need to apologize," he said. "And yes, I am. Don't worry. I'm not going to psychoanalyze you. But it sounds like it was a life-changing experience."

"You could say that."

It was *the* experience that changed my life. It hadn't happened exactly as it did in my dream. Yes, I was in a hut and yes, a dead man was lying next to me, but nobody was pointing a gun at me ... yet. I probably didn't have more than an hour to live, but the rescue came in the nick of time. In my dreams though, I was always shot and killed.

It was my old life and it felt like so long ago. In my twenties and thirties, I had done a lot of international travel, often writing from dangerous hotspots. I found it exciting and rewarding. My work was published in many of the top magazines and newspapers and I was commanding top dollar. And then it ended. It ended in a hut in the middle of nowhere in South Africa.

I was doing a story on the blood diamond trade and got just a little too close to the action. The smugglers I got too close to hated anyone they didn't know, but they especially hated journalists. I was taken prisoner and was within minutes of being executed when a large group of government troops converged on the area, killing most of my captors and rescuing me.

After that, I lost my taste for adventure. My articles these days were relatively tame—some (me included) might say boring—and I was no longer paid top dollar. I was okay with it though. Always frugal, I had accumulated a decent-sized bank account that could easily carry me over in hard times.

As much as this time travel thing scared me, I also found it somewhat exhilarating. Was my adventurous spirit finally returning?

I gave my new friend a brief recap of my last day as a journalist and thanked him for his concern. By then, we were beginning our descent into Boston.

After arriving home from Flagstaff and then dealing with Mitch and his friend, I had given myself a couple of days to rest and catch up on some bills and work. I told myself that I would clear my mind of anything to do with Stan Hooper, but I failed miserably. I had two articles that I'd hoped to finish, but that didn't happen. So, two days later, I hopped on a flight to Boston. That would probably send out all kinds of alarms to the NSA guys, but I didn't care.

I arrived in Boston around noon and took an Uber to my hotel at Copley Place. I had spent a few years living in Boston and knew the city well. I also knew that it would be easier to take the "T"— the subway system—wherever I wanted to go than to rent a car.

Lynn Carter, Stan's ex-girlfriend, lived in an apartment

building not far from Fenway Park. I had called her the day before and asked if we could meet, saying that I was a journalist writing a story on Stan's disappearance. It wasn't really a lie, as I hoped to do exactly that. She had given an audible sigh at the request but said she'd meet with me. We chose a restaurant near her house and agreed to meet at 5:30, right after work. I got the distinct impression that she just wanted to get it over with. I couldn't blame her. She'd been dealing with this for ten years and probably just wanted to move on.

We described ourselves to the other, so when 5:30 came and she walked in the door, I recognized her immediately. I gave her a wave from my seat in a booth in the bar and she walked over. I stood up.

"Lynn?" I asked. She nodded and shook my hand. I gestured to the seat opposite me and we sat. She was a few years younger than me and somewhat average-looking—probably the same way people referred to me. She had shoulder-length brown hair, a small mouth with thin lips, and sad eyes. Or maybe they were just tired eyes.

"Thanks for meeting with me," I said.

"I can't believe you could write anything new on the subject," she said matter-of-factly. "He was here, then he wasn't. The police have no leads at all. It's pretty straight forward."

Or not, I thought. A waitress came over and we ordered drinks. I had decided that meeting for drinks would be better than meeting for a meal. If the interview lasted ten minutes, having a meal to look forward to would create quite an awkward situation.

"Well, I appreciate you humoring me," I said. "I'll try not to make this any more painful than it already must be."

"The only pain," started Lynn, "is having to answer reporter's questions."

I gave her a questioning look and she said, "Stan and I had broken up, and it was never a great love affair to begin with. We lived together for a short time—mainly because he had been evicted from his last apartment. After a few months, I'd had enough. I asked him to leave. He moved out a few days before he disappeared. That was the extent of our relationship. Every article referred to me as his girlfriend. I wasn't."

"If you don't mind me asking, why did you ask him to leave?"

"He was too depressing to be around," she answered. "He was in massive debt, he didn't like his job, he didn't like his life, and..." she hesitated, then brushed away the thought.

"And what?" I asked.

"He was hanging around with someone I didn't like. He was, well, strange. I only met him a couple of times, but that was enough. He used expressions I'd never heard before and expected that I'd know what they meant. I heard the two of them talking in the next room, and he said things like, 'In your world' and 'in your time,' statements like that. Almost like he wasn't from here ... or now. He was just creepy."

"Was his name Herb Wells?" I asked. "And did he disappear around the same time?"

"How did you know about him?" Lynn asked, obviously surprised. "Two men from the government who interviewed me told me to call them if anyone ever asked me that question. Screw them though. I didn't like them."

"Mitch Webster and his bald friend from the NSA?" I asked.

She nodded.

"Don't worry. They've already approached me. They asked me about Herb Wells, too."

"He called me the day Stan disappeared—although I didn't know that Stan was gone at that point. He asked me if I had seen Stan. He seemed worried, but he didn't seem worried about Stan, more that Stan was gone. Does that make sense?"

"It does," I said. "Perfect sense."

I shouldn't have added those last two words. Lynn suddenly looked at me suspiciously.

But she continued anyway, "I didn't think it was strange that I never saw Herb again. After all, he knew I didn't like him. It never occurred to me that he disappeared around the same time. Do you think he killed Stan?"

"No. He didn't kill him," I said.

"You seem very sure of things," she said. "Did you have something to do with his disappearance?"

I laughed. "No. Until a few days ago, I had never heard of him."

"Then why am I getting the feeling that you know more than you are saying?"

How much do I say?

"Did you find it strange that the NSA got involved? Did they ever hint to you why they were looking into it?"

"Yes and no. Yes, I thought it was strange. And no, they never hinted. It would be one thing if it was the FBI—and they did get involved at first, after he'd been missing for a week or so—but as soon as the NSA showed up, the FBI disappeared. The most obvious explanation would be that Stan was into something that involved national security. If you knew Stan though, you'd realize how ridiculous that was."

"Tell me more about Herb Wells," I said.

"Not much to say. He just showed up with Stan one day. I think he was a co-worker of Stan's—a new one. They were very secretive. I have to admit that for a while I thought they might be gay, but it wasn't that. Stan said he stayed the night at Herb's apartment to sleep off a night of excessive partying. It was right after that that I threw him out. He seemed obsessed with the subject of Herb, and I don't know why. He stayed with Herb for about a week after I threw him out. He stopped by a couple of times to pick up his belongings, and he'd always talk about Herb.

He would talk in riddles, saying that Herb was an amazing person who knew unbelievable things. When I would ask for examples, he said he couldn't talk about it. How frustrating is that? There was definitely something weird about Herb though. That night I heard them, Herb was asking Stan all kinds of questions—strange questions. He asked about computers, car engines, TVs..."

"Like he'd never seen them before?" I asked.

"No, the exact opposite. He was kind of laughing at them. I heard him use the word 'antiques' at one point. But he was also intent on listening to what Stan had to say. He asked about animals, too. I distinctly heard him say, 'Oh, are they still around?' as if they shouldn't be. I don't know what animals he was talking about."

I was nodding my head as she spoke, confirming in my mind everything I had discovered to this point. It was firming up in my brain—and getting more compelling. I had my answer about Stan knowing Herb in this century though.

"So what do you know that I don't?" she suddenly asked. She looked me in the eyes as she said it.

Instead, I asked, "Have you ever heard of someone named Alan Garland?"

"No. The NSA men asked me that. Who is he?"

"I have no idea. They asked me that too. I've never heard of him. I was hoping you had."

I was silent for a minute. Lynn didn't say anything. She knew I was considering how much to tell her. How much should I tell her?

"Okay," I finally said. "This is going to sound weird. Hell, it did for me too. Did the NSA guys ever say anything or hint at anything to do with the subject of time travel?"

Her reaction to that would determine where I took it from here. Do I show her a picture of Stan in the Old West?

"Time travel? You're joking, right?"

Nope. No picture. She wouldn't react well to seeing it. In that brief moment, I realized that this time travel thing was going to have to be kept under my hat.

"The reason I bring it up is that I think the NSA is thinking along those lines. They ask weird questions."

"Are you serious?" she asked.

"You know how Hitler was interested in the occult? I think the NSA has a division that checks out strange things like that."

"Is that what you're writing about?"

"Honestly, I don't know. What started as a story about Stan's disappearance is taking on new dimensions. I learned a long time ago that if a story wants to change direction, I need to go with it. This one's going all over the place."

Lynn had a momentary faraway look, then said, "I do remember one really strange thing. That first day I met Herb, I asked Stan if they were good friends. He said, 'Not yet, but we will be in about 95 years.' I remember Herb giving Stan a real angry look, like Stan had said something he shouldn't have. Maybe they were interested in the subject of time travel. Maybe that's why the NSA is asking questions. Maybe Herb—I know it wouldn't be Stan—had a scientific theory about it all that caught their attention."

"Lots of maybes," I said. "Since Herb's not around to pose questions to, I'll have to find some others."

Lynn thought for a moment, then said, "You need to talk to Uncle Jim."

Chapter 11

"Who's Uncle Jim?" I asked.

"I have no clue," she answered. "I think he worked with Stan—and maybe with Herb, too. I heard them bring up his name a few times. They would say something like, 'Uncle Jim will know.' They seemed to put a lot of stock in the guy."

"Where did Stan work?" I asked.

"A magazine called *Antiques Etc.* He did copy editing and a few small writing projects for them. It didn't pay much more than minimum wage, which is why he was always broke."

"Welcome to the writing business," I said, knowing that with my background, I was one of the lucky ones who could actually earn a living at it. Most people in Stan's position were usually hurting.

"Uncle Jim—I have no idea why they called him 'Uncle'— worked there. I don't know Herb's story. At first, I assumed he was a coworker, but that might not be true. I think this Uncle Jim guy was the connection between the two of them. So if you can find him you might get your questions answered. I talked to him once on the phone the day Stan disappeared. He seemed friendly."

She looked at her watch and informed me that she had to go. The meeting was over. I thanked her for talking to me. She nodded and was gone, probably happy to be rid of me. I sat and made some notes while I finished my beer. It seemed I had four major players in this mystery: Stan and Herb, the mysterious Uncle Jim, and the unknown Alan Garland. The first two were out of the picture (or *in* the picture, so to speak). Uncle Jim would be my next interviewee if I could find him. As for Alan Garland, I had no idea where he fit in.

I put some money on the table and was about to get up when a man slid into the booth, occupying the same space that Lynn had just vacated. He was kind of scruffy looking. His dark hair was unkempt, he needed a shave, and his dark eyebrows formed almost a unibrow. He appeared anxious. He looked to be around my age.

"Can I help you?" I asked.

"Why are you looking into Stan Hooper's disappearance?"

"What makes you think I am? And if I was, what business is it of yours?"

The man didn't intimidate me. In my journalist days, I had found myself in a lot of sticky situations. Most I could talk my way out of, but some involved fighting. I could hold my own. I wasn't sure what to think of this guy.

"Drop it. Walk away. It's no concern of yours," he said. He reminded me of a 1930's movie hoodlum.

"That's for me to determine." He had a smell of garlic about him. I realized I had been smelling garlic from the moment I sat down. He must have been behind me in the next booth. "You were eavesdropping on my conversation. That's rude. How'd you know I'd be here?"

"None of your business," he growled. Then it hit me. He was tapping Lynn's phone. But her cell phone? How?

"Well, this conversation is accomplishing a lot," I said. "Anything else you don't want to tell me? Because if not, I think I'll leave now."

"If you continue," he said, "you'll end up dead."

"We all end up dead," I said. "Look, if you want to tell me why I should drop it, I'll listen. But you don't scare me in the least. So either tell me or shut the hell up and let me go about my business."

He seemed at a loss for words. The intimidation move hadn't worked, and he wasn't sure how to proceed.

"You're Alan Garland, aren't you?" I asked.

His lack of an answer was all the answer I needed.

"You don't know what you're getting into," he said, a little more in control.

"So tell me."

"You wouldn't understand."

"Try me."

"I can't."

"This conversation is still going nowhere," I said. "Let me make it easier for you. Does it have something to do with time travel?"

"Of course not. That's ridiculous."

That's what came out of his mouth. His face told a completely different story.

"Stan was just involved in a dangerous endeavor and if you stick your nose in it, you might end up dead."

"Yeah, you said that. I'm shaking in my boots. Who's going to see that I end up dead. You?"

"Maybe."

"So now you're threatening my life. That's a crime. I could call 9-1-1 right now and have you arrested."

"9-1-1?"

"You know. The police?"

"Oh, right." He stood up. "Just stay away from this." And then he left.

Well, that was weird. Especially not knowing what 9-1-1 was.

He didn't have an accent, so he wasn't from a foreign country. Maybe from a different time?

Like it or not, I was becoming convinced that this time travel stuff might be something to consider. Was that rational? Could it be that years from now someone could come up with a way to travel through time? If so, would it mean they could change events? The implications of that were scary.

I fished Mitch Webster's card from my pocket. I figured I may as well give them a little nugget to make them think I was playing on their team.

I dialed and Mitch picked up on the second ring.

"Ray?" Wow, we were on a first-name basis.

"Hi, Mitch."

"What can I do for you?" he asked.

"I'm sure you know that I'm in Boston," I said.

"I didn't."

"Yeah, right," I said. "Well, I am. I decided to pursue the Stan Hooper story. I met with his former girlfriend and didn't get much from her, but after she left, a man dropped into the seat across from me and warned me to stay away from the Stan Hooper case. He said I might end up dead."

"Do you know who it was?"

"I remembered you asking me about someone named Alan Garland, so I asked him if that's who he was. He wouldn't admit to it, but his face gave him away."

"What did he look like?" asked Mitch.

I described him.

"What else did he say?"

"That was the problem," I answered. "He kept telling me to stay away from it, but when I asked him why, he wouldn't tell me. It was the stupidest death threat I've ever received—and I had a few of them in my old profession."

"That was it?"

"That was it," I said. "I just thought you might want to know that Alan Garland really exists."

"Thanks for letting me know. I appreciate the cooperation."

That's all you're going to get, I thought.

I hung up.

It was time to talk to Stan's co-workers.

Chapter 12

I figured I'd look them up in the morning. I went back to my hotel and had a relaxing meal in the hotel restaurant. I wasn't tired when I got back to my room, so I thought I'd look at some more pictures.

There were some short videos, but not as many as I would have thought. Maybe he was concerned with space on the memory cards or maybe it was just easier to take pictures discreetly than it was videos.

There were a lot of shots of the hills from the town and of the town from the hills. They were wasted shots, as far as I was concerned. They didn't add anything to the story. He had several pictures of the cave, as well as one video taken outside the cave. In it, he says, *"This is where I came out. I've tried to go back into the portal, but it's disappeared. I can't get back to the life I led. Maybe I don't want to. I'll find another portal to take me somewhere else."*

A portal? Like a wormhole? And how would he find another portal? Did he have a map? He didn't say *maybe* he could find another portal, he said he *would* find one. That indicated to me that he knew how to find it.

There was a video that showed the front of one of the saloons—*The Miner's Spot.* At first, I wasn't sure why Stan was filming it, but then I heard a lot of shouting and a man flew out of the batwing doors and landed hard on the raised plank sidewalk, rolling off into the dirty main street. A man walked out after him. I recognized him as Max Hawkins, the town marshal I had seen in an earlier picture. He told the man to get out of town. Card cheating wasn't allowed. The marshal had a more refined voice than I would have thought in a dusty cowboy town. But then, people in the west came from all walks of life.

And then came the interesting part of the video to me. After the marshal told the man to leave town, he lifted his head and stared right at Stan, who was across the street. It looked like he was staring at the camera, but I would have thought Stan would have had it well hidden. The video ended, so I have no idea what might have happened next.

In another video, taken with Natalie near a stream outside of town, Stan asked her, *"Would you like to say something for the people back in the 21st century?"* She looked sadly at the camera and said, *"I know you're wondering what happened to me. I am too. Please tell my family that I love them."* She said it in the voice that I had the crush on. She still looked lovely. Sad, but lovely. I felt a little jealous that she was with Stan. How sick was that? Maybe it was time for me to find a girlfriend.

One of the last videos was of Stan repeating what he had written on the scrap of paper, *"Herb stole my notebooks, and I don't know where he hid them."*

What was in the notebooks? And did Herb hide them, or had he destroyed them?

I fell asleep thinking of Natalie, and a little bit of Beryl, Stan, and Herb. What were their stories? It was clear from the video that Natalie ending up there was unintentional. She was wondering what had happened to land her there. What were the others doing there? Where was Natalie's boyfriend, Randy? Was Beryl's presence also unintentional? It had to be something different with Herb and Stan. They were both here and then they were there. It couldn't have been an accident.

Stan and Herb went there for a reason.

What was it?

Chapter 13

Antiques Etc. was located on the second floor of an older building in Brookline. It was a hot summer day and the air conditioning in the trolley car of the Green Line had stopped working. So, by the time I arrived at my destination, I was drenched with sweat.

Unlike when I interviewed Lynn, this time I didn't call ahead. I wanted to see their reactions when I arrived to talk about Stan. It would give me an immediate impression of what they thought of him. I had found that sometimes it was more telling than listening to people struggle to describe in glowing terms someone they didn't like.

I needn't have worried. No one felt compelled to speak nicely of Stan.

Antiques Etc. consisted of five offices—two of them bare—and a corral of cubicles in the middle of a large center room. Three of the eight cubicles were occupied by kids who couldn't have been much beyond high school age. The other cubicles were unused. Not a thriving operation was my guess. The place was warm. Living in Florida, I was used to central air in just about every building. If this building had it, it wasn't very strong. I was going to stay wet for a while.

I approached the receptionist's desk. From the look of the piles of papers in front of her, her role went way beyond that of a receptionist. Her nameplate said, *Joyce Simmons*.

"Hi, I'm Ray Burton," I said. "I'm writing a story about..."

"Let me guess," Joyce said with a sigh, "Stan Hooper."

"I'm that transparent?" I asked.

"You have that look," she said, smiling at me. "Hold on."

She picked up her phone and pressed a button. "Hal, a reporter to talk to you about Stan." She laughed. "Yeah, again."

"Sorry," she said to me. "We get a lot of this. He'll be right out."

"Thanks," I said. "Um, did you know Stan?"

"You should probably go through official channels and talk to Hal," she said politely.

"I'm writing this from a completely different angle," I said. "The 'Stan Hooper disappearance' story has been done to death. I'm looking into his life and his friendship with Herb Wells, who also seems to have disappeared, but with none of the same publicity."

This seemed to grab her attention.

"You know, we mentioned that to the police after Stan disappeared. They looked for him, then told us that there was no record of Herb Wells."

"Didn't he work for you too?" I asked, thinking that they would have had tax information on file, proving he did exist.

"Herb? No. He was here often because he knew a lot about antiques, but he didn't work here. He could even tell what modern items would eventually become valuable antiques—and why. It was kind of spooky. He was a decent guy though. A little strange, but decent."

"Strange how?"

"He gave off an image of a mad scientist type. You could tell that he was smart. No, more than smart. If I had to guess, I'd say he was brilliant. And yet ... I don't know. There was just something odd about him. He knew about everything, but there were simple things he didn't know that anyone growing up in this country, or most countries, would know—DVDs, current movies, current music—lots of things. Just odd."

"What about Stan?"

"A little sleazy. Not to disparage his memory—if he's dead, that is—he was the kind of guy you tolerated." She looked around in a conspiring sort of way. "I didn't like him much. Kind of a dreamer, but a lazy dreamer, if you know what I mean. Always talking big but not doing anything about it."

At that moment, a large man in new jeans, expensive shoes, and a button-down shirt came out of one of the offices and approached us. Casual, with a touch of class.

He held out his hand. "Hal March."

"Ray Burton."

"Follow me," said Hal. "Let's go back to my office." He stopped and looked back at me. "Ray Burton. I know that name. Hotshot journalist?"

"I wouldn't say 'hotshot,' but yes, I was a journalist once upon a time."

"Your stuff was all over the place," said Hal. "*Time, Newsweek,* all the biggies. I haven't heard your name in a long time."

"I gave it up. That life can burn you out." I thought that was enough information for him about my past. "I'm still writing, only tamer stuff."

"I liked your work a lot," said Hal.

"Thanks."

I immediately liked Hal, and not because of the compliments. He came across as sincere, well-read, and an intelligent professional. He was older than me, probably around sixty. He stopped and addressed the young cubicle-dwellers.

"Hey, listen up. This is Ray Burton. If you've never heard of him, look him up. You want to be writers? Read his stuff. This man was at the forefront of many of the big events of the last thirty years. One of the best writers you'll ever run across."

"Thank you, Hal. A little embarrassing, but I appreciate it," I said.

When we entered his office, he closed the door for privacy.

"How's the magazine business these days?" I asked. "Mostly online?"

"Yeah. Somehow, it's not as much fun as it used to be. Or as profitable. We're hanging in there though. Because of the subject matter, we still have decent sales of the physical product—mostly to the older readers—but the online magazine brings in the money. That's why I have my stable of young people. They handle the online version. They are good at it. They just don't have the drive we used to have. That's why I introduced you. I wanted them to see one of the legends."

"Yeah, well, this legend doesn't have the drive he once had either."

"You did, and that's what counts. You deserve to take a rest. But I'm curious," he said. "The Stan Hooper story has been done to death and seems to have no legs. Have you found a new angle?"

Boy, have I, I thought. I liked this guy. Although I didn't want to completely open up to him, if I opened a little bit, it might spur some thoughts on his part.

"Yeah, but you might find it a little strange. I'm certainly finding it strange."

"The sign of a good writer," said Hal. "Grab the reader's interest immediately. You've grabbed mine."

I laughed, then said, "I can't tell you everything, because I'm still trying to figure some things out. I think this goes a lot deeper than just a missing person."

"I'm all ears."

"Have you ever gotten a call from the NSA about this?" I asked.

work had become too much for him."

"Is he still alive?" I asked.

"As far as I know. We stayed in touch for a couple of years, then, as often happens, we lost contact. I can give you the last address we had for him." He went silent for a minute. "You know, now that you've brought up all this, it was Jim who introduced Herb to us. He said they had known each other for a long time. I remember Herb giving a small laugh when Jim said it. I thought it was strange. I just figured it was an inside joke. Time travel would be a real inside joke. Just for the record, Jim didn't like Stan. I could just tell."

"How did he act after Stan and Herb disappeared?"

"Funny that you ask that. He was pissed. I couldn't tell who he was angry at though, Stan or Herb. Maybe both of them. It was like he knew something. I heard him tell the police that he didn't know anything about it. But he did."

He distractedly moved some papers on his desk. I could tell something was bothering him.

"I can't believe in the time travel thing. Or let's say that I'm trying not to. But your visit has brought up a lot of questions. There was something not quite right about the relationship between Jim and Herb. It's like they were sharing a secret. And just before Stan disappeared—and I did tell the police this—Stan was really excited about something. What I didn't tell the police— simply because I didn't register it at the time—was that as excited as Stan was, Herb and Jim were just the opposite."

He looked on his computer, then wrote something on a piece of paper.

When he looked up, he said, "Ray, you are onto something. I have no idea what it is, but there's more to all this than meets the eye."

We stood and he handed me the paper.

"Uncle Jim's last known address. You should talk to him."

Chapter 14

More than anything, I had wanted to show Hal a few of the pictures. I held off. It was more for his sake. I didn't want him to get involved in something that he really couldn't tell anyone about. If I showed him pictures of Natalie O'Brien and Beryl Dixon stuck 150 years in the past, what could he do with it? The information I gave him was more than enough to get his mind working. Maybe somewhere down the line, I could fill him in further. Then again, I didn't even know what I was going to do with the information.

Suppose it was true? Suppose Natalie and Beryl were stuck in time with Stan and Herb (a dead Herb, based on the picture)? What could I do about it? I could write an article or a book, but would I be laughed out of the profession if I did? Experts would say that the photos were forged or Photoshopped and that the story was too unbelievable.

That brought up the question: Why was I doing it? If I'd be laughed at by writing something about it, what was the sense in doing it? It didn't matter. I was in too deep now. I had to find out what it was all about.

*****

I purposely left my phone at the hotel, so the NSA couldn't track me. I brought my laptop and turned off the Wi-Fi and Bluetooth capabilities. Hopefully, it was enough so they couldn't trace it.

Jim hadn't moved. He still lived at the address given to me by Hal, a third-floor apartment in a firetrap of a house in East Boston. I took the train to the Orient Heights T station and walked four blocks to the address.

I pressed the buzzer beside the name Lawrence and waited. After thirty seconds I pressed again. If the man was sick, he might take a while getting to the door.

"Yes? Can I help you?" came the tinny voice over the intercom. The poor quality made it impossible to sense if the person speaking was sick.

"Jim Lawrence?" I asked.

"Yes, what do you want?"

"My name is Ray Burton. I was wondering if I could talk to you about Stan Hooper."

"Don't know him."

"Or Herb Wells?"

A slight hesitation. "No."

"Or Alan Garland? Hollow Rock? Mr. Lawrence—Uncle Jim—I'm not from the government. I'm a writer who stumbled upon something significant. All of my research has led me to you. I'd really like to talk to you."

Silence, then "Okay." A buzzer sounded and I opened the door.

He was waiting for me at the top of the stairs with a scowl on his face. He was a sick man, that much was obvious. He was probably around seventy but looked fifteen years older. He was someone who was once round in physique but had lost much of that weight. He couldn't have been more than 5'6", with wispy white hair and round rimless glasses.

"Up here," he said unnecessarily. He knew I saw him, or maybe he didn't know. Maybe his eyesight had diminished to the point where I looked like a shapeless blob.

I climbed the squeaky stairs. This was a house that needed to be torn down. Maybe it would be when Jim died, which looked to be fairly soon. I reached the third-floor landing and held out my hand.

"Ray Burton."

He stared into my eyes, then took my hand and said, "Jim Lawrence."

He motioned for me to follow him into his apartment. Considering his declining health, the place looked amazingly clean. The living room had shelves stacked with books. One corner had a table that was set up as a workbench. An object was on the table, but it was covered by a towel. Something he didn't want me to see?

"Have a seat," he said, pointing to the couch. "You look hot. Would you like some water?"

"Yes, please."

He seemed a little more pleasant than he had on the intercom. He returned with two bottles of water, gave me one, then sat down in a recliner. By the looks of it, it was his favorite chair.

"What can I do for you?" he asked. "And who gave you my name and address?"

"A couple of people gave me your name. Hal March gave me your address."

"Hal wouldn't have done that unless he trusted you. That's a good thing. How is Hal?"

"He's good. The magazine is still going. He spoke fondly of you."

"What did he say about Stan and Herb?"

"From what I can gather, no one particularly liked Stan. Hal seemed to like Herb—or maybe he was just curious about him. He really liked you."

Somehow, that seemed to satisfy Jim. Maybe he was trying to figure out if I was for real.

"How can I help you?" he asked. He fell into a coughing fit that lasted a full minute.

"Can I do anything for you?" I asked.

"No thank you. As you can probably tell, I don't have a lot of time left."

"Would you heal if you went back in time?" I asked. I'm not sure why I asked it. I was planning to lead into the subject slowly.

"Well," he said. "This conversation just got more interesting. And the answer to your question is no."

His buzzer sounded. He looked at me. I shrugged. He slowly got up out of his chair and walked to the intercom.

"Yes?"

"Jim, it's Alan. I need to talk to you."

"I'm not feeling well. Can we talk another day?"

"No, I need to talk to you now. Open the door."

Jim took his hand off the intercom and looked back at me.

"Go into the bathroom." He pressed the button to let Alan into the building.

I hurried to the bathroom—taking my water bottle with me—and hid behind the open door. I heard Alan come up the squeaky stairs, then walk into the house.

"What's so urgent?" asked Jim.

"You might get a call from someone named Ray Burton. Don't talk to him. He knows something about all this. I'm not sure what, but we can't take the chance of telling him anything."

"I know the rules," said Jim. "I helped make them."

"He knows Stan's name, Herb's name, and he knows my name. I don't know how. I met with him and warned him off, but I don't think it was enough."

"What do you know about him?" asked Jim.

71

"I looked him up. He was some kind of war correspondent and reporter. Very respected. That's not good for us."

"He was a war correspondent, and you think you can scare him off?" asked Jim. "You're crazy. It probably just made him more curious. Who knows? Maybe it is time to tell someone about this."

"What are you talking about?" Alan said in a loud voice. "That could be devastating to the whole project. Hell, it could be devastating to the world. We can't tell anyone."

"Stan knew."

"And look where that led. Old man, tell me now that you won't talk to Ray Burton."

"I can't promise you that. And don't call me 'old man.' You can leave now."

"You think you can break the bond because you're about to die? I won't allow it."

I heard the sound of something being moved.

"What are you doing with the finder?" I took that as Jim's cue to me that something was about to happen.

I left the bathroom at record speed and saw Alan standing in front of Jim with an object about the size of a medium flower vase in his hand. Alan turned at the sound of my approach and I barreled into him. The object fell to the floor and Alan crashed into the thin wall, creating an indentation of his body. I grabbed him by the shirt and pulled him toward me, giving him a ridge hand strike to the neck. He went down like a sack of potatoes. He wasn't unconscious, just woozy.

"Are you okay?" I asked Jim. He was breathing heavily and had his hand over his heart.

"Yes. Just a little out of breath." He looked down at Alan. "What are we going to do with him? We can't turn him over to the police."

"Why not?"

"We just can't."

"Because they might find out something about him that you don't want to be known?" I asked.

"Something like that," he answered.

"When he catches his breath, he's going to come after you," I said. "You'll be safe with him in police custody."

"No, he won't. And I don't think he was going to hurt me. I think he was going to take the object he was holding. He gets a little intense and will do anything to protect the program, so who knows what his intentions were? Please watch him for a minute." He walked into the bathroom and emerged a minute later with a hypodermic syringe and a small bottle. "This will put him under for a couple of days."

"A couple of days?" I asked. "What kind of injection puts someone out for a couple of days?"

"One not invented yet."

There it was. That one comment told me that Uncle Jim was going to spill the beans. I might finally get a clue to what I had stumbled upon. He gave Alan the injection, then asked me to drag Alan into the second bedroom. Alan wasn't a big man—about my size—but the dead weight made it hard to lift him onto the bed. But I did it. We took his shoes off, put the covers over him, and arranged him in a comfortable position. We returned to the living room, where Jim sat back in his recliner. I sat down on the couch and looked at him.

"You came to me," he said. "Ask your questions."

Chapter 15

"I have too many questions," I said. "So let me start by telling you a story. A few days ago, I had never heard of Stan Hooper … or Herb Wells, or the others. I was in Flagstaff to see a dying friend. When he passed on, I took his ashes to scatter out in the desert, and ran across a ghost town…"

"Hollow Rock," interrupted Jim.

"Yes. A heavy rainstorm came, and I took shelter in a cave." I told him the story of finding the trunk, along with pictures, and Stan's notes about dying a hundred years before he was born and of Herb supposedly stealing Stan's notebooks. I then mentioned running into the NSA guys. "I came to Boston to see if there was a story. I interviewed Stan's ex-girlfriend, Hal March, and had a run-in with Alan. So here I am."

"Interesting about the NSA," he said. "Luckily, I never had the pleasure of a visit from them. That might have been awkward."

"Why?"

"Because I work for the NSA, in a manner of speaking."

He laughed when he saw my jaw drop.

"I'll explain later when it'll all make more sense. Could I see some of the pictures?" he asked. He was taking it all in stride and didn't seem at all surprised by my visit. Maybe it was the fact that he knew he was close to death.

I took the laptop out of my backpack and set it up.

"There are about a thousand pictures," I said. "So I'll only show you some of the more significant ones."

I started with Stan's picture by the Hollow Rock sign. Jim cursed under his breath. I had a feeling I'd get an explanation of that soon.

Then I showed him the picture of Stan with Natalie and Beryl.

He sat up in his chair and peered at the screen. "Is that Beryl Dixon?"

"It is."

"Son of a gun," he said quietly. "He did it."

"Did what?"

He thought for a minute, then waved me off.

"For another discussion," he said. Then he chuckled to himself. It must've been one doozy of a story.

"Who is that next to her?" he asked.

"Natalie O'Brien. A movie actress who went missing a couple of years before Stan did."

"Oh yes, I've heard the name." He shook his head and gave a low whistle. "Beryl Dixon. Son of a gun."

"This last picture might be disturbing," I said. "I suppose this is the time to tell you that Herb Wells is dead."

That evoked a reaction. Jim put his hand to his mouth and said, "Oh no. That can't be. Herb and I were colleagues. Oh, that's distressing. So distressing."

"I'm sorry."

"No, you don't understand. Yes, it's distressing that he's dead because he was my friend. But it's worse because I don't have proof that Stan is dead. We only have Stan's note about that, and he was obviously alive when he wrote it."

"Is Stan supposed to be dead?" I asked.

"Not necessarily. If Herb is dead, I would hope Stan is too.

Could I see the picture?"

I showed him. The blood left his face. He closed his eyes and made a motion with his hand for me to turn the computer away from him. I closed it. I handed him his water, but he set it down.

"I need a cup of tea," he said.

I went into the kitchen and found his kettle. It seemed a little old-fashioned, considering where all this seemed to be leading. He told me where to find the peppermint tea. I made it and brought the cup to him.

"Ah, thank you. Nothing like peppermint tea."

I sat quietly while he composed himself.

"Let me ask you a question," he finally said. "What do you plan to do with anything you learn from me?"

"Honestly? I have no clue. When I found the trunk, I was just curious. I didn't know what I had stumbled upon. When I learned about Stan Hooper and had the visit from the NSA, I began to think there might be an article—or even a book—in it. Now?" I just shook my head. "Now I'm just trying to get my head around it. I don't know what fits in where."

"Well then, I'm going to make a request," said Jim. "I can't force you not to write about it, especially since I'm going to explain it all to you—against the code of ethics I helped write and also embraced when I joined this team, I might add. All I ask is that if you do write about it, please make it a work of fiction. You are better off doing that anyway, otherwise, people will laugh at you and instead of forever being known for your journalism, you'll forever be known as the man who got suckered into believing in time travel."

"That's a reasonable request. One question. If you are breaking a code of ethics by telling me, why tell me?"

"Because it's become a mess. When you showed up and started to tell your story, I was going to ask for your help. But now that Herb is dead, I *need* your help!"

Chapter 16

"This doesn't involve me traveling back in time, does it? Because I'm afraid the answer will be no." I said it jokingly, but there was a part of me that was a little nervous. This couldn't possibly be real, could it? A week ago, if someone had said I'd be talking seriously about time travel, I would have referred them to the local mental health facility.

Jim laughed. "No, of course not. I need your research skills. Your reporting skills. I need to find out what happened to Stan Hooper. Did he end up dying, like his note suggested he would? I must know."

"Why?"

"Because Stan's not supposed to be there. The damage he could do—or already did—could have serious repercussions."

I was already overwhelmed.

"Can you start from the beginning?" I asked.

"Easier said than done, but I'll try."

"Why 'Uncle' Jim?" I asked, veering slightly off-topic.

"Of our group, I was the oldest and the most even-tempered. I just became known as Uncle Jim. Compare that to Alan. You've seen what he's like."

"So he's part of your group?"

"Yes. You didn't see him at his best. He's brilliant and very dedicated."

"How many people in your group … and what kind of group is it?"

"It's a scientific group. There are—were—ten of us. Six travelers and four people doing the research."

"Travelers?"

He smiled. "How about you let me tell you without the questions?"

"Sorry. I'm just having trouble processing all this."

"As you may have deduced, I'm not from this time period. We—the group—are from the year 2105."

He gave me a look.

"You don't seem surprised," he said.

"It's a combination of disbelief and acceptance," I said. "The subject of time travel is mind-boggling, but after seeing the pictures and hearing Stan's girlfriend say that, ten years ago, when she asked Stan if he and Herb were friends, he told her that they *would* be in 95 years. I guess I'm just trying to take it in with as much of an open mind as possible."

"Yes, I heard he had said that," said Jim. "Herb was really angry at him."

He took a sip of tea. I noticed that he was regaining a little color in his cheeks.

"Sixty years from now, the initial testing of time travel began. Yes, I know it sounds strange to be talking about the future in the past tense, but for me, that's what it is. There were a lot of false starts and, sadly, some deaths in the testing process. For twenty-five years following that, a lot of progress was made. Our group came together twenty years after the initial discovery. We made great progress in five years and were ready to make safe tests. Herb was the first one of us to travel. Have you caught the significance of his name?"

"Of course," I said, slapping my forehead and feeling a bit

foolish. "Herb Wells. Herbert George Wells. H.G. Wells. No, I missed it completely."

"Our rule is that you have to devise a name. You can't use your real name. It could come back to haunt you later on."

I didn't understand that, but I let it go.

"We were getting reports from him that things were going well," said Jim.

"Reports?"

"We have certain places around the world where our travelers leave reports. Our co-workers in the 22nd-century check for them regularly. Once the traveler leaves a report, it appears, and someone can then read it."

My head was spinning.

"What happens if you go ahead in time? Into the future?" I asked.

"We can't," answered Jim. "We haven't mastered that yet. At least, we can't go into the far future. We can move around in time prior to when we started the project, but we haven't even found a way back to the original time when we started. We're sure the portal—or gateway—exists, but we just haven't found it yet. Remember, this is a scientific group. For us, time travel is in its infancy. There are still things we are figuring out. We don't have all the answers. That's why we need those reports. They are invaluable to the research."

"How do you go back in time?" I asked. "Like the time machine in the old *Time Machine* movie?"

Jim laughed. "Good movie—and book, by the way—but nothing like how it's done. No, it's nothing mechanical. There are time portals all over the world and in different time periods. You walk through the portal. For example, Hollow Rock. There's a portal in that cave you were in."

"Wait," I said nervously. "Do you mean to tell me that by being in that cave, I might have gone back in time and ended up in

Hollow Rock at the same time as Stan? Did I come close to sending myself back in time?"

"Yes. But I'm familiar with that particular portal and that cave. It's deeper in the cave. It's a bit of a squeeze between two close walls, so the chances that you would have gone through it are slim. However, you can see a larger cavern beyond the squeeze, so if you had been curious to explore that cavern, then yes, you would have ended up back in the 1870s."

"At the same time that Stan arrived?"

"Probably not, but close. All of our research indicates that there seems to be a time frame that people access when they go through the portal—that's part of what we are studying. So if our research is correct, everyone who goes through the portal arrives somewhere in the same period, within eight months to a year, give or take."

I was thinking about what he said and was trying to process it all. Jim could tell and was silent while I thought.

"You said the portals were in different places and different times. What did you mean by that?"

"Let's take the Hollow Rock portal as an example. That particular portal only goes to that specific time. So if you go through it, you will be taken to Hollow Rock around the year 1870."

I started to interrupt, but he held up his hand. "And before you ask, portals are only one-way. You can't enter the same portal in the 1870s and end up in this time period."

"Then how would you get back?"

"It's complicated."

"More complicated than this?" I asked.

He laughed. "I'm afraid so. I said before that we can't go into the future. What I meant by that is that we haven't yet found a portal that takes us even as far as 2105, the year I came from. That's not to say that a portal doesn't exist to do that. We just haven't yet found it. There is a portal in 2105 that takes us back here—well, here about twelve years ago. There are hundreds—if not thousands—of time portals all over the world. From what we've been able to determine, they have a limited time span. They eventually collapse—become inactive. For example, the Hollow Rock portal. We know that it existed back in the 1930s..."

"How do you know?" I interrupted.

"Later," replied Jim. "I'll tell you later. We also know that it's active now—or at least it was ten years ago when Stan went through it. It might have already closed up, or maybe it will in ten or twenty years. They are unstable."

"And if someone wanted to go from Hollow Rock in the 1870s to Hollow Rock in the 2020s?"

"They couldn't. It's one-way and there are no other portals there. They would have to find another portal in another location to do that. Herb Wells found a portal to take him back to 1930s America. He was able to return here around 2010 by accessing a different portal. Actually, I believe it was three—maybe four—different portals."

At my questioning look, he said, "It's like taking three different busses to get where you want to go because there is no direct route. It's kind of—how do you say it here—a crapshoot. There is no guarantee that you'll find a portal that will bring you back where you started."

"How do you find these portals?"

Jim pointed to a metal object on the table. "Could you bring me the device that Alan was going to use to maybe bash in my skull?"

I retrieved it from the table. It was fairly light, thinner at the bottom than at the top, and covered in lights. None of the lights were on. I handed it to Jim.

"This is how we find the portals. It's imaginatively called a Portal Finder."

He frowned.

"And I wish we'd never invented it."

Chapter 17

"I thought this was your life's work," I said.

"Oh, it was exciting, for sure, especially when the NSA discovered our project and offered to fund it. Your two NSA friends don't know it, but their division probably helped spur on some of the future time travel experiments. So in a sense, they are at the forefront of the time travel era. That would certainly confuse them," he added, chuckling.

He stared down at the object, then quickly got serious. "I've come to realize that we're playing with fire and there is absolutely no way we can stop it now. I've put my conclusions in my recent reports. What if, over time, there are more Stan Hoopers? People who go back in time without the training to deal with it. And it's bound to happen. This," he said, holding up the object, "is what we use to locate the portals. This one is dead. I've been trying to fix it for a couple of years, but I just don't have the essential parts that are available in the 22nd century. I've tried everything, but I've finally given up."

"So when you go through time, you carry one of these with you to help you find other portals to take you to other places and other times?"

"Precisely."

"Does it tell you where and when the portal leads?" I asked.

"Yes. It also tells you if the portal can't be accessed. By that I mean if the portal is one-way going the other way. In Hollow Rock in 1870, it can find the portal, but it will also tell whoever has it that it's not usable from there. You can only find the portals that are available in that time period. So if you're trying to get back here and now, you'll have to use the Portal Finder to locate one."

"But there might not be one to take you back," I said. "In which case, you'll have to go to different periods until you find one that takes you home."

"Now you're getting the idea," he said.

"That could take a long time," I said.

"It could and it does. A lot of it is hit or miss. Herb had mastered it. He knew where to go to find portals that would take him where—and when—he needed."

"Are the portals always in hidden spots? I mean, could a portal exist in the middle of a busy road? Could people go through them randomly?" I asked.

"Not that we've ever discovered," answered Jim. "And we don't know why that is. It's part of our research. We think it has something to do with the energy of certain locations. A busy city street might create too much energy. Do they appear on lonely rural roads? Again, not that we've found, so we have to figure out why."

"Okay," I said, "here's the big question: Can you change history? That's always been the big issue in time travel books and movies."

"Of course you can," answered Jim. "But should you? It would be easy to go back and try to prevent a devastating fire from happening, or assassinate a particularly despicable world leader..."

"Like Hitler," I said.

"Exactly. Think of the lives saved by killing him early in his reign. BUT," he said emphatically, "we have no idea how that would affect the future. Would that spawn someone even worse? Would it result in circumstances that would someday precipitate a nuclear war that destroys the planet? You might think you are doing the right thing, but since you can't see the results of your actions, you just don't know."

"And that's why you don't want people going back using their real names?"

"Exactly. For example, Herb has been to more times and locations than any of us. What if he was using his real name and he inadvertently did something to change the course of history? The consequences and confusion that he could ultimately create could be enormous. So we go back with made-up names and stay as anonymous as possible. I knew I was going to stay here, so I did research, obtained a Social Security card, and got a job, all under the made-up name of Jim Lawrence."

"What's your real name?" I asked.

"Can't tell you that. One of our rules in case someone like you discovers us."

"Something I don't understand is how two people, like Natalie O'Brien and Beryl Dixon, could have accidentally sent themselves back. What are the chances of them both finding the portal by mistake?"

"Actually," said Jim, "only one of them was by accident. As good a scientist as Herb was, he was also human, and he let his emotions get in the way. He broke the rules."

"How?"

Jim was quiet for a minute. I think he was trying to decide how much to tell me. He threw his hands up.

"Oh what the hell," he said. "I've come this far with you. I just have to trust you. He fell in love. Herb met Beryl when he went back to the 1930s. He never gave me the full story—except that she was in some kind of trouble. For some reason, he gave Beryl the location of the Hollow Rock portal. By going back after Stan, he probably hooked up with Beryl. Maybe you can find those notebooks and it will tell the story."

"Do you age when you time travel?"

"What do I look like to you?" he asked. He started to laugh, then broke into a fit of coughing. He had a sip of tea and when he calmed down he said, "Yes, you age. It doesn't matter where you are or when you are there. Your body ages in a normal fashion."

"Last question," I said. "At least for now. You said there were six of you who did the traveling. I know of you, Herb, and Alan. Have you ever been in touch with the others?"

"We worked out ways to leave messages for each other—too complicated to explain to you. Sorry, it's not that I consider you stupid or anything. It's just that I'm talking about science from the early 2100s. Anyway, two of them are still traveling. The other one is presumed dead."

"Presumed?"

"We stopped getting communications from her, and we knew that she was having a difficult time, psychologically and emotionally. If I had to guess, she probably committed suicide. She was one of our two women travelers."

He shook his head sadly, then looked me in the eyes and said, "Ray, one of the reasons I consider this a big mistake is the toll it has taken on us all. If I'm right, one committed suicide; Herb was killed if the picture is correct; Alan—as brilliant as he is—is on the verge of cracking up. He's become paranoid about the whole thing. I'm dying, but it's just because my body developed cancer. I can't blame the time travel for that. But who knows? Maybe it's another side effect. So, if I had realized the toll it was going to take on us all, I wouldn't have gotten involved with it. As it is, I've left copious detailed notes about the dangers of time travel and have implored them to shut it down and destroy the equipment. They will find the notes a day or two after I leave, so who knows? Maybe they took my advice. Sadly, they probably didn't."

"So what is it you want me to do?" I asked.

"Find those notebooks," said Jim. "It's imperative that we find them if they still exist. And see if you can find some evidence of Stan's death."

I gave him a questioning look.

"Stan Hooper could be traveling all over the place, creating chaos wherever he goes. I have to know whether Stan Hooper is still alive!"

Chapter 18

When I left Jim's house, it was late. He had offered his couch for the night, but I needed to get away from there and clear my head.

I didn't want to be associated with Jim, as far as the NSA guys were concerned, so I didn't call for a cab. I walked back to the T station. I had to wait a while for a train, but I eventually made it back to my hotel and immediately fell asleep. That night I didn't have my usual nightmare. Instead, I had one where I was lost in time. It might have been scarier than my African dream.

I woke up late. It was almost ten and I was famished. I ordered room service and took a shower while I waited. When my food came, I ate slowly, thinking about everything I had learned at Jim's.

There was no longer any doubt in my mind that all of this was real, and that I wished I'd never found the trunk. My life was a lot simpler before I found it.

I could walk away right now. I was under no obligation to go back to Hollow Rock and find the notebook, assuming it even still existed. I had almost decided to walk away when I thought of Natalie. The video of her was heartbreaking. What if I could unearth some way to get her home? Like what? My emotions had taken over. But suppose I could? What if I could send a message through the time portal? If so, what kind of message? Maybe I was fooling myself. Let's face it. I had a crush on an actress I'd never met, who disappeared about twelve years earlier, and was now stuck in the 1870s. Now, there was a relationship with potential.

I tried to tell myself that it had nothing to do with my admiration for Natalie as an actress and that I would try to help anyone in that situation. Since she happened to be the one in the situation, it was a moot point.

I knew what the answer was going to be. I was now in this too deep. Long repressed reporter tendencies were beginning to come alive.

Like it or not, I was headed back to Hollow Rock.

I looked at my cell phone to see if anything had come in while I was gone. A lot of robocalls, a call from one of the magazine editors I did business with, asking if I wanted to take on a new assignment. The short description almost put me asleep. Hey, compared to the time travel stuff, nothing was ever going to come close again. There was also a call from Mitch Webster asking if I'd had any further contact with Alan Garland. Mitch could wait.

While I was checking my voicemails, my phone rang. I didn't recognize the number, but it was a local area code, so I answered it.

"Hey Ray, it's Hal March."

"Hi, Hal. Thanks for giving me Jim's address. I saw him yesterday."

"How's he doing?"

"He's dying of cancer," I said. "It's sad. He's a nice guy. He sends his regards."

"I'm sorry to hear about his health. I'll reach out to him and see if there's anything I can do. Was he helpful at all?"

Again, how much to tell Hal?

"The phones have ears," I said, "and I have to leave town. When this is all over, we'll sit down, and I'll explain the whole thing to you. It's probably safer right now that you don't know a lot about it. But just for the record, everything I was telling you? It's all real."

Hal gave a little whistle. "It's hard to believe," he said. "At the same time, I very much believe it. However, not telling me is probably a good decision. The reason I was calling was to give you a heads up. I got a call from a friend of yours."

"From a company with three initials?" I asked. "One that you told to go pound sand a long time ago?"

"The same. He wanted to know why you had come to see me and whether you had mentioned the names of Herb Wells and some other guy. I told him to go pound some more sand. They are very interested in what you're doing, so be careful."

"Yeah, not the easiest thing to do," I said. "But I appreciate the heads up."

"My pleasure. I won't ask where you're going, but I have a feeling I know."

"And I think you'd be right. Time for more research."

"Good luck," said Hal. "I'll be interested in hearing the whole story when it's all over."

We hung up and I quickly packed. I went online and found a nonstop from Boston to Flagstaff leaving at two. That gave me plenty of time to get to the airport and make it through security.

Or so I thought.

Chapter 19

I walked out of the hotel, directly into the arms of Mitch Webster standing in front of a waiting car. When I saw him, I put up my hands to ward him off.

"No, I'm not talking to you," I said. "I gave you information about Alan Garland out of the goodness of my heart. Now I have a plane to catch."

"If you cooperate, you can still catch it," said Mitch. "You're heading back to Flagstaff."

He said it as a statement.

"Gee, how could you possibly know that?" I asked, rolling my eyes. "And I *have* cooperated with you. I've told you everything I know."

"No, you haven't."

He guided me by the arm to his car. It was a black Chevy SUV. It looked very official, and the back door was open, waiting for me.

"So I don't have a choice. That's what you're saying?"

"That's what I'm saying."

He waited for me to get into the SUV, sitting in the seat next to me. The vehicle smelled new. I could have objected, or I could have made a wisecrack. I decided to do neither. I stayed silent.

My bald friend, Charles Smith, was driving. He barely

acknowledged me. Nobody said anything as we drove through the Boston streets. I had no idea where they were taking me. We drove around for about ten minutes, then pulled up to the Boston Common and parked in a spot marked *No Parking*. That was weird. My hotel was only a few minutes' walk from Boston Common. Why did we drive around?

"Let's get out," said Mitch. "Get some air."

"We could have done that from the hotel," I said, "and arrived here a lot sooner."

"I have my reasons."

"Let me guess," I said. "Not everyone is as convinced about this as you are, and people are monitoring you just like you're monitoring me. We're walking in the Common to stay away from listening devices. You're the NSA. Who are you afraid of?"

"Nobody," answered Mitch. "But this is too sensitive. Absolutely nobody can know about it. Even people within the NSA."

"You think I know about it and you're afraid I'll tell people all about it."

"No. We want to know what you know," he said.

"Precious little," I lied. "I'll admit that there's something suspicious about all this. You think it has something to do with time travel. I think that's quite a reach. But I agree that something is off-kilter here."

"Where were you last night?" asked Mitch, ignoring my time travel comment. But I could tell that it hit home with him.

"In my hotel. I wasn't feeling well."

"We think you weren't in your hotel. Who did you go and visit?"

"I didn't go anywhere. I wasn't feeling well," I said, "so I decided to do some research from the hotel. Like I already told you, I'm writing a story about Stan Hooper. Herb Wells's name has come up—first by you, then by Stan's ex-girlfriend. I've checked. Herb Wells doesn't exist. When Stan went missing, this mysterious Herb Wells did too. And yet, no one looked for him. It's because he didn't officially exist. Why? And something else. Alan Garland doesn't exist."

I wasn't sure if that was true about Garland, but it made sense that he'd be in the same boat as Herb. "You have two people who are physically alive, but for whom no records exist. Could that indicate time travel? Maybe. It could also indicate several options, the obvious being that they are in the country illegally. I'm doing as much research into Herb Wells as I can, but I keep running into dead ends. So now I'm going back to Flagstaff to see what I can find."

I wasn't sure he believed me, but it was the story I was going with.

"Mitch," I added, "I'm good at research. I might be able to dig up some things for you. But I can't if you're not going to give me anything to work with."

Mitch thought for a moment as we walked. Had I convinced him that I didn't know as much as I actually did?

He finally said, "We contacted Stan Hooper and asked for his help. We were pretty sure he would help us."

"Meaning of course," I said, "that you had done your research and knew he could be paid off. Was he expensive?"

Mitch smiled. "He didn't cost as much as you'd think. We could have gone higher. Anyway, we came across Herb Wells and Alan Garland, and knew that Herb had ties to Stan and the magazine Stan worked for."

"You didn't just 'come across' Herb and Alan," I said. "Someone had to tell you about them."

Mitch considered it for a minute, then said, "A man named Hawkins. Max Hawkins."

I felt a shiver.

"Hawkins showed up on our radar courtesy of the FBI. He

had tried to contract with an undercover FBI agent to have Wells and Garland killed. The FBI could find nothing to suggest Hawkins even existed, so they bumped him up to us here in the 'Unexplained Phenomena' division. We worked on him for many days until he finally told us a strange story of time travel. Of course, we didn't believe him at first, but as he went into more detail, it had a ring of truth. We knew he was holding back a lot more information, but we couldn't get much more out of him than that. He mentioned Hollow Rock, and that it held some importance. We had to make some deals with him to even get that much. To make a long story short, we gave him a little rope and he slipped out. He did tell us where Wells hung out, and by putting two and two together, we made the decision to contact Hooper. He took our money, was in contact with us for a few days, then he disappeared. We were never able to talk to Wells before he disappeared. So, with Hooper, Hawkins, and Wells all gone, Alan Garland is our only hope of getting the rest of the story."

"I wouldn't count on him, based on the few minutes we talked," I said. "He was fanatical about whatever he was trying to scare me away from. And now I know. It was this time travel crap."

"You don't believe it?"

"Of course not," I replied. "Don't tell me you do?" I was trying to be convincing.

"It's just our job to investigate," he said noncommittally.

I was anxious to leave him. I had to ask Jim a question.

"So what did Stan tell you?" I asked.

"He didn't know about Garland, but he had already talked to Wells and insisted to me that the time travel stuff is real."

It was interesting that Uncle Jim's name hadn't come up. He was a nice guy. Did he have such an effect on people that they didn't want to get him in trouble?

"While I'm researching the Stan Hooper story, I will continue to try to locate either Wells or Garland. And if you find something else about Hollow Rock, let me know and I will investigate it. Suppose I do locate Wells and Garland, and you haul them in," I asked, "what exactly do you want from them, instructions on how to build a time machine?"

I was waiting for the lie and I wasn't disappointed when it came.

He gave me a condescending smile. "No," he said. "one or more of them is in possession of an object—a very dangerous object—and we need it. Hawkins mentioned it."

"What kind of dangerous object?" I asked.

"Let's just say that it could destroy life as we know it."

What a liar he was. There was no doubt about what he was looking for.

He wanted the Portal Finder.

Chapter 20

Mitch offered to drop me off at Logan so I wouldn't miss my plane, and I took him up on it. What he didn't know was that I had no intention of catching that flight. I had something to do first.

I turned my phone off. I had read that the NSA could track your phone even if it was turned off, but I decided to take the chance that at the local level, Mitch wouldn't be able to. If they'd had lockers at Logan, I would have just stashed it in there, but in this new, dangerous world, they had done away with them.

I changed my ticket for a later flight to Flagstaff. The only one I could find had me going through Chicago. I didn't care. I had a question to ask and I needed to ask it now—and in person.

An hour later, I walked up to Uncle Jim's front door, having once again taken the T to his house. He buzzed me in, showing surprise that I had returned.

"I'm sorry to bother you," I said.

"Not at all," answered Jim. "Come in. Alan is still asleep."

"That's good," I said. "I don't care much for him."

I pulled out my computer and opened Stan's pictures.

"I just spent an hour with my NSA friends. They asked all kinds of questions about Herb and Alan. They don't seem to know about you."

"Yes, everyone was willing to keep me out of it."

"They did it well. The NSA has no clue. I did find out what they are looking for. It seems Stan was informing on Herb Wells for them."

Jim made a face. "I'm not surprised. I never liked Stan."

"They paid him for information. He must have liked you though. He didn't tell them about you. What they are looking for is a Portal Finder. But that's not why I'm here."

I opened the pictures to one of Marshal Hawkins and showed it to Jim.

"Does he look familiar?"

"Max! That's Max Hawkins. How the hell did he get there?"

"The NSA guy, Mitch, told me that they were tipped off to Herb and Alan by someone named Max Hawkins, who told them stories of time travel. I remembered seeing a picture of someone the newspaper referred to as Marshal Hawkins. Before leaving for Flagstaff, I had to see you to find out if my suspicion was correct."

Jim was shaking his head. He looked at me with a pained expression. "Why would Max have told them anything? He was as dedicated to this as anyone."

"Mitch said they had him in for questioning for several days. Maybe he just couldn't take it any longer. He said they gave him a little freedom and he gave them the slip."

"He never stopped in here," said Jim. "Everyone knew where I was." He rubbed his chin in thought. "Did he know about Stan?"

"I don't think so. They said they located Stan after learning about Herb. Stan seems to have thrown a monkey wrench into everything," I said. "And here's a disturbing piece of information. The reason the NSA had him was that he tried to contract with someone to have Herb and Alan killed. The FBI picked him up."

"I can't believe that. Why would he do that?"

When I didn't answer, he changed the subject.

"When I told you that Stan using the portal could have

devastating consequences, I meant it," he said. "If I had to guess, I'd say that Herb went after Stan right away. Maybe Max did too. I don't know."

"Which now makes Hollow Rock a very busy place," I said. "Why the Hollow Rock portal?" I asked.

"It's the closest one," answered Jim. "Some time periods and places have a lot of portals. Not here at this particular time. There are a few in Europe, Africa, and Australia, but the only outgoing portal here in the U.S. is in Hollow Rock. We have a few incoming portals—one here in Boston, to be exact—but Hollow Rock is the closest outgoing portal."

"So, Beryl arrived in Hollow Rock, followed by Natalie, then Stan, Herb, and Max. Do I have that straight?" I asked.

"Actually, no, not necessarily" answered Jim. "Remember, a portal delivers you to a specific period but in a less specific time frame. The window can be up to several months. So there is no way of knowing which one of them got there first. If Max was the town marshal, it could be that he got there first. There's no way of knowing."

"Is it easier to blend in the further back in time you go?" I asked. "Nowadays, you need so much identification."

"Yes, it is easier, but not too far back in time. The easiest period is from the late 1800s to about the mid-1900s. It's fairly simple to stay anonymous. If you go back much earlier than the late 1800s, you run across speech and language issues. You begin to stand out from the crowd."

"Thank you again for your help," I said. "I'll see what I can find out—if anything. Watch yourself. The NSA wants one of those Portal Finders, and I don't know how far they'll go to get it."

"Thank you. I'm not worried. Mine is dead, never to come back to life. Alan has his hidden someplace safe. Max probably still has his, and he may be somewhere else in time now. If Herb is dead, as the picture indicates, Stan probably stole his. Who knows where it—or Stan—could be. That's the one that I'd be concerned about."

I thanked him, and when I was turning to walk away, Jim grabbed my arm.

"Ray, be careful. Alan is a fanatic about keeping this secret. He may come after you. He doesn't know how much you know. With the whole Stan Hooper state of affairs, he's getting desperate to keep it all hidden."

He lowered his voice to a whisper.

"Your life might be in danger."

Chapter 21

As I walked to the T station, I thought about what Jim said. Of course, my life was in danger. I wasn't overly worried about Alan, but then, you never know how far someone will go if they are fanatical enough. I was more worried about the NSA. They would go to great lengths to get their hands on a Portal Finder. If I was in the way, they wouldn't hesitate to squash me.

I arrived at the airport in plenty of time to eat something before catching my flight. It was going to be a long day of flying. The restaurant wasn't crowded, so I asked for a corner booth. I knew I shouldn't do what I was about to do, but I couldn't help myself. While I waited for my food, I opened my laptop, made sure my Wi-Fi was still off, and hooked up my headphones. I inserted one of the memory cards and scrolled through the Hollow Rock pictures until I found the video with Natalie O'Brien. I played it.

"Would you like to say something for the people back in the 21st century?" said Stan. Natalie's sad expression was breaking my heart. *"I know you're wondering what happened to me. I am too. Please tell my family that I love them."*

I played it again … and again. I didn't notice when the waitress brought my food. She touched my shoulder and I jumped.

"I'm sorry, sir," she said. "Here's your food. Hey, is that the missing actress, Natalie O'Brien? Wow, I've never seen that video. What's she saying?"

Shit! I had turned my laptop enough that she was able to see what was on the screen when she tapped my shoulder.

"Uh, just something personal. A friend of mine was good friends with her, and she had recorded a video for him many years ago."

"I'm sorry. I didn't mean to see it."

"That's okay," I said, giving her a big smile to let her know that I wasn't mad. "My friend died recently, and this was in his belongings. It's very personal."

"I'm sorry about your friend," said the waitress. "And I'm so sorry about Natalie. I wonder if we'll ever know what happened."

She moved off to another table.

I had to be a lot more careful. I was starting to understand what Jim meant about the danger of going back in time if you weren't trained. Even looking at the video could have been dangerous if it had been a different person who saw it. Luckily, the waitress seemed innocent.

The plane was only a half-hour late by the time we took off, and I settled back in my seat. I pulled out the copies I made of the Hollow Rock newspaper. I'd go through them word for word. Maybe a clue to Stan's supposed demise would be revealed. But it wasn't just Stan I was interested in, was it? No, it was Natalie. What a horrible experience it must be for her to be stuck in a place and time so foreign. I tried to get her out of my head while I looked through the newspapers.

Beryl wrote most of the articles. Marshal Hawkins was mentioned quite a few times—pretty mundane stuff though—but there was never a mention of Stan or Herb—except for Herb's death—and only that short piece on Natalie doing shows. And what about Natalie's boyfriend? The one who disappeared with her? What was his story? Did they break up? Was he killed? I ran across a story of someone finding the bones of a dead guy about a mile outside of town. He'd been bushwhacked and robbed. Animals had gotten to him, making him virtually unrecognizable. Could it have been Randy?

I woke up with a start. I must have fallen asleep. I furtively looked around to see if anyone was looking at me. No one was. Whew. I hadn't yelled out. But I wasn't having my usual nightmare. I had been dreaming about Natalie. What if I could get a message to her? I could throw something into the portal. I could at least make her aware that someone knows where she is.

Would that be stupid? And would it break the rules of time travel? Hey, I didn't make the rules. All of a sudden, I knew I had to get a message to her. Did she ever go back to the cave? If I threw a bottle with a note into the portal, would she get it? *A bottle with a note?* I couldn't do better than that? I'd have to think about it.

When I finally arrived in Flagstaff, it was mid-evening. I rented a car and drove to the same hotel I'd stayed at earlier. I locked my laptop and luggage in the room and went for some takeout. I brought it back to my room and began to think about a plan. I had to find Stan's notebooks. Did they still exist? And I had to get a message to Natalie. I had decided that I was going to do it. Who cares what the rules of time travel say? I started a note to her:

Hi Natalie. My name is Ray Burton. I come from the time period you left. In my world, you've been missing for 12 years. I ran across a trunk left by Stan. Maybe you'll get this before he even leaves the trunk. Time travel is confusing, to say the least.

I've run across friends of Herb Wells and Max Hawkins. One of the friends explained things as well as he could, but it's still a bit overwhelming. What I do know is that there might be a way to get home. It involves using the Portal Finder and coming back in a roundabout way: going to one time period, which brings you to another, and so on. I don't know if Herb or Max would share that information with you.

I will keep trying to find a way to get you home, but I can't guarantee success.

Try to hang in there.

Yours,

Ray

Chapter 22

I slept well that night. It was either the fact that it had been an exhausting day, or that I had made the decision about contacting Natalie.

I quickly showered and dressed, then picked up a fast-food breakfast. I stopped at a Home Depot and bought a heavy-duty bright red plastic container. In it, I put my note, a picture of myself—just so she knew who was trying to help her—and some copies of articles I'd written. I wanted her to know that the person behind the message was someone she could trust. I wrote her name on the top with a black Sharpie, then I headed for Hollow Rock. I parked in the same place I had parked before and walked the half-mile to the town.

As I stood on a hill overlooking the ghost town, I suddenly had a sinking feeling in the pit of my stomach. I was never going to find the notebooks. This was stupid. If Herb had stolen them and hidden them someplace in town, they would be gone—wiped off the earth with the rest of the town.

Recognizing the futility of searching the town, I made my way over to the cave. I stood outside the entrance and threw in some rocks in case something had moved in while I was gone. It was quiet, so I ducked into the darkness. I turned on my flashlight—a real flashlight this time—and took a frantic look around, just in case an animal had ignored the announcement that I was coming in. The cave was empty, except for a couple of old empty cans I hadn't seen the first time. I could read the word "smoke" on one of them. A smoke bomb. Maybe to clear the cave of varmints? Had it been used by Stan, Herb, or Max all those years ago?

I went over to where I had found the trunk. Jim was right. To the left of the trunk, in the area I hadn't investigated, was a thin opening. If I squeezed, I could make it through to the room on the other side. There was no way I was going to do that. I wasn't ready to make such a life-changing one-way trip.

Instead, I knelt and slid the plastic box through the opening and across the smooth floor. Suddenly, it was gone. It had disappeared. It wasn't like it evaporated in a flash of light or anything. It was so natural I didn't even see it disappear. Like throwing it into a fog bank, except that there was no fog.

I looked around the cave some more, but there was nothing there. Other than to deliver a letter to Natalie that I wasn't even sure she would see, it had been a wasted trip. Thanks to Herb, Stan's notebooks no longer existed.

I went back to the hotel in a funk. I was at a total loss. I had come out here hoping I could find a clue to the whereabouts of the notebooks, but other than indulging in a teenage type of crush, I had accomplished nothing.

I still had some of the afternoon left, so I made my way to the library to read more copies of the *Hollow Rock Gazette*. I spent a couple of hours reading through them and found a few interesting tidbits, but nothing that helped me at all.

I learned that Beryl's articles ended suddenly with the issue that Stan left in the trunk. There was no mention of her after that. Marshal Hawkins left around the same time and just dropped out of sight. The newspaper didn't offer an explanation. Much later, there was a story about the closing of the mine and the residents escaping the dying town. Finally, there was a one-page edition announcing the closing of the newspaper.

So, what had happened to Beryl and Max? And to Stan? Had he really died, as his note suggested? More importantly, what had happened to Natalie?

I arrived back at the hotel with some Chinese food. I took a shower and sat down to eat, opening my laptop to get the news of the day. I was feeling down, and I wasn't sure why. Was it because I felt bad about Natalie? Was it because I really wanted to read those notebooks? Was it because I had started something that now I couldn't finish? Yes, to all of them.

I drifted away from the news and opened the pictures again. I looked at a lot of them without really seeing. Then I came to Natalie's video and watched it three or four times. I was wallowing in my self-pity. I was about to close the laptop when something caught my attention. There was another video after Natalie's. It couldn't be. There were only a few short videos. I had looked through the pictures enough times to know that.

With hands shaking, I clicked onto it.

It was Natalie. She was all alone. The camera wasn't moving as it would if it were being held. She had put it on a rock or a tree branch. She had a coat on, and it looked cold outside.

"Hi, Ray." She was talking to me!

"I got your note. Thank you! I was going to get the camera from the trunk Stan left, and I saw the red container. I'm so glad you know where I am. I can't imagine though that you will ever be able to rescue me from this God-awful place. Just the fact that someone knows where I am gives me a good feeling. Stan is gone, as are Beryl—she died—and Herb. If you've seen the pictures, you know what happened to Herb. Even Max Hawkins is gone. I'm the only one left here who knows what life is like beyond Hollow Rock and the 1870s."

There was a tear rolling down her cheek.

"I am so lonely. I've thought about suicide, but I don't think I can *do that. The battery of this camera is almost dead, so I have to say this quickly. Stan made notes about life here. It gives the whole story up until the last couple of weeks, which I filled in. You should probably read them. Also, Beryl wrote a book while she was here. If you can get it published, I know it would've meant a lot to her. I've put them in the cave. Maybe you've already found them. There's a small shelf of rock above Stan's trunk. I put them there for you. I always knew where Herb had hidden the notebooks when he stole them from Stan. Also, I put...*

The battery must have died at that point.

I had to go back to the cave.

Chapter 23

It was too late to go tonight. I'd have to wait until morning. It was going to be a long night. However, it wasn't too late to hit up a phone store. There was one nearby, so I hid my computer, locked up the room, and headed out. An hour later, I was making a call on my new prepaid phone. I was sick of worrying about the NSA listening in. This seemed to be a good decision.

Jim answered on the third ring.

"Hello?" He said it tentatively.

"Hi, Jim. It's Ray."

"Oh, hi Ray."

"I picked up a prepaid phone so I can't be traced. Is everything okay at your end?"

He caught on to the question immediately.

"Yes. All clear here. Alan finally woke up. He was beyond angry with me that I talked to you, but I don't care. I didn't tell him how much I revealed though. There was no reason to bash my head in since the damage was already done, so he left. I have no idea where he went, and I don't care. I haven't heard from your friends, so I think I'm still an unknown quantity to them. It doesn't matter. I think I'm reaching the end."

I had noticed that his breathing seemed heavier.

"You don't sound good," I said. "I only saw you a couple of

days ago. You were sick, but you didn't seem this bad."

"I have a few good moments, but the end is near. I've destroyed the Portal Finder I had. Even though it wasn't working, I didn't want it to fall in the wrong hands. Alan agreed with me on that point anyway. How's your progress?"

Tell him or don't tell him about contacting Natalie? I'm sure he wouldn't be happy with me for doing it, but I kind of needed to tell him that aspect to tell him the rest.

"I'll know tomorrow," I said. "I went there today but couldn't find any notebooks. However, I made a decision. I sent Natalie O'Brien a note through the portal."

I could hear a gasp on the other end.

"I figured you wouldn't be happy, but hear me out. After sending her the message through the portal, I arrived back at the hotel to find that another video had been added to the collection. It was from Natalie. I know it goes against all the rules, but then, she wasn't breaking any rules when she accidentally went through the portal, so it wasn't her fault."

Jim was silent. Maybe he just no longer cared about the rules.

I told him what she said about the others. He didn't respond.

"You still there?" I asked.

"I am. I'm just waiting for the punch line. I know you're ending with something big."

"How do you know that?" I asked.

"I've read your work. You know how to tell a story."

"You're right about the punch line," I said. "But I'll find out tomorrow if there is one. She said she knew where Stan's notebooks were and said she'd leave them for me on a rock shelf above where I found Stan's trunk. In her world, Stan's trunk is still there, where Stan left it. If this video appeared after I sent the note, then I have faith that the notebooks will be there tomorrow."

"Maybe, but don't get your hopes up," said Jim. "Time is a strange thing. It can play a lot of tricks on you."

"Well, I'll let you know tomorrow," I said.

"If I'm still here."

"Don't talk like that. You will be."

"We'll see. Do let me know if there's anything of interest in them, but to be perfectly honest, the closer I get to death, the less I care."

We hung up soon after that and it suddenly occurred to me that with the passing of Jim, I would be all alone with the knowledge. Technically, Alan was still out there somewhere, but he wasn't exactly someone I could go to for help. For the first time in this adventure, I was scared. I think I was mostly scared of the awesome responsibility I was going to have if I found those notebooks. Did I want to take that on? It was a little late to be asking that question.

As expected, I didn't get one wink of sleep. I *did* watch Natalie's video about thirty times, however. When the sun rose, I was out the door. I didn't even stop for something to eat. I had snacked on leftover Chinese food all night.

I parked in my usual spot near Hollow Rock and made my way to the cave in record time. It was cold in the desert at that time of the morning and I hadn't brought a jacket, so I was pretty chilled by the time I arrived at the cave. I rubbed myself to get warm. It didn't help much.

I did my usual routine of warning anything that might be waiting for me in the cave but got no response, so I entered. I rounded the small bend to the wall where I had found the trunk.

On the rock shelf above the now-empty space was a package!

It had the name "Ray Burton" written on it in large letters. I grabbed it. It was heavier than I thought it would be. Then I looked around to make sure Natalie hadn't left something else. The package was it.

I headed out the cave entrance and almost ran the half-mile to my car, paranoia attacking me from all directions. However, I needn't have worried. I made it back to the hotel in one piece.

Once I had calmed down, I carefully opened the package. It had been sitting there for about 150 years, but it was in surprisingly good condition. Natalie had packed it well. The papers were covered in cloth, which was covered by a rain slicker. On top of the rain slicker was something else. I knew exactly what it was. I had already seen one. It was a Portal Finder!

Since I didn't know what to do with it, I set it aside. Could I get Jim to tell me how it works? Before he died, of course.

I peeled away the rain slicker, then the cloth, revealing a batch of papers on top of two full notebooks. With the papers was a note:

Thank you, Ray, for caring! She followed that with a drawn heart. I felt a lump form in my throat. *On top of the notebooks is the book Beryl wrote. She wrote it while she worked at the newspaper office. It's typewritten and she signed it to validate its authenticity. You can just tell people you found it in a trunk in an attic or something. I guess her fans will be thrilled to see it.*

As for Stan's notes: It's all pretty accurate. Truth be told, I never really liked Stan, but he was my link to the 21st century. He liked to think that we had something going, but we didn't. Otherwise, he tells a good story—and all of it true. I made notes in the margins for things that needed clarifying, and I added a little bit at the end.

The other item is the Portal Finder you mentioned. You were right, Herb and Max wouldn't tell me how to use it. Don't send it back through with instructions for me if you do figure out how to use it. It might appear before all this and Max or Herb might destroy it. I stole it from Herb after he died.

Ray, I don't hold out a lot of hope of being rescued from here, but if you do come across a way to get me home, I would be forever in your debt. Much love, Natalie.

Holy cow. This was just all too much.

I put aside Beryl's manuscript—I'd look at it later—and

opened the first of Stan's notebooks. There was an inserted piece of paper at the very front. It read:

To whoever finds these notebooks, as hard to believe as it might be, every word is true. My name is Stan Hooper. The year is 1870. I was born in 1970. In 2011, I entered a time portal and was transported here. While here, I found four other people who had been transported here (one I had known back in 2011). Not all of them were forthcoming with information, but I was able to piece together facts that weren't given to me directly. Some of us wanted to be here and some didn't, and we all arrived for a variety of reasons.

These are our stories…

PART TWO

Chapter 24

STAN HOOPER
BOSTON, MA—2011

It was a cold night, the perfect night to be in a warm bar, surrounded by lots of people he didn't know. He preferred people he didn't know. They couldn't complain about his laziness at work, his piss-poor job at being a boyfriend, his money problems, or his adolescent desire to run away from it all. January in Boston sucked. There wasn't any other way to describe it. The holidays were over—not that Stan ever put much attention on the holidays—and it was just frigging cold. And dark. It always seemed to be dark.

He was on his third beer, the third of what he predicted would be many. He was in the doghouse with Lynn ... again. He hadn't produced his share of the rent—for the third month in a row—and she was pretty angry at him. This relationship was going the same way all his others had. Too bad. He really liked Lynn. Why was he such a loser?

"You look like how I feel."

Stan turned to the man sitting next to him. It was Herb Wells. He was a friend of Stan's coworker, Jim—affectionately called Uncle Jim by everyone. Herb was often seen around the office talking to Jim. Although Stan hadn't talked much to Herb, he was aware that the man knew a lot about antiques. Hal March liked it when Herb visited, as the man often made suggestions for articles. But there was something about him that was "different," but he couldn't put his finger on it. For that matter, Jim shared some of Herb's "different" qualities.

"Sorry?" he asked.

"You look like how I'm feeling. Things kinda gack, don't they?"

"Gack?"

"Sorry. Suck. Things kinda suck."

"Yeah, you could say that," said Stan. He saw that the man's beer glass was empty. "Buy you another?"

"Thanks. I appreciate it."

Stan motioned the bartender for two more.

They drank in silence for a while, then the man said, "Herb. Herb Wells. We haven't really met. I'm a friend of Jim's." He awkwardly held out his hand to shake. His palm was facing the floor.

"It's about time we officially meet," said Stan. "Stan Hooper." He grabbed the man's hand and turned it the right way. "You don't seem to be from around here."

"Is it obvious?"

Stan suddenly realized that Herb was quite drunk. Holding his own for the most part, but pretty wasted.

"The way you held out your hand to shake," said Stan. "I've never seen that before. And the word 'gack.' Where are you from?"

"Awe, you'd never believe me."

"Try me."

Herb swayed a bit as he moved closer to Stan until their heads were almost touching. Stan's hunch was right. The man had had a lot to drink already. A lot! If Stan lit a match, the man's head would go up in flames.

Herb's voice dropped to a drunken whisper. "From the future."

"Well, it was nice talking to you," said Stan, turning away.

"You don't believe me," said Herb.

"Of course I believe you. I meet people every day from the future. They're all drunk, of course. And so am I."

"I'm not supposed to tell anyone," said Herb. "Sometimes it just gets lonely being so far from home. Don't tell Jim. He wouldn't be happy."

"Is Jim from the future too?"

Herb put his finger to his mouth. "Shhh."

"You say you are far from home. Where is home?" asked Stan. He would put up with Herb for another couple of minutes before making his escape.

"Boston."

"Well then, you're not far from home, are you?"

"Boston from 21 ... 05," he said, burping in between the numbers.

"The year 2105?" asked Stan.

"The same."

"Uh-huh. Okay, I'll bite. And what are you doing here and now?"

"I've been traveling. I'm tired of it. I'm trying to find my way home ... to my own time."

"And where have you been traveling?"

"Mostly Europe and the U.S.," said Herb. "At different time periods, of course."

"Of course."

"Wanna see proof? I've got some right here."

He dug into his pockets and came out with some change. He squinted at it, then pulled out a quarter and handed it to Stan.

"A quarter, from 1928."

"Anyone can buy a quarter from 1928," said Stan. "You might even find one in your change."

"I bet you've never seen this," said Herb. Stan had a feeling he was going to have to catch him when he fell in about a minute.

Herb pulled out an oblong coin and handed it to Stan. It said 4.00 on the back and had a picture of a building he had never seen. He turned it over. The date on the front read 2103.

"What is this?" asked Stan.

"A four-dollar coin. I keep it with me as a good-luck piece. You believe me now?"

"No. You could have had that made."

"No. It's real." Suddenly, a shocked expression came over Herb's face. "I've gotta go. I've said too much."

Stan felt a little sorry for the man. He was about his own age—forty—but he had a better physique than Stan, who had started to fatten out from a bad diet, too much alcohol, and not enough exercise. As opposed to Stan's mop of black hair, Herb had longish thinning light brown hair that hadn't seen barber scissors in a long time.

"You're not going to make it home," said Stan. "Let me drive you."

"I only live a couple of blocks away," said Herb, slurring "couple of blocks."

"Then I'll walk you home."

Herb stared at him for a moment, then said, "Thanks."

Stan took his arm and guided him out of the bar. It was more like three blocks, and by the time they arrived, Stan was exhausted. Between the cold, the alcohol, and Herb's increasingly dead weight, Stan was happy it wasn't any farther. Unfortunately, Herb lived on the third floor. He helped Herb up the stairs, then took Herb's keys from him, unlocked his door, and helped him into the apartment. He carried Herb down the hall to his bedroom and let him fall on the bed.

"Thank you," said Herb. He seemed a little more awake. Probably from the cold air. "You need a place to dish tonight?"

"Dish?"

"Uh, crash. I think that's how you say it, right? When I'm drunk, words from my own time tend to creep out."

"Ohhhkay." Stan rolled his eyes. This was too much. He looked at his watch. It was 1:30. Lynn would be even more pissed than normal if he showed up drunk in the middle of the night. "I'll take you up on that if you don't mind. I can take the couch."

"Good." And Herb was asleep a moment later.

Stan made his way to the living room. The house was pretty sparse, but a bookshelf against the far wall had a few books and numerous other items. Most of the other objects were antiques. They were all small, but Stan recognized some of them as being very old. Most were in surprisingly beautiful condition. Working at *Antiques Etc.,* Stan was familiar with valuable items versus pieces of junk. These were the real things. There were also some items he didn't recognize: a watch that seemed overly complex and a few other shiny objects. Next to the bookcase was a table on which sat a box. In the box was a gadget about the size of a medium-sized flower vase. It was covered in lights and switches.

What the hell could that be? He thought.

On a table next to the couch was a framed photo of a pretty woman who looked vaguely familiar. She was wearing clothes from a different era—the 1920s? 1930s?—and the photo was from that time. Stan had seen enough old photos at the magazine to know that this one was real, and from that time period. However, despite its age, it was in beautiful condition. The inscription read: *To my beloved Herb. Until we meet again. Love, Beryl.*

Holy crap! That was Beryl Dixon! He'd know that face anywhere. But it couldn't be … could it?

He was too drunk to think about it right now, so he laid down on the couch and fell asleep.

He was awakened by someone shaking him. Light was pouring through the window.

"You can't be here!" It was Herb, and he had a frantic look on his face.

It took Stan a minute, but then clarity returned. He looked up at the items on the bookcase, then over at the box on the table, then over at the picture on the table. The picture was gone. Herb had taken it away.

A realization dawned on him.

"You really are from the future, aren't you?"

Chapter 25

Herb's mouth dropped open.

"What do you mean?"

"Everything you were telling me last night. It's all true."

"What did I tell you?" Herb said slowly.

Stan relayed the gist of the conversation, then added, "Before I went to sleep, I looked around. You have some very new-looking antiques. Hard to find them in that condition. Then you have some items that don't belong in this world. And that thing," he said, pointing to the object in the box, "certainly doesn't belong here. Then, of course, there's the now missing photo of Beryl Dixon."

Herb looked down at the floor. When he looked up, Stan noticed that his eyes were swollen. Was Herb about to cry?

"I knew I said too much, but I didn't know how much. What I told you last night was something I had sworn never to reveal. I have to ask you not to say anything to anyone."

"It's just between you and me," said Stan. "So what are you, some kind of scientist? And is Jim part of this?"

"Oh shit. Jim. He's going to kill me."

"Don't worry about it," said Stan. "I have your back. So, are you a scientist?"

"That's exactly what I am," answered Herb with a sigh.

"There's a team of us—but only six who actually do the traveling. And yes, Jim is one of us." He proceeded to tell Stan a story about time portals, leaving notes for each other, and some of the technicalities involved in time travel. When he was done, Stan found himself believing him, despite it being an unbelievable subject.

"If you are sworn to secrecy," said Stan, "why are you telling me?"

"I've been traveling for about ten years, although," he said wryly, "it's sometimes hard to keep it all straight. That watch on the shelf over there keeps the time, so I accurately know how long I've been gone from home." It was the futuristic item that Stan had seen the night before. "It's a lonely life," continued Herb, "and you have to pretend to be someone you're not. You also have to learn the speech of the time—and learn it quickly."

"Your use of the words 'gack' and 'dish,' and turning your hand the wrong way to shake hands?"

"Exactly. Hey, where I'm from, that's how we shake hands. You see what I mean. There have been a few times when I just didn't fit in. I had to leave that time period quickly. Getting back to your question, it gets very lonely. You just want to tell someone. You, being only ninety-five years or so from when I left, can accept it better. Imagine me trying to tell a mine worker in Britain 200 years ago. Do you think he could understand something like this? Not at all. And," Herb added, "the alcohol last night didn't help."

"Have you ever told anyone else?" asked Stan.

"Only one other person. I fell in love. Things got a bit dicey and I had to leave, but I'm hoping to see her again."

"The famous Beryl Dixon? The one who disappeared?"

"Ugh. Yes. Please, I implore you, forget that name and forget you ever saw that picture. Just having you mention it to someone could change history. Please?"

"I'll forget it if you answer this question: You'd go back there, even with it being dicey?"

"No. Someplace else. I told her how to get there if she needed to escape her situation. I'll probably go there at some point to see if she chose to go."

"I promise not to tell anyone what you've told me, as long as you tell me more."

They talked for a couple of hours, Herb telling Stan stories of his travels and explaining how time portals worked. Being a Saturday, Stan didn't have to go to work. So he texted Lynn to tell her that he spent the night on a friend's couch and that he'd be home later. She didn't respond.

"How do you know where to find the time portals?" asked Stan.

"This," said Herb, holding up the object in the box. "It's a Portal Finder. It can find all the portals that work during your time period. Portals only work one-way. For example, there is a portal out west that can lead to the year 1870, give or take a few months. That portal exists for anyone to find after 1870—well, a few years after. You probably can't go through it in 1871 and go back to 1870. Maybe you can in 1880. We haven't quite figured out the time frame yet. You can enter it to take you back to that time. In 1870, there will be another one—I say one, but it's really dozens—to take you to another time. Some go backward in time and some go forward. Most seem to have a limit of a couple of hundred years. I would never find one to take me back a thousand years or forward a thousand years. We don't know why that is. Probably just as well that we can't. The Portal Finder will help you find the right portal to take you where you want to go. Sometimes you have to go to different time periods before you can find what you need. I haven't yet found the right portal that will take me home. I might never find it."

It was a lot of information, and Stan was drifting in and out as

Herb talked. Mostly, he was thinking about the money he could make going back in time and bringing items back that would sell for a fortune. He tuned back in and when he'd absorbed enough of Herb's story, he asked, "So, what now? Are you going to stick around here?"

"No, it's time to go. I've been here too long already. I'll stay another couple of weeks, and then I'll go."

"Where?"

"To see if I can find my love. To see if she made it."

"Made it where?" asked Stan.

Herb looked at Stan with a sad expression.

"Hollow Rock, Arizona."

Chapter 26

"Hollow Rock, Arizona?" asked Stan.

"It's a ghost town now," said Herb, "but for a while back in the late 1800s, it was a thriving community. I researched it."

Stan scratched his head. "So how does it work? You just go there and hope you find the portal?"

"No. The Portal Finder will give you a general idea of where it is, but the closer you get, the more you can pinpoint its location. In the case of this portal, it's in the back of a cave above the town."

"I thought you said you have to get closer to get specifics."

"I did. It was back in the 1930s. When I fell in love with Beryl. I was with her in L.A. for a few weeks. The Hollow Rock portal existed then. She was having some problems, so I took a trip out to Hollow Rock and, using the Finder, located the entrance to the portal. I went back and told her where it was, in case she had to escape her troubles. There was a chance she was going to go through it, so I went out there a few weeks ago intending to access the portal." He stopped and looked at the floor.

"What happened?" asked Stan.

"I chickened out. It's the first time it's ever happened. It just shows that I'm burned out. I could go back to the 1870s, but what happens if she's not there? I'll then have to look for another portal, one that will get me home. There's no way to know until you are in that time period."

"And if you did go back there?"

"From everything I've read, travel from place to place in the west wasn't the easiest thing back in the 1800s. What if I get there and she's not there? I could wait a while to see if she suddenly shows up—since the portal can deposit you anywhere within a few months—or I could check the Finder to see if there's a portal that might get me home. If there is, how am I going to get there? Stagecoach? Wagon train? And what if the next portal is in another country? There was a time when that wouldn't bother me. I would just keep on going until I found a portal that appealed to me."

Herb trailed off. He was done talking, so Stan suggested they go to a local diner for breakfast. He then convinced Herb to come home with him. He had an ulterior motive for that suggestion. He knew that Lynn would be on her best behavior if Herb was there and she wouldn't take her wrath out on Stan for all of his mistakes of the last couple of days.

Lynn was marginally polite to Herb, although it was clear that she didn't think much of him. Herb, in return, seemed awkward with the situation. Herb stayed for a couple of hours, and he and Stan talked quietly in Stan's room. Stan had more questions. Stan knew that Herb felt trapped, but Stan didn't care. He was going to make full use of the information Herb had divulged.

When Stan made a joke in front of Lynn, saying that he and Herb would be friends in 95 years, Herb looked seriously pissed and announced that he had to go. After he left, Lynn told Stan that he had to move out. The relationship was over.

For Stan, it was just another sad event in an increasingly sad life.

"Oh, and this came for you," she said.

Stan glanced at it and felt his heart sink. It was from the IRS. He knew his past was catching up with him. He opened the letter, read it, and let it drop to the floor.

"What's wrong?" asked Lynn.

"A few years ago, I made some creative adjustments on my tax return."

"Creative adjustments?"

"I didn't think they'd catch it."

"Obviously they did," said Lynn. "What did they send you?"

"A bill," Stan said quietly. "I owe over $10,000 in back payments and penalties."

"Oh, Stan." Lynn wanted the relationship over, but she still had a few feelings left for him. "What are you going to do?"

"I don't know. Do you have any money I can borrow or anything you can sell?"

"Me?" The few feelings she had for him suddenly disappeared. "Stan, this isn't my problem. And we're not a couple anymore. I've spent a lot of money on you, helping you through your various financial crises. This has been a very one-sided relationship. You're a taker and I can't have a taker in my life. Please leave."

There was nothing more for either of them to say, so Stan gathered a few of his belongings and told Lynn he'd be back in a few days for the rest of his things. Where was he going to live? Maybe Herb would take him in. He'd ask him. If Herb refused, he would insist. After all, he had something over him. It would only be for a few days anyway. Just until payday. A plan had been evolving in the back of his brain since he found out about the time travel, and it was time to put it into motion. It was kind of a fantasy thought before. But he really had no choice now.

He called Herb. The man was seriously annoyed about Stan's comment, but Stan tried to smooth it over. He asked Herb if he could stay with him just until Friday. Then he would find other arrangements. Herb was stuck and he knew it. He grudgingly agreed.

Just as he hung up with Herb, Stan got a mysterious call from someone saying he was with the NSA and had to talk to Stan immediately, and that he should tell no one of the call. Having just received a bill from the IRS, any government agency with three letters automatically scared the hell out of him, so he agreed to meet.

Mitch Webster from the NSA was thrilled to learn that Stan would be living with Herb for a week, and he immediately agreed to Stan's demand of $1000 upfront. Stan had a feeling he could have demanded a lot more, but that, plus his paycheck, would be enough to get him where he wanted to go.

He spent the week generally being an annoyance to Herb and passing on fairly useless information to his NSA handlers. Even though he was using Herb, he liked the man and didn't want to see him in any trouble. He also didn't want to give the NSA any information that could screw up his plans.

He had to leave, and he had to leave without anyone knowing where he was going. Friday was the day. He went to an ATM and took out $450. That left $50 in the account. He'd just had his pay direct deposited the day before, and it was usual for him to take it out the next day, always leaving $50. When he was packing his backpack at Lynn's, he included his camera and two memory cards he'd bought months earlier. The only other items were a few shirts, some jeans, underwear, and $100 he stole out of Lynn's purse when she was in the bathroom. Between the pay, the stolen money, and the advance from the NSA, he had over $1500— enough for his plans.

He had nobody to say goodbye to, so he made his way to South Station and caught a bus to New York City. He considered Springfield or Hartford and ultimately decided that he would be less likely to be remembered in New York.

From New York, he bought a ticket to Flagstaff, changing busses in St. Louis. He could have flown more cheaply, but he'd be more anonymous taking a bus.

A little over two days later, he found himself in a cheap room at a bedbug motel in Flagstaff, with a little over $1000 left in his wallet. He went to a store and bought a couple of thick notebooks. He'd had time to think on his way west and decided that he'd write a book about his travels. Then he went to a thrift shop and found some inexpensive cowboy boots, a well-used cowboy hat, and a flannel shirt. *How in the world did cowboys wear flannel shirts in the hot weather?* he thought. Then he visited a rare coin shop and spent most of the rest of his money on bills and coins that could be used in 1870.

The next morning, Stan hitched a ride to a spot about a half-mile from Hollow Rock. His stomach was in knots. Was he really doing this? And if he was, could he find the cave? And if he found the cave, would it just turn out to be a massive joke played on him by Herb?

He found the town of Hollow Rock without any trouble. There wasn't much to it—some mining equipment, some building foundations, and even a couple of wooden walls that wouldn't last much longer in the elements. He walked along what was once the main street. He tried to imagine what the town looked like when it was alive. Well, maybe he'd soon find out. Was he just conning himself? He was beginning to have doubts about the whole thing. It *had* to be a joke by Herb. Time travel couldn't really exist … could it? Herb wasn't the joking type.

He shaded his eyes and peered up at the hills overlooking the town. *That must be where the cave is,* he thought.

He climbed the hill and walked along a thin trail on the side of a rocky cliff. There were a few holes, but nothing that looked like a cave. And then he saw it. Hidden behind some bushes was a hole that had to be a cave entrance. He threw in a handful of pebbles and heard an angry snarl in reply. Not good.

He was prepared. At an Army-Navy store, he had purchased

a couple of smoke bombs. He was told it would clear out any varmints from caves. He threw one in and stepped back against the wall. Whatever critter was in there was going to be angry when it came out. Staying out of sight might be a good thing.

A moment later, a scared bobcat shot through the cave entrance and ran down the hill. Stan waited for the smoke to clear before entering the dark hole. He turned on his flashlight and hurriedly looked around, just in case the bobcat wasn't alone. He looked in every corner and along every inch of the cave floor, walls, and ceiling. Nothing.

Now he looked around without fear. The cave walls were smooth, and the edges of rock outcroppings were rounded. Stan figured that at one time—and for a long time—this cave had been underwater.

Around a corner was a sharp turn leading to a second room. It was a tight squeeze to get into the other room, but he was able to wiggle through by taking off his backpack and dragging it behind him. Once in the second room, he shone his flashlight all around. The room was only about 10 x 10, and it was empty, with no other offshoots or corridors leading anywhere else.

"I can't believe I fell for this," he said, his voice echoing in the empty chamber. The wrong words used in the conversation ... the shaking of hands in a strange way ... it was all a big joke.

He angrily pushed his backpack through the tight opening, then followed it. He was feeling crushed, knowing that he had fallen for such a juvenile prank. *If I ever get my hands on Herb ...* he started to think. Just then he heard the faint sound of a tinny piano. There were other noises too. Some yelling, some laughing and something else ... cows, maybe? In the far distance, he heard a gunshot.

What the...?

Stan reached the cave entrance and looked out.

Below him on the desert floor was a town. A living, breathing town.

And it was full of people.

Chapter 27

HERB WELLS
BOSTON, MA—2011

He was so stupid! Letting himself get so drunk that he told someone about the time travel. That was all part of the training—don't get drunk! The wrong things are always said when you're drunk, he was taught. He believed it too. He'd been around enough bars in various centuries. Nothing changed. The clientele was the same no matter where or when you were. There was always someone in there who'd had too much to drink and was telling his life story to anyone who would listen—which was usually nobody.

Now he'd done it. He'd run off at the mouth. Unfortunately, someone *was* listening. What was he going to do about Stan? Should he tell Jim? He was going to have to. And then there was Alan. He had just shown up recently. Alan was the only one of the group Herb had never really liked. He was too intense about everything. Alan showing up was another reason Herb wanted to leave and go home. Max had been around for a short time, but then he disappeared.

Now Stan was staying with him for the week. Ugh. That could be a good thing though. Maybe he'd be able to impress upon him the importance of keeping it all under wraps.

But he wasn't drunk the previous morning when he explained how the portal worked. What was his rationale for that?

Weariness. He'd had enough. He just didn't care anymore.

*****

The week went pretty well. Stan promised him he'd keep quiet, but Herb was still suspicious.

On Friday, Stan said he had to leave the house early. Herb didn't think about it until later that Stan was leaving with his backpack. The reason became apparent when Herb arrived at work and Stan wasn't there.

"Where's Stan today?" he asked Jim.

"We don't know," said Jim. "He has a project that needs to be finished. I thought he was staying with you."

"He is, but he left early."

That wasn't good.

He confided his transgression to Jim, who took it fairly well. Jim was level-headed. He knew that keeping something like that a secret forever was impossible.

"Do you think he went to the Hollow Rock portal?" he asked.

"I only gave him a vague description of where it was," answered Herb. "But it's possible."

"Well, let's see if he shows up," said Jim. "In the meantime, I'll try to get in touch with his girlfriend … ex-girlfriend. Maybe she knows something. I think I have her cell phone number somewhere." He gave Herb a sour expression. "You realize I'm going to have to tell Alan all this? We all know the rules. If there's a breach of any kind and one of our team is in that time period, we have to tell them. You'll also need to write up a report and put it in the transfer location. They have to know back home."

"I know. I know. I'm just kicking myself. It's bad enough

telling anyone, but telling Stan is even worse."

Herb was already carrying around the guilt of his 1930s love affair. Telling the others about it had been embarrassing.

He decided to look for Stan. He first went to Lynn's apartment. She'd be at work, but maybe Stan let himself in. As expected, no one answered the door. He then checked in at the bar where he had seen Stan a couple of nights earlier. He was just leaving the bar when his phone rang. It was Alan.

"You stupid idiot!" yelled Alan. "How could you have done that? How could you allow yourself to get drunk and tell a complete stranger?"

"Hi, Alan. Nice to talk to you, too."

"How could you?" Alan's voice was still at a yelling pitch.

"Gee, I don't know, Alan. You've never done anything stupid in your life?"

"Not like this."

"Okay," said Herb. "I get it. I did a stupid thing. I'm out looking for Stan right now."

"What are you going to do when you find him?" asked Alan a little more calmly.

"I have no idea. I'm open to suggestions."

"Do you think he went to Hollow Rock?" asked Alan, sounding almost reasonable now. Herb knew that Alan would calm down once he let off steam.

"I'm beginning to think it's possible."

"I would give it another day, then you know what you'll have to do, right?"

"Yeah," said Herb with a sigh. "Go after him."

"And?"

"Alan, you know I'm not capable of that."

"It was part of your training. We can't—under any circumstances—allow someone to go back and change history. If he went through the Hollow Rock portal, it could have devastating effects. You know that. Herb, if he's back there, you have to take care of it."

"What if I arrive months after him? You know we can't control when I arrive. He could have already screwed up something in that time."

"And you might arrive before him. Either way, you have to kill him."

Herb sighed. "I know. I'll let you know if I find him." He hung up.

His phone rang a minute later. It was Jim.

"I talked to Lynn," he said. "She has no idea where he is and couldn't care less."

"And he could be anywhere," replied Herb.

"Yes, but I'm thinking he headed for the portal. Lynn said that he got a letter from the IRS telling him that he owed them $10,000. She said there was no way he'd ever be able to come up with that much…"

"…Unless he had it in his head that he could go back in time and collect valuable things and come back and sell them here," interrupted Herb. "When he was in my apartment, he looked at the trinkets I've collected and made mention of how much things from the past would be worth now."

"Hmm, I wasn't thinking along those lines," said Jim. "I suppose it's a possibility. I was thinking more that he might have wanted to escape this life and start fresh. We got paid on Thursday at the magazine and Lynn says that a hundred dollars from her purse suddenly disappeared. She assumes it was Stan. The man was always broke, so between his pay and Lynn's money, he might have made it to Flagstaff."

Herb went back to his apartment in a funk. He wasn't particularly happy where he was now. He'd like to find his way home, but he hadn't yet found the portal that would take him there. The next best thing would be to find Beryl. He hadn't known her for more than a few weeks before he had to leave. She was sad that he left, but she understood that he had work to do. Besides, things were getting complicated for her and she didn't want to get him involved. Could it be she made it to Hollow Rock? He had traveled there after leaving her. He found the cave using the Portal Finder and he called her with the directions. She might have gone there. After all, historically, she did disappear. Was it because those who were after her did away with her, or had she escaped to another time?

Well, there was only one way to find out. Between his need to find—and kill?—Stan, and his desire to find Beryl, Hollow Rock seemed his only choice.

Herb made arrangements with Jim to empty his place, and he packed some clothes, a few mementos of his travels, and of course, his Portal Finder. It was because of the Portal Finder that he was going to have to rent a car. He would never be able to get it through airport security.

Having heard nothing from Stan, he started on his way the next morning. There was no reason to rush. It wouldn't make any difference with the portal. What time he arrived in Hollow Rock was strictly random. It would most likely be in a span of a few months, but would it be before or after Stan? For that matter, if Beryl had decided to go there, he might even arrive before her. He liked the fact that it was random with the parameters of a few months. All of the portals were like that.

He arrived in Flagstaff three days later, anxious to be done with the long drive, but equally anxious to go back in time. He'd had a lot of time to think about it during the long drive and he now found himself happy to be leaving the 21st century. He was feeling a bit of his old adventurous spirit. If Beryl was there, he could take care of the Stan situation and then either live a quiet life with her in Hollow Rock, travel the world in the 1870s with her, or find another portal with Beryl as his companion. He was beginning to have fantasies of traveling through time with her.

He returned the car to the rental agency that night. The next morning, he paid a young guy to take him out to Hollow Rock. He trudged the half-mile to the cave, seeing footprints in some of the sandier sections. Stan's?

There were boot prints as he approached the cave entrance. Had Stan bought cowboy boots? Good. It meant that he was thinking things through, knowing he had to blend in. Herb had done the same thing that morning.

He checked the cave for varmints, then went through the opening. The cave had a strange faint smell. Then he saw the reason. A smoke bomb. Stan had definitely been there.

He looked at his Portal Finder to see exactly where the portal was in the cave. He followed it to where he had to squeeze through the narrow entrance to the back room.

He took a deep breath to calm himself. He was always a little nervous going through a portal. There was so much that was unknown on "the other side." But he was more nervous than normal this time. He really had no choice though.

He stepped into the room.

Chapter 28

MAX HAWKINS
HOLLOW ROCK, ARIZONA—1869

Max Hawkins emerged from the cave above the bustling town of Hollow Rock, Arizona. This wouldn't have been his first choice as a destination, but he was desperate. He had spent days as a "guest" of the NSA. When they finally let him go, it was with the warning not to leave town. Well, not only was he leaving town, he was leaving the century.

There were other portals that he could have accessed, but there was only one outgoing portal in the U.S. in the year 2011. There were plenty of incoming portals, but to reach another outgoing one, he would have had to go up to Canada or down to Mexico, and he couldn't chance getting stopped at the border. That left Hollow Rock. He really had no interest in the American wild west, but he didn't have the same choices he usually had. It was Hollow Rock in 1870 or talk more with the NSA in 2011.

He glanced down at the date on the Portal Finder: December 13, 1869. He missed 1870 by a few days. Well, he had learned that the portals weren't the most accurate, timewise, to say the least. And did the date really matter?

How was he going to explain any of this to the other members of the team? He wasn't. It was embarrassing enough that he'd been captured by the NSA—or the FBI, then handed over to the NSA—but the fact that they broke him and got him talking was humiliating. And somewhat ironic. The whole reason they caught him was that he had taken it upon himself to kill Herb and Alan for revealing their missions. Or rather, find someone to kill them for revealing their missions. And now, he had committed the same lack of judgment.

Max was one of the leaders of the research team, and the self-appointed rules cop. He was a stickler for the rules, and when he found out that Herb had blabbed to Beryl Dixon back in the 1930s, he knew he could no longer trust Herb to travel in time. The only way to stop him was to eliminate him. And then he found out that Alan—who always thought he was more rules-conscious than even Max—had also told someone. Like Herb, Alan's indiscretion came in the 1930s, but in his case, it was in Germany to a government official in 1937. He didn't know the man was a government official, of course, but it didn't matter. He shouldn't have talked. Unfortunately, this man was a confidante of Adolph Hitler and passed on the information to Germany's leader. Hitler, with his fascination for the occult, seized upon the information— and almost seized Alan. Alan made it out of Germany by mere hours to spare, making his way to France, to England, and eventually Boston, where he found the portal to take him to 2010-2011 Boston—a designated meeting spot for travelers needing a break.

Max learned of Alan's mistake a few days after learning of Herb's. At that point, Max knew that Herb and Alan both had to go. They had broken the most important rule: NEVER tell anyone about time travel. Once they were gone, he would have to decide whether it was still advantageous to keep the program running.

His efforts at eliminating Herb and Alan had gone wrong, and now he had done the very thing that he despised—told someone. He could argue that in his case it was coerced, but it would have been a weak argument. Telling is telling, no matter the reason.

The other ironic thing about it was that it was the NSA that funded their project. It could very well be that their interest in time travel started with Max revealing it to them in 2011. Better not to think about it. It was one of those mindbender types of situations that could give you a headache.

So now he was in Hollow Rock, Arizona, in December, freezing to death. Well, not for long. He opened his travel bag and pulled out a coat. Everything he wore and everything in his bag was authentic to the American West in the late 1800s. He even had some money and a Colt .45 in a holster. He grabbed the holster from his bag and strapped it on.

He had learned to shoot during his last assignment—France during World War II, where he ended up helping the French Resistance. One of the Resistance fighters taught him how to shoot and he wound up quite skilled at using handguns. And before joining the time travel team, he had spent years studying martial arts. So Max was feeling confident in his abilities.

What was he going to do about Herb and Alan though? Nothing. There was nothing he *could* do. He had no idea when— or if—he would ever see them again. No, he lost his opportunity to deal with them.

He walked toward the town. He already had his story. He'd use the name Hawkins again. It wasn't his real name, of course, but he'd used it several times and he liked it. Technically, he was only supposed to use a name once, then change it for each subsequent travel location, but he knew he wasn't the only one to latch onto a name. Herb and his stupid H.G. Wells obsession being a good example. As long as it hadn't been compromised somewhere (or some*when*) else, it was okay to use it again.

He reached the edge of town and was seen by two men

hanging out in front of the hotel.

"Hey mister, where's your horse?"

"I was set upon by some outlaws a couple of days ago. They stole my horse and my whole rig. I didn't have a chance. They were nice enough to leave me my pistol. Too bad for them. I winged two of them as they were riding away. They won't make that mistake again."

"That's just not right. We've been having problems with outlaw gangs. You hungry?"

"I could eat a horse." Max wasn't even sure if they used that expression back then, but it sounded good. Truth was, he'd eaten just before he passed through the portal, but this would be a good way to get to know people."

"C'mon into the saloon. They got a Mex cook and he makes a mean bowl of chili."

The two men were Cy and Homer. *Decent sorts,* thought Max. The men were townies. They did odd jobs and kept busy but spent most of their days relaxing in front of the saloon. They both looked to be around fifty and both had fought in the war. Max didn't ask which side. Did it really matter?

The chili was good—very different from the chili he'd been used to in the 21st and 22nd centuries. It was spicier and tasted fresher.

"You lookin' for work?" asked Cy.

"Might be," answered Max.

"You ever do any marshaling?"

Max knew he had to be careful with his answer. They must need a town marshal, and it was something Max could do, with his gun and martial arts skills. If he said yes, they'd ask where, and it was too easy to check these things. There was always someone who had been through a town he might mention. And then it hit him.

"Not here in the states or territories, but I did some police work over in France."

He said it for several reasons. First, they would never be able to verify it. Second, it sounded impressive. And third, it was logical. Many men—and women—of the west had spent time in—or had come from—Europe, so it wasn't all that unusual.

"We got us an opening," said Homer. "The last marshal just left. Pulled up stakes overnight and took off. The job pays okay, and this is a pretty quiet town. Usually just corralling a drunk or two on payday at the mine or when the herds come through. We can talk to the mayor."

"I'd like that," said Max.

A day later, Max was installed as the town's new marshal. He hired both Cy and Homer as his deputies. They weren't hotheads, so he knew they would emit the calmness he wanted, but they'd fought in the war, so he knew they were tough. When he found out that they had both been cowpunchers for several years, enduring the tough life of a cowboy, he knew he had the right men.

On his second day on the job, he was sitting in his office ruminating on his life. He'd gone from scientist in the 22nd century to town marshal in the 19th century. How did that happen? He found himself chuckling. Could it get any stranger than that? Then he realized that he kind of liked it. Where (and when) he came from was a busy and mentally exhausting place. The more he traveled, the more he realized how much had been lost by the time the 22nd century had arrived.

The world was overpopulated, despite the colonization of Mars. And because Mars was so enticing, many of the world's scientists and leaders in social, economic, political, and spiritual movements had moved to Mars, leaving the less-educated, the poor, the starving, and the undesirables of society inhabiting the earth. Everything was automated, leaving precious few jobs. Socialization was now an awkward and forgotten way of life.

Here, it was real. No one knew of computers, holograms, space travel, instant communication, overcrowding, or worldwide poverty. Here, people helped each other and cared about each other. Yes, for most it was a hard life, but they were willing to put in the work and they took pride in accomplishments, no matter how small.

He liked it here. Would he get bored? Maybe. If so, he could just move on and check out other small towns or even some of the cities. He was tired of the time travel. He wasn't getting any younger (despite going back in time) and was now in his late forties. It was time to call it quits.

He would never see any time travelers again. That made him happy. He was done with that life.

Two weeks later, it all changed.

Chapter 29

"Boss, there's a crazy woman in town. And the man with her ain't much better."

Cy was standing in the doorway of the marshal's office.

"You'd better come see this."

Max had found in his short time as marshal that he didn't need to hurry for most things.

"You should see what she's wearing. Hoo-eee, she's half-nekked."

That got him moving a little faster

When he reached the door, Max said, "Oh shit," under his breath. One look was all he needed to know that the portal had been breached.

He grabbed his coat and pushed past Cy, running to meet the couple. The woman was in her late 20s to early 30s and had the looks of a model. The man was a tall skinny guy of about the same age. He wasn't nearly as good looking, with straggly shoulder-length hair.

The man was wearing jeans and a t-shirt—the t-shirt advertising Star Wars. But it was what the woman was wearing that was catching the attention of the townspeople. She had on a top that ended just below her breasts—exposing her whole midriff—and shorts and sneakers.

Being a cold day, there weren't a lot of townspeople on the street. Max considered it a saving grace. However, the few women who saw the newcomers had their hands over their eyes or were turning away and muttering things to each other. The men in the saloon were piling out to see the sight.

Max reached the woman and threw his coat over her shoulders.

"Put this on and follow me," he said.

"I don't understand," cried the woman. "This town wasn't here a few minutes ago. And it was hot. Why'd it get so cold? What's happening?"

The man was just looking around without saying anything. His expression told the story. He was in shock.

"Come with me and I'll explain everything," said Max. He hurried them into his office and sat them down by the woodstove. They were both shivering. Max poured two cups of coffee for them. They just held the coffee in their hands, soaking up the warmth.

"Cy," he said to his deputy, "go over to the saloon and see if they have any chili today—or stew. Whatever they have that's hot, bring me back two bowls. That'll warm them up."

"Okay boss. Where do you think they came from?"

"I have an idea, but I've got to talk to them. After you bring the chili, go ahead and take a break. Get some lunch. I need to speak to these two alone."

Cy didn't question it and ran off to the saloon. Max locked the door.

"Warming up?" he asked.

The woman nodded, but the man stared at the floor.

The woman looked up at him with pleading eyes.

"What happened?" she asked.

"This is going to sound unbelievable. Or maybe not. You already know that something is wrong. Did you enter a cave in the hills above town?"

The woman nodded.

"I'm sorry that happened to you," said Max. "You entered a time portal. It's transported you back to the year 1870. January 2nd, 1870."

"Bullshit," said the man.

"Sadly, no. Could I get your names?"

"I'm Natalie O'Brien and this is Randy Brown.

"Natalie O'Brien," said Max. "Where do I know that name?"

"I'm an actress…" Natalie began.

"Ah yes, the actress who mysteriously disappeared."

"What?"

"If I remember my history, you disappeared in 2009. Is that the year it was when you stepped into the cave?"

"That's the year it is now," said Randy.

"I'm afraid it's not," answered Max. "This town is real. The people are real, and like it or not, it really is 1870. I came through the portal a few weeks ago. I entered the cave in the year 2011. The difference is, I knew what I was doing. It wasn't an accident as it was in your case."

"Who are you?" asked Natalie.

"My name is Max Hawkins. I'm a time traveler. I started my traveling in the year 2105 and have been to numerous places and times, most recently Boston in 2011."

"Bullshit," repeated Randy.

Max frowned at him. *This guy's going to be trouble,* he thought. "Listen," he said. "I know this is a lot to digest, but you'd better start believing it quickly, because you have no other choice. You're in a time and place you shouldn't be. Anything you do can affect the future. You're going to have to come up with new last names, just to be safe."

"Assuming what you say is true…" began Natalie.

"Nat, you don't really believe this guy, do you?" interrupted

Randy. "Come on. This is just bullshit. This is just a set, and someone is playing a joke."

"Randy, shut up," said Natalie. "Did they build it when we were in the cave for fifteen minutes? Did they change the weather from 90 degrees down to 30? I don't know what's going on any more than you do, but we need to at least listen to Max." She turned to Max. "If we came here through the cave—the portal, you call it—can't we just go back in to return to 2009?"

"You would think so, but no," answered Max. "The portals are all one-way. You'd have to find a different portal to take you back. Finding one that would take you back to the exact time you left ... well ... that's another story altogether." Natalie opened her mouth to ask another question, but Max stopped her. "Let me try to explain."

Max spent the next hour talking about time travel and the program. A few minutes into it, Cy arrived with two large bowls of chili.

"Guys at the saloon asked me about them two," he said, gesturing toward Natalie and Randy, "but I didn't say anything."

"Good, thanks. They've been through a bad time. I'll explain it to you when I hear more of the story. Now, take off."

"Okay, boss. See you later."

When Cy had gone, Max said. "We're going to have to come up with a logical story for how you showed up the way you did. That's for later. For now, I'll continue to explain what's going on. Eat up. It's the best chili you'll ever have."

When Max was finished explaining about time travel and Natalie had finished her chili, she asked, "So you're really a scientist?"

"I am."

"How'd you become marshal?"

"You try to blend in wherever you are. In this case, they asked me, and I accepted. We'll have to find a way for you to blend in."

"I just want to go home," said Natalie, her eyes filling up.

"I know," said Max tenderly. "It seems unfair. It wasn't like you purposely came here. I'll try to figure out a way for you to get back, but I can't guarantee anything. Meanwhile, I'll do my best to help you adjust while you're here."

He patted her shoulder. Randy, who hadn't seemed much interested in Max's explanation or interested in the chili, suddenly perked up.

"You touch her again and I'll kill you."

Max stared at him until Randy averted his eyes.

"Son," said Max, "you're going to be trouble, and I don't need trouble. I can lock you up and throw away the key and just tell people that you're crazy. Or I can take you out to the middle of the desert and leave you there. You've got to understand something: you're not supposed to be here. The wrong words or actions and you could disrupt history. It's up to me to make sure you don't do that. Trust me, I take that responsibility seriously."

Randy gave a sullen nod. Max knew he'd won that round, but he still felt that Randy was going to have to be dealt with. Natalie, as badly as she wanted to go home, seemed smart enough to adjust as she had to.

As for Randy, Max could only see one outcome.

Chapter 30

Over the next week, Natalie O'Brien—now Natalie Fox—was able to fit into life in Hollow Rock. They came up with the story that Natalie was an actress in a traveling troupe and Randy was the manager. The troupe was set upon by an Apache war party, and everyone scattered. Natalie was in the middle of changing clothes when the attack happened. She and Randy were able to escape with some blankets, which they lost close to town when they were attacked by animals. It wasn't a foolproof story, but it was the best Max could come up with.

Max took all the clothes they were wearing and stored them in a safe place. He didn't want someone a hundred years from now finding a Star Wars t-shirt a few years before the movie was released, or a pair of sneakers before they were invented. However, he had found from experience not to dispose of clothes in case you find yourself traveling to a place where they could be used and not attract attention. He had the owner of the general store bring over clothes for the two of them, then helped Natalie figure out all the details that went into women's clothing in the 1870s.

Max got Natalie a job in the saloon, waiting on tables and singing at night. She had a good singing voice, but now just had to learn a lot of the songs of the day. Max let it be known that she was not to be touched by the clientele.

Randy was another situation altogether. Max didn't trust Randy to keep his mouth shut, so he hired him to keep the jailhouse clean. Max hated the idea of having Randy around, but he couldn't think of any other way to keep watch on him.

Max wasn't going to be able to keep Randy in the marshal's office forever, so he had Cy spread the rumor—which was true as far as Cy was concerned—that Randy wasn't "right" after his experience with the Apaches, and that he sometimes said strange things. That allowed him to let Randy out more frequently. Meanwhile, he had Cy and Homer keep tabs on Randy, and report back to Max regularly.

Things went relatively smoothly for a few weeks. Natalie would often stop by Max's office to talk. She was settling in well enough but needed the company of someone who knew about the times she was from.

"I notice that you and Randy spend less and less time together," he said to her about a month after Natalie and Randy had arrived.

"Randy was never right for me," she replied. "He was fun to be with when we first met, but as time went on, we had fewer and fewer things in common. The trip to Arizona was his idea—I think a desperate attempt to keep us together. I agreed to it because I felt bad for him. In retrospect, the worst decision I ever made. I told him last week that we are done. It sucks to be dumped a hundred and forty years from home, but I have to get on with my life. I don't want to be here anymore than he does, but I *am* here, so I have to deal with it." She looked at Max with a tear running down her cheek. "But I'm scared for Randy. He's become unstable. He carries a gun now. I'm afraid he's going to do something. I don't know what, but something."

"I know," said Max. "That's why I have my deputies watching him."

Max and Natalie spent many hours talking about life and loneliness. Max taught her to ride and as the weather warmed up, they would spend afternoons a few times a week roaming the hills. They occasionally slept together, but they both knew that it wasn't out of love, but the need for some close physical contact.

The longer he knew Natalie, the lonelier Max became. He'd had enough of time travel, and he didn't want to go back home to a deteriorating world. He also knew that he would soon tire of the 1870s. It lacked the stimulation his brain needed. When he did tire of it, he would use the Portal Finder to locate his next destination, but he wouldn't tell Natalie. She wanted to go back to the 20th century. He didn't. If he had a second Portal Finder, he could leave it with her and let her find her own way home. He had no doubt that she'd be able to handle herself through the ages, and she knew enough now to travel incognito.

Yes, Natalie could handle herself. Randy was a different story.

A couple of months was all he could tolerate Randy for, and evidently, it was all Randy could tolerate too. It was time to end it.

"My deputies tell me that you've been talking about the future again," he said one morning as Randy was sweeping the jail.

"What I say is my business," replied Randy.

"I still don't think you have any idea how your actions can affect the future. It's dangerous."

"I don't care. I didn't ask to be here."

"I have an idea," said Max. "Part of the problem is that you can't appreciate where you are. Let's go riding. I've taken Natalie out riding and I think it has helped her."

Randy thought about it. If he suspected anything, he didn't voice it, but Max was relieved when Randy finally agreed.

"Good. I'll grab a couple of horses."

An hour later, they were riding into the hills. Randy had

ridden a bit when he was young, so he was comfortable on a horse. They rode for a couple of hours, not saying much, before stopping on a butte that overlooked the desert.

"Beautiful, isn't it?" asked Max.

"If you say so," answered Randy.

"Why are you so angry?" asked Max. "I get it. You don't want to be here. Natalie doesn't either, but she's adapting. You're more like a petulant teenager. Face it. This is your life. You have to embrace it at some point."

"Who says I do? I know you're sleeping with Natalie. I was in love with her. You've taken that away from me."

"It didn't have to be that way," answered Max. "She just couldn't be with you the way you are. But she's worried about you. As for Natalie and me, we're not in love. We just need some physical contact now and then. That could have been you, but you chose a different path."

"Shut up. You have no idea what you're talking about. I had a life and now that life is gone. So I'm going to be whoever I want to be and you can't do anything about it."

Max sighed inwardly. He knew it was coming to this. He pulled out his gun and pointed it at Randy. Randy's eyes opened wide.

"You've given me no choice, Randy. You're too dangerous to the future and you don't seem to care."

"You ... you're going to kill me?"

Max pulled the trigger and the gun bucked in his hand. The sound of the shot reverberated against the surrounding hills. Randy fell to the ground, clutching his chest.

Max moved fast. He pulled Randy's gun from the dying man's holster and shot a round into the sand. Again, the sound seemed to go on forever.

Randy was dead. Max searched his pants and shirt for anything that didn't belong in this time period. Satisfied, he rolled

Randy the four feet to the edge of the cliff and pushed him over. The story was that Randy accused him of sleeping with Natalie, and pulled a gun and shot, missing him. Max defended himself by shooting back, getting Randy in the chest. Randy rolled off the side of the butte. It wasn't a perfect story, but everyone liked Max, and no one liked Randy, so no one would question it.

Natalie would know. There was no way she would believe that story. But she wouldn't say anything.

Natalie didn't believe it, of course, when he told her, but she understood and didn't ask any questions. After that though, she no longer rode with him or slept with him. That was when Max decided that it was time for him to leave.

And then Herb showed up.

Chapter 31

"Another stranger walking into town," said Cy.

It was only a week after Randy's death. No one had even questioned Max's account of the shooting, and Randy was immediately forgotten. Max was sad that Natalie no longer stopped by for talks, but it didn't matter. He'd be leaving soon.

Max got up from his chair, hoping that it wasn't another innocent victim of the portal.

He stepped outside the door just as Herb was passing. Herb looked up at him and did a double-take.

"Max?"

"Hi, Herb. Welcome to Hollow Rock."

"What are you doing here?"

"I'm the town marshal. C'mon in. Cy, we're going to need some privacy."

"Gotcha boss. I'll go make my rounds."

When they were alone, Herb said, "What happened to you? You suddenly disappeared."

"I was picked up by the NSA." Then he lied, "I have no idea why they chose me, but they had some information about time travel. They wouldn't say where they got it."

Max decided that telling Herb the truth: *They picked me up because I put out a hit on you,* wouldn't go over well.

"They had me for a few days. When they finally let me go, they told me to stick around. There was no way I was going to do that, so I skipped town as quickly as possible. I didn't check in with Jim, just in case they were following me. I headed for the closest portal, which was this one. I've been here for a few months. What about you?"

"I screwed up," said Herb. "I got drunk and told someone. He suddenly disappeared and I knew where he was headed, so I decided it was time for me to follow him. Has he appeared yet? His name is Stan Hooper."

"Haven't seen him yet," said Max. "I'll keep my eye out for him. You came back just for him?"

"Well ... not exactly. You remember I told you about Beryl Dixon?"

"Yeah, your other screw-up."

"Don't judge. You know as well as I do that this is a tough life. We're going all over time and we have to pretend we're people that we're not. I fell in love with Beryl. When you fall in love with someone, you can't keep secrets."

Max thought about his experience with the NSA. He had vowed never to talk, and yet, he had. For Herb, it was love. For him, it was pressure. He couldn't judge Herb anymore. And yet, Herb had revealed secrets on two different occasions. Were there more he hadn't mentioned?

"I assume Beryl isn't here?" asked Herb.

"No. Is she coming?"

"I don't know," Herb answered. "I guess I'm hoping that she will show up. She was in a tough situation—literally a life or death situation. She didn't have much choice. If she stayed, she would probably be killed."

"So you have two people to look out for. We're going to have more time travelers in this town than original residents." He told Herb about Natalie and the late Randy.

"When Stan makes it here," Max added, "don't let him know who I am. I want to be able to keep an eye on him."

"Good idea," said Herb. "Just a warning, he's a little squirrelly."

Max rolled his eyes. "Of course he is. Well, now that you're here, we have to find you a job. What's your plan? Are you staying long?"

"Depends on Beryl, and whether or not she comes. You?"

"No. I'm tired. I want to go find a place—and time—to live out the rest of my life in peace. I was going to leave soon, but with Stan and Beryl possibly coming, I'll give it a while longer. Hey, do you want to be my deputy? One of my guys, Homer, just told me that he has to quit. His rheumatism is getting worse and he has trouble walking."

"I've never shot a gun much."

"I can teach you. Besides, this is a quiet town. Nothing much happens here. *Besides,*" he thought, "*I may be tired, but I still have a responsibility. I have to decide whether you live or die.*"

Chapter 32

BERYL DIXON
HOLLYWOOD, CALIFORNIA — 1932

It might be time to leave, thought Beryl. *How ironic was this? A mystery writer getting caught up with just the sort of lowlifes she writes about?*

She couldn't help it if she liked to live the high life. *Paying* for the high life, on the other hand, was something she needed to work on. How much debt was she in now? The amount was staggering. The worst part about it was to whom she owed the staggering amount. It wasn't banks and other legal institutions. The worst they could do to her would be to repossess her mansion and put a lien on all of her possessions. *Her* lenders, on the other hand, had other ways of extracting the money.

How did it come to this? She was a successful mystery writer, the author of more than two dozen books. At forty, she was attractive and desirable. She always considered herself one of the lucky ones who survived the '29 crash virtually unscathed. But she really didn't. It just didn't hit as quickly as it had for others. Book sales had dropped considerably in the past couple of years. Books were a luxury, and people weren't thinking in terms of luxuries.

By the time she realized just how much her income had dropped, she found herself heavily in debt. Nobody else was thinking of luxuries, but for Beryl, luxuries were almost necessities. Luxury was who she was. It was the image she projected and the image her fans expected. They needed someone through whom they could live vicariously.

She found some men more than willing to lend her the money to stay afloat and to live the life to which she had become accustomed. She didn't pay much attention to their terms. After all, she was Beryl Dixon, a world-famous mystery writer. They'd get their money.

Well, she didn't have their money, and they were getting rather insistent. Their veiled threats weren't really so veiled. They didn't care if she was a world-famous author or Joe Schmoe. They wanted their money, and she didn't have it. She thought about selling her mansion to raise the money, but she was told by the bank that it wasn't an option. She had bought it for cash but had taken out a mortgage soon after to help pay for a business venture that went bust almost immediately. Since the stock market crash, housing values had plummeted, so she now owed more on it than the house was worth.

And now she feared for her life.

She had an option. Maybe. It was extreme if it was even real, but it *was* an option to consider.

Herb Wells had come into her life a few weeks earlier. She was giving a book signing in downtown Los Angeles and he was in line for a book. She noticed him immediately. There was an appealing oddness about him. He wasn't particularly handsome, but he had an intelligent look. He seemed somehow out of place. When he stood before her, book in hand, he said the strangest thing, somehow verifying her opinion of him.

"This one is good," he said. "My favorite is *The Sleeping Death*."

"I haven't written one with that title," she replied sweetly.

"You will. You're probably working on it right now. It takes place at a mansion in the south. A body is found in a swamp..."

That was the story she had just finished and was about to send to her publisher. She just hadn't titled it yet. *Hmm, that was a good title though.*

Had this man been in her house? That was the only possible way he would know what her new book was about. Not even her editor knew yet.

"How could you possibly know that?" she asked. An edge had come into her voice.

"It's a long story," he said, "and I'm not sure you would believe it. Rest assured, I don't follow you, I've never been to your house, and this is the first time I've ever seen you."

"Then how...?"

"Let me take you to dinner and I'll tell you the story. I guarantee it'll be worth your while. At worst, it'll be an entertaining evening."

He had a strange attraction, so she agreed. She had gone out with men for lesser reasons. He waited at the bookstore and took her to a restaurant when her signing was over. Her fame allowed her to request—and receive—a private dining room.

He told her he had read all her books and proved it by talking intelligently and enthusiastically about them. He was charming and witty—and a wee bit mysterious.

"So how do you know what my new book is about?" she asked.

"Because I've read the finished product." He then told her a strange story about time travel, time portals—whatever they were—and the fact that he was from the year 2105. While it was all unbelievable, he was so convincing she found herself wanting to believe him.

"Something I don't understand," she said. "Well, lots of

things I don't understand about the science of it all. Regarding you: on one hand, you tell me that you are not allowed to tell anyone what you do and that you never have. And yet, you are telling me, a perfect stranger. Why?"

"I've been a fan of yours since I was a teenager and started reading your books. There's also a mystery concerning you that I can't tell you about right now. So when I had the chance to come back here, I made it my mission to meet you. I have to say that you are everything I imagined."

"I hope that's a good thing."

"A very good thing."

She smiled. "You know how to charm a lady."

"I feel as if I've known you for a long time."

Beryl invited him home and they slept together that night—not an unusual occurrence for her. That night, for a short time, Beryl felt content. Her life had just begun to unravel with the loan sharks and for one peaceful night, she was able to forget them.

Dawn was breaking and Beryl was lying in Herb's arms. They hadn't slept a wink and in between the lovemaking, she would ask him questions about the future and about time travel. By that time, there was no doubt in her mind that he was telling the truth.

"You mentioned a great mystery concerning me," she said, snuggling in closer to him. "I'm glad people still remember me in the 21st- and 22nd-centuries, but what is the mystery? Do I die? Do I have a death that would fit into one of my books?"

"No, but if I tell you, it might change history."

"Honey, we've made love three times tonight. Hasn't that changed history? The minute you met me and told me who you are you changed history."

"Point taken. Okay, in early 1933, you disappear, never to be heard from again."

Beryl unwrapped herself from his arms and sat up in bed. "Then I'm going to die."

"You don't know that," he said. He sat up and put an arm around her.

"Something I haven't told you," she said. "I owe a lot of shady people a lot of money. They've already threatened me." She told him the story of stupidly going to them for loans to keep her luxurious life flowing.

"If I remember the stories I read about you, there were rumors of that," said Herb. "But the gangsters they interviewed at the time said they had no reason to kill you. You were no good to them dead. I have to agree. It wouldn't serve their purpose to get rid of you."

"No. There are two in particular who know I'll never be able to pay them back. They would kill me just to send a message to other famous people in their debt. Herb, I will never be able to pay these people back. I'm going to be in their debt for the rest of my life. The things they are going to demand of me will ruin my life. They may as well kill me."

Herb laughed. "Then maybe my coming back here hasn't changed history after all. Maybe I'm the reason you disappear."

Beryl raised her eyebrows questioningly.

"What if you could leave this life?"

Chapter 33

"What do you mean?" asked Beryl.

"Suppose I provided you with a way to leave this life and start fresh somewhere—and sometime—else?"

"But you would change history."

"Would I? In my world, you disappeared in 1933. If you still disappear in 1933, am I changing the past?"

"Are you saying that I will disappear no matter what?" asked Beryl.

"Maybe. Maybe you are destined to disappear in 1933. But is *how* you disappear destined?"

"Uh..."

"We're still learning about this. Maybe some things don't change, no matter what. Or maybe your disappearance resulted from me going back in time. Maybe it didn't. What I'm getting at is this: We don't know why you disappear. Maybe if I never showed up, one of your gangster friends would kill you and dispose of your body. Because I showed up, maybe you still disappear, but with a different option ... or outcome. So we're not changing history, because history has you disappearing. I know the exact date that you are reported missing. If you leave on that date, it changes nothing historically."

"So what's your idea?"

"Unfortunately, in this time period, there aren't a lot of portals to choose from. Most take you too far back in time. But there is one portal that takes you back to 1870 in Arizona. If you're willing to start a new life, that's one option."

"So I could be killed by gangsters if I stay or gunslingers if I go."

They both laughed.

"It's just something to consider," he said. "I'll drive to Flagstaff to check it out. I will write down precise directions to the location, in case you decide to go."

Beryl took his hand. "From what you're saying, it sounds like you are not planning to stay here."

"I can stay a week or two, but believe it or not, I am working. I have a few more places to visit and document for the people back home. But..." he hesitated. "When I finish with those, I was considering checking out Hollow Rock, Arizona, of the 1870s. If you decide to escape your enemies here, you might find me coming to Hollow Rock."

"If I decide to go, I'll look for you," said Beryl tenderly.

*****

Herb stayed almost two weeks and then departed for someplace in New Jersey that held the next portal. He told Beryl that he was going back to the late 1700s. He planned to visit Philadelphia, New York, and observe the construction of Washington DC. Beryl almost asked if she could accompany him, but then changed her mind. This was his journey, not hers.

For the next several months, she was able to keep the wolves at bay. She managed to pay the minimums that the loan sharks insisted on, but she knew that she wouldn't be able to keep it up. They knew it too.

She arrived home from a New Year's Eve party late at night to find three men in her kitchen. It was the help's night off and there was no one else home. The men informed her that their boss was not happy with her payments and that the debt was to be paid in full by the end of the month. When Beryl informed them that she didn't have the money, they beat her, choosing areas of the body that wouldn't reveal the bruises if she was fully dressed. She was told that it was a preview of what was to come if she didn't pay—and that the next beating would be long, painful, and bloody, resulting in a slow death. Although it was probably not in their instructions, the men then raped her. She was left lying naked in the corner of her kitchen sobbing.

Long after the men left, she laid there, trying to cope with what had just been done to her, the emotional trauma being almost worse than the physical. She finally picked herself up hours later, retrieved her ripped clothes, and made her way to her bathroom. She took a long, hot bath, and began planning her escape.

Beryl had a box in a hidden location in her house that contained several thousand dollars in cash. It was money she refused to touch to reimburse her lenders. Anyway, it wouldn't be enough to satisfy their demands. Over the next several days, she stayed inside the house and made her plans. She put most of the money in envelopes for her staff, on the condition that they never speak of it, even to the police. She gave her chauffer some money to buy her a cheap vehicle—something untraceable. Where she was planning to go, she would need very little luggage, so she packed a travel bag with a few extra clothes and some personal items. A week after she was beaten—on the date Herb told her that history had her disappearing—Beryl stole out of the house in the middle of the night, after being assured by her staff that the house wasn't under surveillance. She gave each of her staff a hug and thanked them for their service and friendship and then drove off into the history books.

Beryl stopped only when she needed to, and for short increments of time. She had disguised herself well, knowing that she would never be recognized. She arrived at the ghost town of Hollow Rock near dawn a few days later. There were no other cars on the road, so she took her time staging the scene. She opened the hood, making it look like her car had broken down. Since the car couldn't be traced, no one would ever know who it was who broke down and left their car. The owner of the broken-down vehicle would never return for it.

She gathered her travel bag and made sure she hadn't left anything in the car that would identify her, then she began to walk toward Hollow Rock. She arrived at the town to find a half dozen broken-down buildings. A couple had signs that had been washed out from the elements and were impossible to read what the signs had once advertised. One looked as if it had been a saloon. She waited until the sun was fully up before climbing the hill to the cave.

She had read Herb's instructions so many times, she knew them by heart. She found the cave easily, and using her flashlight, entered it and found her way to the back room. She was shaking. Was this real? Would she find out that Herb was nothing more than a liar who was having a big joke at her expense? She didn't think so. She could read people and he was genuine.

If she went through the narrow opening, she was saying goodbye to a fulfilling career as a world-famous author. Was she ready to give that up? She had thought about approaching her friends to help her out with her debt, but she knew she'd be unsuccessful. Everyone was hurting these days. And even if she did find some friends to help her, it would be an embarrassment she'd never be able to live down.

No, it was time to leave.

She took a deep breath and squeezed herself through the opening.

She was now in the small cavern. She didn't feel any different. Herb said that each portal was different. He wasn't sure if she would land outside the cave or would then have to exit the room and go out of the cave entrance.

Must be the latter, she thought. She squeezed back through the opening and approached the cave entrance. She took a breath and stepped out.

It was real.

Chapter 34

HOLLOW ROCK, ARIZONA—1870

Beryl had once spent a day on a movie set, back when she was dating an actor. It was a realistic-looking western town, one that had been used as a backdrop in many westerns. Everything in that town was a façade. The scene in front of her was no movie set. It was real. There were real buildings, real dust, real horses, and cattle, but most importantly, real people. Herb was telling the truth. She had gone back in time.

She felt a little dizzy. Was it coming back in time or was it the emotions of the moment? Either way, she needed to sit down. She found a rock, brushed off some of the dirt, and sat on it. The rock was hot. She looked up at the bright sky. The sun was hot. When she left 1933, it was January. Now it had to be early summer. She looked down at her clothes. She was dressed too warmly. She had some jeans in her bag. Maybe she should go back to the cave and change.

She was feeling better, so she entered the cave and changed into jeans and a summer shirt. Was the shirt appropriate for this time period? How about her shoes—fashionable high-tops? Well, they were the only shoes she had, so they'd have to do. She could buy others if she had to.

Before she left, she'd had the foresight to visit a coin dealer, where she bought some coins and bills from the late 1860s. It wasn't much, but it might be enough to get her some new clothes, a room, and some food.

Where to? She could go into town and find the hotel. What if she was asked how she got there? This wasn't the 1930s. She couldn't say that someone had dropped her off. She couldn't say she came on the stage. They would already know who was on the stage. Did they even have a stagecoach come through here?

All of a sudden, it dawned on her how little she knew about the old west. Herb had told her as much as he could about time travel, and he told her to prepare for the period she was traveling to, but he hadn't told her anything about what to expect in Hollow Rock. It made sense. After all, he had never been to Hollow Rock himself. How could he have prepared her?

Well, she couldn't very well stay up in the cave. She decided that if anyone asked her how she got there, she'd say that she was riding from St. Louis and her horse died and that she'd been walking at night to avoid the heat. It was weak, but it was better than nothing.

Beryl looked around. There was nobody in the vicinity. She saw a rider about a half-mile away, but everyone else seemed to be in town. She slowly slid down the hill. The town was only a few hundred yards away. She could walk that pretty quickly, although the heat had already tired her out.

She heard a horse and looked around. That rider was now a lot closer. It seemed to be a woman on the horse. The horse was now in a gallop and coming toward her. She stopped. A moment later, the rider stopped in front of her.

The woman was beautiful. She had shoulder-length brown hair that glistened in the sun, clear skin, and eyes that seemed to dance. The woman stared at her for a minute, then smiled.

"You must be Beryl Dixon."

Chapter 35

That was the last thing Beryl expected to hear.

"I recognize you from your pictures in magazines and books."

Beryl was momentarily speechless. How could that be? She wouldn't have even been born yet. Finally, trying to keep her composure, she asked, "And who are you?"

"My name is Natalie O'Brien. Here I'm known as Natalie Fox. You're going to have to give yourself a new last name."

Beryl just stared at her.

"I came through the portal too," said Natalie. "In my case though, it was an accident. I came through it in 2009."

At Beryl's obvious confusion, Natalie added, "Herb told me to keep an eye out for you."

"Herb? Herb is here? When did he get here?"

"About a month ago. He said he entered the portal in the year 2011. He was hoping you'd come. He didn't know if you'd already be here. The time you arrive can be within a range of a few months. He came through almost ninety years after you and arrived before you. Yeah, I know, it's all strange. Hop up on the back of my horse. I'll take you to Herb."

This was all going too fast.

"I ... I don't understand. It's a little overwhelming."

"Yeah, it is. At least you came through the portal with the

intention of coming back here. Imagine walking through by accident as I did."

"How long have you been here?" asked Beryl.

"About five months. And I didn't have anybody to help me through this." She reached down to help Beryl up behind her on the saddle, but Beryl shook her off. She wasn't ready yet. "Mostly, people around here don't know what to make of me. I kind of made a scene when I first arrived."

"What were you doing going into a cave alone?"

"I wasn't alone," said Natalie. "My boyfriend was with me."

Natalie's voice took on a different tone, prompting Beryl to ask, "I'm sensing something happened to him."

"The marshal shot him. I wasn't there when it happened, but the marshal said that Randy tried to kill him. It doesn't sound like something he would have done—although he did have a temper—but since I didn't witness it, I couldn't very well dispute it."

"I'm so sorry," said Beryl.

"We had already broken up. I know, it's hard to imagine that two people thrown back in time together couldn't stay together. You'd think we'd need each other for support. It was kind of the opposite though. This experience brought out the worst in Randy." Natalie glanced over at the town. "C'mon. We have to go. Hop up."

Beryl had never been on a horse before, so climbing up onto the saddle behind Natalie turned out to be a chore requiring several attempts. Once up, she put her arms around Natalie's waist. Natalie spurred the horse on and said, "I'm going to try reaching Herb's place by going around the town. Better that you're not seen in town yet. While we're riding, come up with a last name."

"Christie," said Beryl. "Agatha Christie is another mystery writer who's getting pretty well known. I think she's going to be big. What a better way to show my respect. Beryl Christie. That's my name."

"She became really big," said Natalie. "One of the most famous in history."

"That's good to hear. I'm happy for her."

Natalie managed to reach Herb's house with only a couple of people seeing them. Herb lived in a new house—hastily put together—on the edge of town. Natalie helped Beryl to the ground, then dismounted. The house—more of a shack—didn't have a porch. Natalie knocked on the door.

"Visitors," she called out.

Herb answered the door in a white undershirt, loose-fitting trousers, and suspenders. Beryl noticed that he had aged a few years. His hair was longer than before and somewhat unkempt, but he was clean-shaven. He greeted Natalie, then saw Beryl standing behind her.

"Oh my God! Beryl."

She flew into his arms.

"Finally," he said, smothering her in kisses. "It's been so long."

"It's only been three months," said Beryl with a laugh.

"Three months for you," he replied. "Five years for me."

"How?"

"I've been to six different places—and times—since I last saw you. Those six places took five years to accomplish. Remember, my body still ages naturally."

"Yes, you have a few extra lines in your face since we last saw each other," admitted Beryl. "But you still look good."

"I look tired is what I look," he answered.

He does look tired, thought Beryl. *And sad.*

"What's wrong?" she asked. "You look happy to see me, but you don't look happy."

"I'll take this opportunity to leave," said Natalie. "I'll be back in a couple of hours to get you."

Beryl looked at Herb. "I can't stay with you?"

"Not yet," he said. "They're a little straight-laced around here about single people living together. In some western towns—the wilder ones—it wouldn't matter. There's a bit of a religious undercurrent running through this town. Until we figure out how to work this, it would be better for you to stay with Natalie."

Natalie said her goodbyes and promised to be back before dark to get Beryl. After she left, Herb took Beryl in his arms and kissed her deeply.

"I'm sorry," he said.

"Sorry for what?" asked Beryl, holding onto Herb tighter than she intended.

"I'm sorry I told you about this portal," he said. "This is no place for you. When I mentioned it, I had romantic visions in my head—the old west, starting over, it just seemed idyllic somehow. It's really not. It's dirty, it's rough, and it's dangerous. There are some really bad types here. You're not safe."

"I always heard that if a man assaulted a woman in the old west, it was the worst thing he could do. They would hang him from the first tree they came to."

"Maybe, but it doesn't stop them from trying. There are also marauding bands of Apaches. Most of all, there's ignorance here that I'm not used to. This is the furthest back in time I've ever gone. I never made it back to the 1770s. I guess I wasn't ready for how primitive it is here. I was in the year 2011 when I decided to come back. I was getting up the courage to come through the portal to see if you were here, but then circumstances made it imperative that I come."

"What circumstances?"

Herb explained about Stan and his mistake in telling Stan about time travel. "I've been waiting for him to come through, just as I've been waiting for you—at once wishing you were here, but at the same time hoping you stayed where you were."

"You know I couldn't do that," said Beryl. "They were going to kill me."

"I know. But I'm not sure this is going to be much better. All I can say is that I'm happy I got here before you. I realized once I arrived that I hadn't prepared you at all. It must have been so frightening for Natalie to show up here all alone."

"I thought she was with her boyfriend," said Beryl.

"Yes, she was," answered Herb, without offering anything else.

Beryl, sensing that there was more to the story, said, "Natalie said he was shot by the marshal. Why? And don't say it was self-defense. I'm smarter than that."

"Randy—Natalie's ex-boyfriend—was going around telling people he was from the future. Our marshal, Max, is one of my partners from the future. I'm told that Max tried to get him to shut up about it. Even Natalie tried, but he wouldn't. He was telling people what was going to happen in the future. Luckily, most people thought he was just deranged. Finally, Max had to eliminate him."

"You mean kill."

"Yes. He rode into the desert with him. The story is that Randy pulled a gun on him and Max had to kill him. I know that didn't happen. Natalie doesn't know the reason, so please don't tell her."

"Natalie is smart. I saw that immediately. I'm sure she knows it. But I won't say anything. What about Stan Hooper? What are you—or the marshal—going to do about him when he arrives?"

"That all depends on Stan."

"Would you kill him?"

"As I said, it would all depend on Stan."

Herb took a sip of lukewarm water from a scratched glass.

"But yes, I would kill him if I had to."

Chapter 36

STAN HOOPER
HOLLOW ROCK, ARIZONA — 1870

Stan looked down at the bustling town. Everything Herb had told him was real! Now that he was here, he realized that as much as he had *hoped* it was real, a big part of him didn't believe it. Well, he believed it now.

He pulled out his camera and took a few shots of the town from the hills above. He was going to have to be careful with the camera. If anyone saw him using it, it could become problematic.

Stan looked down at his clothes, feeling a little embarrassed. He'd gone out and bought clothes that would fit in with the times, but everything looked too new. The thrift shop he got them from had done a good job of cleaning them. Too good. How was he going to explain walking into town from the desert in sparkling clean clothes?

He climbed down the hill to the desert floor. He set down his bag and laid down in the dirt. He spent the next few minutes rolling around and covering himself with dirt.

When he was done, he patted himself off. Well, it would have to do. He picked up his bag and walked toward town. When he came across the Hollow Rock town sign, he looked around to make sure no one was nearby, and he took a selfie of himself in front of the sign and the main street of the town in the background. He was going to have to get good at taking pictures surreptitiously.

"Where'd you come from?"

The voice startled Stan.

A man had come out of a doorway of what looked like a restaurant.

"Uh, my horse threw me a while back, so I've been walking."

"Never seen so many people walkin' into town. Unheard of," said the man. He was older and looked like he'd spent his life in the sun. His skin was leathery.

"Is there a hotel in town?" asked Stan.

"Of course. Got one in the center of town. Prob'ly got some rooms available. A dollar a night. What's your name?"

"Stan. Stan Hooper. I'm from Boston."

"Boston, huh? Never been there. Never been east of St. Louis. My name's Cy. I'm one of the deputies here. Let me take you to meet the marshal. Always good to do that if you're new in town. Follow me."

Stan felt that he really had no choice, so he followed Cy. When they got to the jail, Cy opened the door and asked someone if the marshal was there.

"Gone for lunch," came the reply. The voice sounded familiar to Stan.

"New guy in town. I thought he should say hi to the marshal."

He motioned for Stan to follow him into the office.

"The marshal ain't here, but this is the other deputy, Herb Wells. Herb, this here is Stan Hooper, from Boston. Says his horse threw him. Walked into town like you did."

Stan entered and stood in front of Herb. Herb didn't look happy.

"I gotta go visit the outhouse," said Cy. "I'll be back in a while."

As soon as Cy left, Stan said, "How'd you get here?"

"You idiot," answered Herb. "You used your real name?"

"Oh, right. You said to make up a last name. Sorry."

"Sorry? Do you think this is some kind of joke, Stan?"

"Hey, what are you getting mad at me for? I just wanted to check it out. I'm in a real financial bind. I owe the IRS $10,000. I figured I'd pick up a few rare coins and antiques and bring them back and sell them."

"Bring them back where?"

"Back home. Back to Boston."

"Did you not listen to a word I said?" asked Herb angrily. "That portal is one-way. You can't get back home through it."

"Oh God, I forgot. You threw so much information at me. It's hard to remember it all. I was just thinking about getting myself out of debt. How *do* I get home?"

"I have no clue. You just have to find the right portal, but that could take you years."

"Can't you use your magic Portal Finder?"

"Yes, but you might have to go to a lot of different periods to find one that will get you home. And even then, it's not guaranteed that you'll arrive back anywhere near the same time."

Stan's face dropped.

"You mean I'm stuck here?"

"Yeah, and I'm stuck here with you. I came after you to make sure you didn't screw anything up. You've already given your real name, so you've screwed up already."

A woman stepped in from outside.

"Herb, have you seen Beryl? We were going to go for a ride. Oh, I'm sorry. I didn't see that you had a guest."

"He's not a guest. He's the bane of my existence. Natalie from 2009, meet Stan from 2011."

"Oh My God! You're from the 20th century?" asked Natalie.

"I recognize you. Natalie O'Brien. You disappeared in 2009."

"She's not Natalie O'Brien anymore. She's Natalie Fox," said Herb. "She came here by accident, and yet, she was still smart enough not to use her real name."

Stan was smarting from Herb's rebukes.

"Okay, I'm sorry! This is turning into a really bad day. I didn't know I couldn't go back through the portal."

"I told you at least three times. What the hell were you doing while I was talking?"

"I was listening, but I was also thinking of the things I could bring back. I'm sorry. That's just how my mind works."

Natalie was getting visibly uncomfortable with the angry discussion.

"I'll leave you to your business. I'll go try to find Beryl."

"Beryl Dixon?" asked Stan. "She did come. Wow. I'm looking forward to meeting her. And Natalie, I'd love to get together with you to talk about life in the 20th century."

"We'll see, but I'm quite busy most of the time." At Stan's crestfallen look, she added, "I'm sure we can make it happen."

As Natalie left, a big man stepped into the room.

"Ah," said Herb. "The marshal is here. Stan Hooper, meet Marshal Max Hawkins."

Max looked Stan over with a critical eye.

"Passin' through or settling down?" he asked.

"I'm not sure yet," answered Stan.

"We always welcome newcomers, as long as you don't bring trouble with you."

"No sir. I'm not trouble."

"The hotel is just up the street. You have cash?"

"I do."

"You go get yourself settled. The hotel ain't much, but it's clean. Stop by later and we'll talk."

"I'll do that, marshal." He nodded to Herb. "Thank you, deputy."

When Stan was gone, Herb said to Max, "Ain't?"

"I wanted to sound authentic," said Max. "I assume you didn't tell him about me."

"Not a word."

"You're right," said Max. "Squirrely is a good description of him. He's going to take some watching."

"And if he crosses the line?"

"We eliminate him."

At Herb's frown, Max said, "Hey, he decided to come here. You said you told him all the reasons for not traveling…"

"It turns out he wasn't listening," interrupted Herb. "He didn't know that the portal was one-way, even though I told him three or four times. Who knows what else he didn't hear?"

"That's his problem," said Max.

They discussed the problem that was Stan Hooper for the next half hour, with little progress. He was going to have to be watched closely.

They heard the pounding of feet on the wooden sidewalk, and one of the locals stuck his head in the door.

"Marshal, we got a fight at the saloon. Some new guy in town is gettin' beat up."

Chapter 37

Max and Herb rushed over to the saloon, only to find a bloody Stan lying on the floor. While Herb went to help Stan, Max asked in a commanding voice, "Okay, what happened?"

The bartender pointed at Stan. "This guy tried to pass off some foreign coin as money. A couple of the boys wanted to see it, but he suddenly got all excited-like and told them to give it back. Hell, we just wanted to look at it. We never seen it before."

"What was it?" Herb whispered to Stan.

"A quarter from 2007," answered Stan. "I didn't even know I had it. I just wanted it back, that's all. They wouldn't give it back."

Herb helped him to his feet.

"C'mon, let's go see the doc. Happy you came back in time?"

"I've been happier."

After Herb and Stan left the saloon, Max asked for—and received—the coin in question. He looked it over and grunted, to feign a total lack of interest.

"Hell, I know what this is. They had an exposition back east in Boston. They gave these out. It was advertising something—I forget what. I got one myself. People carry them around as a good luck charm. Probably why he was so crazed to get it back."

"It didn't bring him no good luck," yelled out one of the patrons. That got a laugh from the others in the saloon.

"Hey, cut him a break," said Max. "He told me this is his first time out west. Easterners can get pretty confused out here. Next time he comes in, someone buy him a drink to show there are no hard feelings."

*****

The next few weeks passed uneventfully. Stan healed from his beating and the next time he visited the saloon, he was treated well, with numerous people buying him drinks. However, he had a nagging feeling that he wasn't respected. He couldn't help but think that behind his back, they were secretly laughing at him. He mentioned it to Natalie when they finally met over lunch—after Natalie couldn't put him off any longer. So they could talk freely, Natalie suggested they take a picnic lunch to a grassy knoll on the edge of town. It was within walking distance—a necessity since Stan had never ridden a horse. It was a sunny day, but not too hot, and Natalie had made some sandwiches.

Natalie wasn't sure of what to expect from Stan. She'd heard Herb's opinion but preferred to make her own judgments. Right away, though, she could tell what sort of person Stan was.

"Wow, I'm sitting and having lunch with the famous Natalie O'Brien," he said.

"No, you're having lunch with a regular woman named Natalie Fox. Natalie O'Brien doesn't exist. You have to start accepting some things. For our safety, we can't give any hints about our previous life."

"Yeah, I know. But this is not what I expected," he said.

"At least you came here willingly. For me, it was a total shock."

"You seem to be coping," said Stan.

"What's the alternative?"

"You don't have people laughing at you," he said. "You don't

179

have people calling you greenhorn. I want to do something big with my life, and it's not going to happen here."

"What do you mean by 'big'?" asked Natalie.

"I want to be known for something. You're an actress. Everybody knows your name."

"Not here they don't."

"Doesn't matter," said Stan. "In 2011, when I left, everybody knew your name."

"And that's what you want?" asked Natalie. "You want everybody to know your name?"

"Is that too much to ask? I planned to come back here, collect some valuable antiques, and go back home a rich man. I'd make my mark on the world. But Herb never told me that the portal was only one-way."

Natalie was quickly tiring of Stan and his shallowness—and now of his lying. She knew that Herb had told him about the one-way portal numerous times.

"Stan, you're here now. You have to accept that. The chances of us making it back to the twenty-first century are slim, at best." As she said that, she could feel her heart drop.

"Can I tell you a secret?" Without waiting for Natalie's answer, Stan said, "I brought a camera with me. I won't let anyone see it though. I saw how freaked out they were when they saw my quarter from 2007. No one will see me taking pictures. I also brought some notebooks with me. I'm going to write a book and have the pictures to back it up—to prove it's true. If I can get home, I'll publish it. If I can't, I'll find a way to preserve it and have someone open it in the 21st century."

Natalie knew that was bad news, but she remained silent.

"Hey, what's with that marshal?" Stan asked, changing the subject. "He's always watching me. It's kinda spooky."

"He just cares about the town," said Natalie. "He's a good man."

They awkwardly talked about a few inconsequential things, but when Stan asked her if they could go on a date sometime, she knew the lunch was over. She knew what "date" meant to someone like Stan.

"Stan, things are different here and I'm still trying to fit in. I'm not ready to even think about things like that."

She made an excuse that she had to get ready for work, and left Stan sitting in the grass. Once in town, she immediately sought out Herb. He was with Beryl at his house.

When Herb let her in, she said, "You might have some problems with Stan."

"I've had nothing but problems with Stan," he said. "What now?"

She told him.

"Oh, it figures that he would've brought a camera. I'll talk to Max about it. I guess we'll let him alone for a while, then when the time is right, we'll confiscate the pictures and the notebooks."

"He also asked about Max. He's worried that the marshal is showing a little too much interest in him."

"I'll let Max know. At some point, we'll probably have to tell Stan the truth about Max. That'll royally piss off Stan."

"Max wouldn't kill him as he did with Randy, would he?"

"As you know, I wasn't here, but from what I heard," said Herb, "Randy was becoming dangerous. I don't think Stan is there yet. Maybe there's still time to get him to see things correctly."

"Good luck with that," said Natalie, opening the door to leave. "I don't have a good feeling about him."

*****

Surprisingly, Stan behaved himself for the next several weeks. He got a job helping out at the newspaper. It gave Beryl a chance to keep an eye on him, and she reported back that he was flying straight. Any pictures were taken in secret, except for a couple that he took of the two women. They found a shack for him to live in. It was rundown, but it didn't seem to bother him, as it cost him almost nothing.

Despite the relative calm, Natalie was convinced that it wasn't going to last. There was a feeling in the air: Stan had turned around too quickly; she was becoming aware that Herb and Beryl were now beginning to have problems; and Max kept threatening to leave. It was all a ticking time bomb.

And then it exploded.

Chapter 38

When she thought about it after it was all over, Natalie realized that the demise of her friends was inevitable. The stress of being stuck in Hollow Rock, Arizona in 1870, was just too much for any of them to handle.

It started with Max telling Stan that he was really from the future. Herb was right in thinking that Stan would be upset. He felt betrayed by everyone—they all knew but hadn't bothered to share the information with Stan. Natalie realized that for a man with an already fragile ego, it was the ultimate insult.

Natalie was the only one—much to her dismay—that Stan would talk to, and even that relationship was strained. He would rant about the others every time he was near her and she found herself avoiding him as much as possible.

Her friendship with Beryl was the one thing that had become stronger, and they would often ride together, stopping at a favorite stream for hours to talk. That's where Natalie found out that Beryl was sick, and where Beryl confessed to her that her relationship with Herb was ending.

Beryl had developed an occasional cough, but over a few weeks, it had become much more pronounced. Beryl didn't know what it was, and the town doctor—who she said must have decided he was a doctor because the shingle outside his office said so—couldn't figure it out. She called him devoid of any real medical understanding. Was it pneumonia? Tuberculosis? Some sort of viral infection? Without a real doctor or real medicine, it was impossible to know.

During those weeks, Herb was becoming increasingly restless and was hinting at leaving. However, none of those hints seemed to include Beryl.

Herb had also had enough of Stan, and one day when Stan was at work, he went into Stan's shack and stole his notebooks. Stan had his camera with him, so Herb was limited to the notebooks. Herb was also suggesting that it was time for Stan to go, and when Stan got word of it, he knew what that meant. He was furious at Herb for stealing the notebooks, but he was now also scared. It was time to leave. But where? And how?

And then he hit upon a plan. He would steal a Portal Finder. He knew how they worked. He watched once as Herb explained it to Beryl. It was simple. There were two Portal Finders in town—one belonging to Herb and one to Max. He would figure out which was the easiest to steal, and he would head west. He already knew from listening to Herb explain it to Beryl that the closest portal was in California.

He spent the next week planning his escape and avoiding Max and Herb. He was now fearing for his life in a big way, and he knew he had to get out of there. He wouldn't be able to take a stagecoach without them knowing—and then they'd never let him go—so he contracted with a local farmer to take him to the next town that had a stagecoach. He still had a fair amount of money that he brought with him from the coin shop in 2011, and he offered the farmer more than was necessary, on the condition that he kept quiet about it.

His chance came unexpectedly a few days later. The relationship between Herb and Beryl had deteriorated badly. Beryl was now quite sick. Herb told her he was leaving, and she accused him of abandoning her when she needed him most. He tried to explain that it had nothing to do with her illness, that it was just time for him to go. Regardless of the reason, their relationship was over, and anyone who knew them could see it.

Stan was keeping his eye on Herb when he saw him enter the saloon. He knew that Herb was leaving on the stage the next day and he was probably going in to say goodbye to people. Stan had been waiting for the opportunity to check out Herb's house for the Portal Finder, and now he had his moment. Then he saw Beryl coming down the road toward the saloon. She had lost a lot of weight and was pale. Stan knew she was sick, but this was the first time he thought that death was probably coming shortly. She stopped on the road outside the saloon. She asked a passing man if he would go in and get Herb. Herb came out and approached Beryl on the street. Stan saw her lift a gun from the folds of her dress. Herb didn't even have time to react when she shot him twice—one bullet in the chest and one that took off half his face.

Stan knew he had to get a picture of the event. When Max arrived, he determined that the killing was in self-defense. He knew that Beryl's claims that Herb beat her were bogus, but he also knew that it was better left alone. The last thing they needed was a trial. Besides, it was clear to him that Beryl was dying. What good would it do to put her in jail?

Stan saw his chance. He went to Herb's place to steal his Portal Finder, but he couldn't find it. While he was there, he also looked for his notebooks, to no avail. Later, he asked Beryl if she had seen them, and she said she hadn't. He knew she was lying, but he couldn't do anything about it.

He also saw Max looking at him and he knew that Max had made his decision. It was time to run. He filled a trunk with mementos, as well as the camera and memory cards, and left it in the cave. If he made it back to his own century, maybe he would find it in the cave.

He still needed a Portal Finder. It was time to check out Max's house. That was always his second—and most dangerous— option, but now he had no choice. He waited until he knew Max was in town and he broke into his house. It took him almost an hour—a stressful, fear-packed hour—before he finally found it. Then he snuck out of town and walked to the farmer's house. He stayed the night with the farmer and was on the road early the next morning, his freedom awaiting him.

*****

Beryl died two weeks later in Natalie's arms. Whatever sickness she had was just too strong for her to fight.

"I should have stayed and taken my chances back home," she said. "Thank you for taking care of me, Nat. You're a good friend. I hope you find a way to get home. I have Herb's Portal Finder, along with Stan's notebooks, and a mystery I wrote while I was here." She told her where they were. "Maybe you can use the Portal Finder to get home. If you do, could you give someone my new book?"

"I'll be happy to, Beryl."

But Beryl never heard the words.

Chapter 39

She was alone. Completely alone. Lost in a foreign century, with no way to get home. If a producer had approached her with that theme as a movie idea, she might have considered it. It would have sounded romantic.

There was nothing romantic about this. At least when Max, Herb, Beryl, and yes, even Stan were around, she had connections with people. They were all gone now. All within a few weeks. And what did she have left?

She had her job at the saloon. She was respected there. In the beginning, Max had to lay down the law about men getting fresh—or worse—with her. But now, her clientele protected her. And there was always Cy, who took over after Max was gone, who was chasing after Stan. Cy was a pretty capable marshal, and people liked him and listened to him. No, she was safe enough. But then what? What was beyond safe?

Nothing. Absolutely nothing.

Herb never told her how to use the Portal Finder, so she couldn't use it to find a way home. Her clientele protected her, but they didn't understand her, and the other women in town barely tolerated her because she was different. Taking Randy up on his request to accompany him to Arizona was the worst decision she had ever made. There was no use crying about it now. She was here and this was her life.

No. She wouldn't accept that. If she was going to be stuck in this century, she was going to do something about it. She'd get out of Hollow Rock, for starters. This was about as dead-end as it got. She'd hop on a stage and head west to San Francisco. She had been frugal and had saved her money in the few months at the saloon. She'd have enough to get to San Francisco and find a place to live. Getting a job there would be easy.

San Francisco would be interesting—certainly more interesting than Hollow Rock—but it would still be the 1870s.

When Natalie needed to think, she'd saddle up a horse made available to her by the blacksmith and she'd go riding. Sometimes she'd ride for hours. Every once in a while, she would stop at the cave and go into the room that transported her here and see if it would transport her back.

After all, Max and Herb said that they were still learning about the portals. So far, they had always been one-way. Who was to say that they couldn't change and suddenly work both ways? Suppose it suddenly changed direction and she never checked it?

It was no different this day. She entered the cave, passed with disinterest the trunk that Stan had left, and started to squeeze through the opening into the back room.

And then she stopped. There was something in the middle of the floor. Something red and plastic.

Goosebumps appeared along her arm, and she could feel them along her spine. It was something from another time. But when? At least the 1960s? She remembered the famous line from *The Graduate*: "Plastics." It wouldn't have been any earlier than that. Could it be from her time?

She continued to squeeze through the opening. She picked it up. It had her name written on it!

She was shaking as she opened the box. There was a note, and it was addressed to her. It was from someone named Ray Burton. Wasn't that the name of some big-time correspondent?

Hi Natalie. My name is Ray Burton. I come from the time period you left. In my world, you've been missing for 12 years. I ran across a trunk left by Stan. Maybe you'll get this before he even leaves the trunk. Time travel is confusing, to say the least.

I've run across friends of Herb Wells and Max Hawkins. One of the friends explained things as well as he could, but it's still a bit overwhelming. What I do know is that there might be a way to get home. It involves using the Portal Finder and coming back in a roundabout way: going to one time period, which brings you to another, and so on. I don't know if Herb or Max would share that information with you.

I will keep trying to find a way to get you home, but I can't guarantee success.

Try to hang in there.

Yours,

Ray

Someone knew she was there!

Included in the box were some articles by Ray, probably to help her get a feel for who he was.

She had to let Ray know that she got his note. But how? And then she remembered Stan's camera. When he packed it in the trunk, he said that the battery was almost done, and it was his last battery. Was there enough for one last video? She could tape her response to Ray and include it in the trunk. Would it appear after he'd already seen the other pictures? If so, would he even see it? It was all too confusing.

Well, she had to try. She dug through the trunk and pulled out the camera. It showed about two percent charge remaining. Maybe. Just maybe.

She thought about what she was going to say, and a few minutes later, made the video. The battery died before she finished, but she hoped it would be enough to let Ray know that she got his message.

She put the camera back in the trunk and rode back to town to gather Beryl's manuscript, Stan's notebooks, and the Portal Finder. She decided to read Stan's account before leaving the notebooks for Ray. She spent almost a full day reading and making notes. Stan had done a good job, but there were things he left out, or just didn't know. When she was satisfied with the additions, she returned to the cave and placed them on the shelf above the trunk. Would he get them, or if she put them there now, will he have seen them when he found the trunk? Based on things Max and Herb explained, she was pretty sure he wouldn't find them at the same time he found the trunk since her message was added later, but it was impossible to say.

Now the final decision. Her original plan was to leave as soon as possible for San Francisco. Should she leave, or wait and see if Ray emerged from the cave? There was only a window of a few months or a year that he could arrive. Max arrived at the beginning of the year. She arrived soon after that. Then Herb, then Beryl, then Stan. There were only a few months left, most likely, when Ray could appear that would still be in the window.

What if he arrived earlier? Could he arrive before she even left him a message? She didn't think so, but it was way too mind-boggling to think about.

She made her decision. She would stay another month or so, then go to San Francisco. She had to go before it became too cold, and she had no way of knowing if he'd even come. He never said he would. All he said was that he'd try to find a way to bring her home.

She'd give it a month, and then she was gone.

PART THREE

Chapter 40

RAY BURTON
FLAGSTAFF, AZ—2021

I closed the notebook and let out a sigh. Wow. I looked at my watch and realized why I was so hungry. It was 7:30 pm. I had been reading all afternoon. More to the point, I had been reading and imagining all afternoon. Stan was a good writer—probably better than he gave himself credit for—and he had drawn me into the world of Hollow Rock.

As I read it, I also looked at the pictures on the computer to enhance my reading. The one picture I kept returning to was that of Herb, with half his face shot off. There was something about that picture that haunted me.

Stan must have asked a lot of questions to be able to fill in the story so well. Natalie had added comments—and sometimes complete paragraphs—in the margins. The comments clarified—and occasionally disputed—Stan's observations. After all, Stan wasn't there when the others arrived, so he had to have written the accounts based on stories he heard.

What to do now?

I carefully placed the notebooks in my travel bag. Tomorrow, I would buy some plastic wrap and secure the notebooks. Time had made them brittle in places. For now, they would go to the bottom of my travel bag with the other items, covered with dirty laundry and hidden under the bed.

I looked at the Beryl Dixon manuscript. I knew what I was going to do with it. I'd send it to Hal March. He'd know how to handle it. If I cared about money, I'd sell it. Hell, it must be worth a fortune. Let Hal have the money.

I picked up the Portal Finder. Did I even want to know how to work it? If I called Jim, would he tell me? Suppose he did? What would I do with it? I certainly wouldn't use it to go back in time … would I? Of course not. Then I thought of Natalie, all by herself in Hollow Rock.

I laughed. All by herself? Earth to Ray, that was 150 years ago. She's dead.

But she wasn't dead. I had just heard from her. She sent me a video. Okay, she made the video 150 years ago, but we were in a conversation.

I was beginning to think I was cracking up. I needed a break.

I put Beryl's manuscript and the Portal Finder in the bag and took it with me out to the car. I headed to one of the better restaurants that did take-out and ate it in the car in the restaurant's parking lot. I just needed to be out of my room, but I didn't want to be around people—and I didn't want to be away from the notebooks and Portal Finder. This seemed like a good compromise.

Herb Wells was dead. There was no doubt about that. I had the pictorial evidence. Beryl Dixon was dead, or so it said in the notebooks. Natalie O'Brien was the last of the group, and she was alone. So, what happened to Stan Hooper and Max Hawkins? Stan's note said that he was dead (or more accurately, *would be dead*), but after reading the notebooks, I was pretty sure he didn't die at Hollow Rock. Max disappeared at about the same time. Was it related to Stan's leaving? Jim wanted evidence that Stan was dead. I couldn't give him that. Could I give him evidence that he was alive beyond Hollow Rock? Tomorrow I'd go online and see if I could find any evidence that Stan (who was not the sharpest knife in the drawer) made his mark on history. I was hoping that he hadn't.

*****

I slept well that night. I must have been mentally exhausted from reading the notebooks. But I was up early. I wasn't ready to do any research on Stan (or Max, who I was pretty sure was too experienced to leave a trail), and I wasn't ready for breakfast. So I did the only thing I could think of ... I drove out to Hollow Rock.

I made the now-familiar trek from my car to the hill above town where the cave was. Out of habit, I checked the cave for a new message. Seriously? The Hollow Rock cave Twitter feed? Nonetheless, I felt a pang of sadness that there wasn't something waiting for me.

I sat on the same rock I sat on that first day I'd visited Hollow Rock, and I looked out over what was once the town. I wasn't sure why I was there, but it just felt right. I tried to imagine the town in all its glory, with people going about their lives. I could almost smell the horses and the cattle.

And then I heard Natalie. She was calling out to me for help. It was the voice I had heard many times before in her movies.

I didn't really hear her voice calling to me, of course, but she was there. She was right below me in town or riding by on a horse. She was there. I could almost feel her.

We were occupying almost the same space ... 150 years apart.

Chapter 41

I didn't want to leave my place on the rock. The fact that it was a beautiful morning was secondary. From all appearances, I was at peace. But it wasn't peace, it was emptiness.

I should be self-destructing. I had run across the most spectacular discovery in history; I had the NSA looking over my shoulder; I was falling in love with a dead woman (okay, that sounded particularly icky, but I knew what I meant); and locked in the trunk of my car was a device that could take me through time.

I should be a mess, but I wasn't.

I closed my eyes and let the morning warmth envelop me. I was no longer imagining Natalie, with her look of despair, or Herb with his face shot off. I was thinking of myself. More specifically, I was thinking of my life and my career. I had led a full life—an exciting life. I had cheated death more times than I wanted to remember. I had reached the pinnacle of my career. For a few years, I was almost a household name. I had received almost every writing award available.

And what was I doing now? Writing fluff pieces. Okay, not exactly fluff pieces. It's not like I was writing stories of dancing dogs. Some of them were on important topics, and most required in-depth research. But they would never be what they once were.

My near-death experience in the hut did something to me. I had been in bad situations before, but there was something about this one that shook me to the core. Maybe it was the blood sprayed across the wall with the embedded brain and skull fragments. Whatever it was, it did a number on me, one that signaled the end of my career. As fulfilling as that career was, my new career was the exact opposite.

And that's what I was feeling, lying there and soaking up the sun. I was feeling unfulfilled. What did I have? I had no family. I had no one to share things with. My previous lifestyle dictated that. Sure, I'd had relationships, but they were all short-term. And I went into them knowing that they would be. The women with whom I was in a relationship probably knew it from the start as well. It was all in the name of an exciting career.

Well, now I didn't have an exciting career anymore and I still had no one in my life. It was all rather depressing.

I sat up. The sun was getting hotter and I was doing myself no good by whining about my life. It was time to get to work. I slid off the rock and trudged through the sandy soil to my car. It was quiet where it was parked, so I turned on the engine and sat, letting the AC wash over me. I needed to talk to someone, so when I cooled down, I pulled out my pre-paid phone and called Hal's cell phone.

"Hal March."

"This is your friend out west," I said. "I'm calling on a disposable phone."

"Hello, friend. As far as I know, no one is listening in here."

"I didn't think so. The disposable phone is really so our mutual friends have less to question me about."

"Are you making any progress in your search?"

"I am. I found the notebooks I mentioned to you. Fascinating stuff."

"Real?"

"Very," I said. "I had another experience that confirms it. I'll tell you about it when I return. I'll tell you everything when I return … if you want me to."

"I'm looking forward to it."

"Yeah, well, think really hard about it. Your life won't be the same when you know all the details."

"Yeah, I kinda figured that."

"In the meantime," I said, "I came across an item I'll be bringing back for you. I'm telling you in advance so you can prepare for it. I'm giving it to you as a gift, so do with it what you'd like."

"Oh?" I knew I had piqued his interest.

"I have a manuscript written by Beryl Dixon."

"Are you shitting me? Original manuscript? For which of her books?"

"No, you misunderstand. An *original* manuscript. The book has never seen the light of day."

"Holy cow! Where did you find it?"

"That will have to come later. It'll come with the rest of the story."

"Do you know when it was written?" asked Hal. "That might shed light on what happened to her."

"Uh, well, that's the other thing. It was written in 1870."

"That's impossible. She wasn't even alive in…" He stopped. I could almost hear the wheels churning in his brain. "Are you telling me that that's what happened to her?"

"I am. And there's more to it than that. Stan and Herb, as well as another cohort of theirs, ended up there, as well as another famous missing person—Natalie O'Brien."

"How do you know?"

"Pictures, notes, and … um … I've been in touch with her."

There was silence on the other end. Finally, he said, "If you weren't who you are, I'd tell you to go stuff it and I'd hang up on you. But unless you've suddenly gone loony, I have no choice but to believe you."

"I'd rather not believe it myself," I said. "It would make things a lot simpler. Unfortunately, I'm in too deep. That's why I want you to seriously consider whether you want to hear the full story."

"I have to. I'm hooked. When are you flying back? Need me to pick you up?"

"I'm driving back. One of the other items I uncovered would never make it through airport security. I'll come to Boston first, before heading back to Florida. I'm going to spend the day doing some research on our friend, Stan, and I'll leave here in the morning."

"Be careful," said Hal before hanging up.

Those were two words I was going to have to take under serious consideration, now that I was in possession of a real live Portal Finder.

I was going to head to the library to do my research on Stan using one of their computers, but then it occurred to me that the NSA had the name Stan Hooper flagged, so it didn't matter what computer I used. I might as well use my own. After all, they already knew that I was investigating his disappearance. By using the library computer, it might seem as if I was trying to hide something from them—which, of course, I was. So I headed back to my hotel.

Hours later, I closed the laptop. I was exhausted, but I was also sure of something.

Without a doubt, Stan Hooper had survived beyond Hollow Rock.

Chapter 42

For whatever reason, Stan chose to use his real name when he went through the portal. By those actions, one would think that no one had told him about the need to use an assumed name. But from what I gathered from the notebooks, he was told about it by Herb after he arrived. However, he kept on using his real name even after he left Hollow Rock. Was he just being stupid or lazy, or was there a part of him that craved some notoriety? I was beginning to think the latter.

It wasn't very hard to find mention of him. I just had to go a few pages deep on Google. No one who looked up Stan online after his disappearance had any reason to check out a Stan Hooper from England in the 1940s, or from California in the 1960s. He wasn't born until 1970, and he disappeared in 2011. Since Stan Hooper was a pretty common name, it would be natural to skip over anyone with that name who didn't fit the parameters.

Had I found the right Stan Hooper? There were dozens of them listed on Google, and I very methodically copied the links to the various articles. Once I had a couple of dozen to work with, I clicked onto each link. A lot were easy to discard, as they had a picture of the Stan Hooper in question, looking nothing like the picture of Stan I was used to seeing.

I skimmed through the articles that didn't include pictures. In most cases, I was able to eliminate that particular Stan Hooper immediately, but there were a couple that needed a little closer attention.

The "ah-ha" moment came in an article in the *San Francisco Chronicle* from 1969, focusing on fringe spiritual groups. It included everything from mediums to gurus to crackpots. One of the crackpots was a man named Stan Hooper, who insisted that he could see the future. Among other things, he talked about phones that allowed the user to see the person on the other end and the fact that almost everyone would own a computer early in the 21st century—and that they'd be small enough to sit on your lap.

Oh, Uncle Jim wasn't going to be happy about that.

That was the only reference to Stan I could find from that time period. Hopefully, it meant that he was laughed at and sent packing.

In the articles that needed closer attention was one from 1965, but the article's author was referencing something that he had observed during World War II in London. The writer was a low-level military man assigned to 10 Downing Street. A man named Stan Hooper tried to get access to Winston Churchill to let him know that May 8, 1945, was the exact date the war in Europe was going to end. He also said that the Allies were going to invade the shores of Normandy on June 6, 1944, starting the downfall of the Nazi Regime. This was in 1942, long before the invasion was even in the planning stages.

The man was sent away without meeting the prime minister, but the writer of the article remembered the two dates clearly. In the article, he wondered whatever happened to the man, and how did he know these things?

So where was Stan now? When he left Hollow Rock, did he go to the 1960s first, or the 1940s? Where else might he have gone? And why was he bragging to people about his knowledge of the future?

Oh yes, Jim would *not* be happy.

Just for fun, I looked up Max Hawkins but could find nothing at all about him.

I ended the session feeling disturbed. I could understand why Jim was so anxious to know if Stan survived. The man was going around bragging about future events. If he came across the wrong person or situation, he really could change history.

And then I had another disturbing thought: If he did change history, would I even know it? After all, if it changed, how would I know? Had he already changed history?

The man had to be stopped.

*****

I was on the road in my rental first thing the next morning. I planned for a long drive that day. The more miles I could put in each day, the sooner I'd be in Boston.

Within an hour of leaving Flagstaff, I knew I was being followed. It was a nondescript white car of recent vintage— probably a rental. It was staying quite far behind me—at least a half-mile—but I knew it was following. It just had that feel about it. I had been followed numerous times in my old life in countries where there were people who weren't thrilled that I was there. This had the same feeling.

A couple of times I drove as slowly as I could and still be safe (and legal), and the car would get dangerously close before realizing that I had slowed down. They would suddenly go even slower. It was never close enough for me to see who was in it.

The NSA was the only logical conclusion.

I stopped in rest areas a few times, only to have the car scream past on the highway. The tinted windows and the speed made it impossible to see in.

It was definitely following me. An hour later, it would be

behind me again.

About fifteen hours after departing Flagstaff, I pulled into a decent-looking hotel off the highway in Tulsa. Before getting out of the car, I waited. Nothing. Had my pursuer given up?

Once I got settled, I called in a pizza to be delivered. They said they'd deliver it to the front desk. I took a hot shower while I waited. Finally, I got the call from the desk that my food had arrived, and I went to retrieve it.

I returned and opened the door to the room. Someone was sitting on my bed. He had a gun in his hand and was pointing it at me.

It wasn't the NSA.

Chapter 43

Alan Garland looked much the same as the two other times I had seen him, but more tired—much more tired. And whereas before he just seemed angry, now he looked scared.

"I told you to stay away from all this," he said.

His voice almost had a growl to it. Then I realized why. He was sick. His eyes were puffy and red, his face was pale, and the hand holding the gun was shaking.

"How'd you get into my room?" I asked, not caring about the answer.

"I have my ways."

"You look like shit," I said. "Have you slept?"

"None of your business."

"I bet you haven't eaten either." I opened the pizza box. "Want some pizza?"

He did. I could tell from his expression. He hadn't eaten or slept for a long time.

"No, I don't want pizza."

"Yeah, well, I think you're lying." The pizza parlor had included napkins and paper plates. I put a slice each on two plates and put one on a table near him. "Eat. I'm not going anywhere."

"I should kill you right here," he said.

"Why?"

"Because you know too much."

"You might find this hard to believe, but me knowing too much is actually a good thing for you. I know things that you don't—things that you need to know. Killing me would accomplish nothing, except to get you locked up for the rest of your life in a time period you probably don't even want to be in. Plus, you're sick. Your hand is shaking. You'd never hit me with your shot. It would go through the wall and probably hit some innocent person. Do you really want that?"

At Alan's silence, I said, "Put the gun down. I'm no threat to you. Eat some pizza. I've got a six-pack of cold water. You need to be hydrated."

He just couldn't do it anymore. The gun hand dropped, and he laid the gun on the floor. I moved quickly and picked it up. He gave me a questioning look.

"Just in case you change your mind," I said. "I don't like having guns pointed at me." My thoughts went back to my dream of the hut. I shut them out.

He picked up the pizza slice and hungrily devoured it.

"When was the last time you ate?" I asked.

He shrugged his shoulders. I put another slice on his plate.

"Why?" I continued.

"Worry. Stress. Fear. You name it."

"How did you know I was here?" I asked.

"In the restaurant that day, I tapped into your phone…"

"So you listen to my phone calls?" I was happy I had called Hal on the burner phone.

"No. This only *tracks* your phone. A little 22nd century gadget. Actually, a 21st century gadget that was perfected in the 22nd century. You just hold it close to another phone and it picks up the signal for tracking."

He knew enough about me to feel comfortable mentioning time travel.

"When did you get here?" I asked, wondering if he knew I had gone to the cave.

"Yesterday."

So he didn't know about the notebooks or the Portal Finder, or that I'd been to the cave. I glanced at my luggage while he was eating. It hadn't been touched. The items were still hidden.

"Jim told me that you're the worrier of the bunch—the stickler for details. Is that why you're so stressed? You see the whole thing unraveling and you can't do anything about it?"

If he was feeling better, he probably would have looked at me in surprise. But he was just too tired and too sick.

"Jim talks too much," he finally said.

"Don't blame Jim. I knew much of it before I visited Jim. You can blame Stan Hooper."

At the name, Alan groaned. "What a mess this is," he said. "You knew him?"

"No. Stan left notebooks detailing his time in Hollow Rock. I discovered them by accident. That's how I ended up involved in all this."

"Do you have them here?" he asked with less enthusiasm than I would have thought. The poor guy was almost asleep.

"No," I lied, "I sent them home. If you really want to blame someone, I suppose you could blame Herb Wells for getting drunk and telling Stan. At least, that's how I understand it. I think there are a lot of people at fault, but that's moot at this point. More importantly, Stan Hooper is traveling through time and he has to be stopped. I get it. I know Herb Wells went after him, but Herb is dead."

"What?" That woke him up.

"I have some pictures that Stan took and left with the notebooks. I'll show them to you when you're feeling better. There's a lot to go over but now isn't the time. You need sleep. What you should know is that I did some research and found that

Stan is still traveling—or was, anyway. I found evidence of him in California in the '60s and England during World War II."

Alan let out a groan.

"Take the second bed," I told him. "Sleep. Maybe you'll feel better after you've rested."

He didn't object. He crawled up to the pillow. I pulled down the blanket and covered him with it.

"Hey," he said, minutes from sleep. "I'm sorry."

"For?"

"Threatening you. Treating you like the enemy. You don't understand. It's just all so hard."

"Don't worry about it," I said. "We'll sort it all out when you wake up."

He didn't hear me. He had fallen asleep.

*****

Alan slept through the night. I felt his head from time to time. No fever. It just must have been a lack of sleep and nutrition. I felt for the guy. What they were involved in was something major. There was a lot of responsibility hanging over their heads, and Alan seemed to take it particularly seriously.

Alan woke up the next morning at eight. He didn't look a whole lot better, but he said he felt better. While he showered, I loaded the car. I had come to a decision. When he was dressed, I shared it with him.

"Since you're going to follow me to Boston, why don't you just drive with me. It'll save us both a lot of hassle. We can talk about what I know, and what to do about Stan Hooper. You can return your rental here in Tulsa."

He seemed pleased with that solution and quickly agreed.

"Meanwhile," I said, "you need food. Let's go eat, then we can return your car."

Two hours later, we were on the road. He asked me what I knew, so I told him everything. Well, not everything. I failed to mention my communication with Natalie. It was none of his business and it would just further upset him. I also didn't say anything about Hal March or Beryl Dixon's manuscript. Why complicate things?

"Uncle Jim gave me a pretty good overview of the program and the responsibility that goes with it. I have a question for you: Do you regret getting involved?"

"I didn't for the longest time. It was exciting. It was groundbreaking stuff. I was one of only a half dozen people ever to time travel. That comes with bragging rights..." He trailed off.

"But?" I asked.

"I'm realizing that it's not so great."

"You say that you're one of only six people to time travel," I began, "but if this is a success, there are, or will be lots of people traveling. Wouldn't that make it ripe for abuse?"

"Exactly. And that's what I've come to realize. When I sent my last report in—did Jim tell you about us leaving reports?"

"He did."

"Did he tell you that we could get responses to our reports after we leave them?"

"No, he didn't." *But I found out on my own,* I thought.

"When we leave a report, they can read it. We've tested it by having them send a response through the portal—remember, the portals are one-way. When we realized we could do that, it created a whole new line of communication. Anyway, in my last report, I suggested closing down the project, and I listed all the reasons. Well, they were way ahead of me. They had already figured it out. The NSA, who was backing the program, was none too thrilled and ordered them to keep it going, or at least provide them with all the documentation. You probably have never dealt with the NSA..."

"Actually, I have," I said, interrupting him. "In fact, I thought that it was the NSA who was following me yesterday. Unpleasant people."

"Then you know that they don't take no for an answer. So, I'm told that our team back home destroyed everything. Supposedly, no records exist of the project anymore. They didn't tell the NSA about the locations of the reports, so they are still monitoring them. They are hoping that everyone comes home. So far, no one has found the right portal to allow us to go back. We might never find it."

"There were six of you traveling, right?"

"Right," Alan answered.

"You, Herb, Jim, Max Hawkins, and I don't know the others."

"Two women. Simone and Hanna. The last I heard, Simone was in bad shape mentally and emotionally and was talking suicide. That was the last anyone heard from her. Hanna, we haven't heard a word from. God only knows..."

"And we know that Herb is dead," I said, "and that Jim is dying. That leaves you and Max."

"And Max could be anywhere in time," said Alan.

"I don't think so," I said. "From what I understand, Stan took Max's Portal Finder. Max is stuck in 1870 somewhere."

"What about Herb's Portal Finder?"

Lie or don't lie. How about a half-lie?

"I have it. Well, not with me. It's in a safe place though. I don't know why it was packed in the trunk, but it was."

He looked at me warily. "What are you going to do with it?"

"I don't know. But I can promise you this: No one—and I mean NO ONE—will ever get their hands on it. I understand its significance and I understand its danger. I'm not a Stan Hooper."

"Which brings up the question..." began Alan.

I finished the question.

"What can be done about Stan?" I asked.

Chapter 44

We hadn't even digested breakfast when trouble showed up. I picked up the tail about a half-hour outside Tulsa.

Alan saw me looking in the rearview mirror.

"Problem?" he asked.

"Yeah, and if it will make you feel better, you're better at tailing than whoever's behind us."

"NSA?" asked Alan.

"Probably, but they must have played hooky on the day they learned tailing."

I was making a joke about it, but in reality, I was scared. I wasn't scared that they would physically harm me—well, maybe a little—but I was terrified that they'd find the notebooks, and more importantly, the Portal Finder. We passed a sign for a rest area coming up in three miles. I also noticed that there was an exit for a town shortly after the rest area. Time for some quick planning.

Our tail was about a quarter-mile behind us. I crossed my fingers that this would work. As soon as we reached the exit to the rest area, I took it. If all went well, our tail would pass it by, not wanting me to know that they were following. A moment later, the car sped past.

Was it following us, or was it my imagination? And if it was the NSA guys, what was the purpose of following us? Assuming it was them, I guess that they were late to the party or I would have seen them yesterday. They were probably assuming we'd find a hotel for the night. They planned to hit us then.

Alan hadn't said a word. He knew I was figuring it all out.

I took off out of the rest area and took the first exit off the highway. I was sure our tail wouldn't have taken it. It was a suburban area, so I knew there would be what I was looking for. Sure enough, I found one within minutes—a storage facility.

"If we are being followed," I said, "I need to relieve myself of some cargo."

"Let me guess," said Alan, "you really didn't ship the notebooks and Portal Finder home."

"I did not. And the last thing I want—or you want—is for the NSA guys to get their hands on it."

The whole process took less than a half-hour. I rented the smallest unit they had, bought a lock, and locked up the notebooks and Portal Finder.

"Now I just have to remember the name of the town so I can get the items later," I said, laughing.

"That was smart," said Alan. "I like someone who can think on his feet. If anyone from this period has to know about the time travel, I'm glad it's you."

"I'm not so sure I am," I replied. "I can understand your stress. It's an awesome responsibility."

"Tell me about it."

We left the storage facility and got back on the highway. I felt a little more at ease. If they approached us, at least I no longer had anything they'd want.

*****

As expected, there was a knock on our hotel room door that evening. Alan and I looked at each other knowingly—and with just a bit of fear. I opened the door to find my two friends standing there.

"Hi Ray," said Mitch. "Can we come in?"

"Like I have a choice?" I responded.

"We all have choices," said Mitch, walking into the room. Smith, the bald one, closed the door and stood in front of it. Yeah, like we were going to try and escape.

Mitch looked at Alan and said, "You must be Alan Garland. You're a hard man to find."

"You found me," said Alan.

"So we did." He looked at me. "Were you lying to us about him? You said you only met him the one time."

"That was then, this is now. No, I wasn't lying to you."

Mitch said to Alan, "I have some questions for you. I'm from the NSA."

"I'm thrilled for you," replied Alan. "But I have nothing to say to you."

"Tell us about time travel," said Mitch.

"Tell me about the internal combustion engine," said Alan.

"Huh?"

"I figured if you wanted to ask me a random question, I'd ask you one."

"Tell me about Max Hawkins, Stan Hooper, and Herb Wells," said Mitch.

"Never heard of them."

"Really? That's not what Max says."

"Then talk to him."

"He's gone. I suspect he's somewhere in time. The others are gone too. So now all we have is you."

"Somewhere in time? Are you a loon?"

Mitch was silent for a minute, then said, "Look, we can play this game all you want. We can haul your ass back with us to Washington, where you'll be put in a room. That's where you'll sit until you talk to us.

"I don't think so," I said. "You don't think I prepared for this? I spent my life in the hot zones of this planet, dealing with some of the worst scum this world has ever seen. Do you think I can't handle you? I have documents out there that will go public letting everyone know that the NSA is obsessed with time travel. Your agency will be the laughingstock of the world. You and bullethead over there will be working at a burger joint washing dishes when this is all over. If I disappear—or hell, if I'm just in a bad mood— they'll be released. Alan is going nowhere. Ask your questions. If he doesn't want to answer, then get the hell out of here."

Mitch knew I had him. His division was super-secret. If word got out about it, the media would light up like a Christmas tree. So he took a different tack.

"Do you want to know why we had your friend Max in custody?"

"Don't know the man," said Alan.

"He was picked up by the FBI for putting a hit out on two people. You want to know who those two people were?"

Alan was silent. He was staring at the floor.

"Herb Wells and you."

That got a reaction. Alan's head shot up.

"You want to know why?"

Silence.

"Something about the two of you breaking your code and telling people about things you shouldn't be telling them." He said in a softer voice, "Talk to us."

"You can leave now," said Alan.

Mitch was slow to stand up.

"Just know," he said. "We will get information from you, threats notwithstanding," he added, looking at me.

They left the room, giving me a mean stare as they left.

"I'm done," said Alan, after I locked the door. He was

hanging his head. "I no longer care about Stan Hooper. I've reached the end of the line. If you want to worry about him, you can."

He looked up at me with tears in his eyes.

"I just want to go home."

Chapter 45

I felt sorry for the guy. When he signed up for the time travel program, he was probably a dreamer, full of enthusiasm for the coming adventure. But ten years of traveling had left him tired and worn out. The reality had hit him: time travel was just too dangerous to the world and it carried too much responsibility for the traveler.

And then to find out that one of your colleagues wanted you dead! I couldn't imagine what was going through his head. It sounded as if Alan, like Herb, had said something he shouldn't to someone he shouldn't. I didn't bother to ask him what it was. It was his cross to bear. If he felt like talking about it, he would, but I wasn't holding my breath.

I don't think either of us slept much that night—whether it was the appearance of Mitch and friend, or whether we were each going through our own crises.

Alan was done. What was he going to do? Keep traveling until he found a portal that would take him home? I guess he suspected that he'd never find it and was now grappling with the decision of whether to try to find a portal home or just give it up and pick a place (and time) to live.

For me, it was something else. It had been in the back of my mind for a couple of days. Do I go back in time to Hollow Rock and try to help Natalie get home? What were the odds of that succeeding? Slim? Nonexistent? It's just that my heart ached whenever I thought about her plea for help. And if I went back, was I prepared to spend the rest of my life caught in time? Would it be any worse than the lack of direction I was now feeling?

Suppose I did make that decision? Could I set up a communication link with Hal? Portals only go in one direction, to one time period. So any message from Hal would go only to that place and time. Somewhere outside the portal, in a hidden spot— whenever I arrived—I could leave things for him to pick up in his current time. Just like Stan, and then Natalie did for me. My gut told me that Jim had a lot of information on existing portals. He would have gotten it from Max, Herb, and Alan in their travels— not to mention his own travels. He could help me find a time period that might be a busy spot for portals. The Grand Central Station of portals. A place that we (assuming Natalie was with me) could get to from time to time to leave messages for Hal in our search to bring Natalie home. Could it work?

And that's why *I* didn't sleep. My mind was going at a hundred miles an hour.

We arrived in Boston the next afternoon. Alan wanted to go straight to Jim's house, but I let him know that it would be safer to go there indirectly.

"We don't know where Mitch and his friend are," I explained. "We didn't see them behind us today, but it doesn't mean they weren't there. Jim is the only one of you they don't know about. I'll reserve a room back at my hotel and we can park there. Then we can take the train to Jim's place."

Alan seemed to appreciate my caution.

By the time we parked, stored our stuff in the room, and caught the train, it was almost evening when we arrived at Jim's. I pressed the buzzer and had to wait a long time for Jim to answer. I could imagine him painfully trying to get out of his chair and make his way to the door.

"Hello?" His voice was weak through the intercom.

"Jim, it's Ray. And I have Alan with me."

If he was surprised that the two of us were together, his voice didn't convey it. I doubt if he had the energy to be surprised. He buzzed us in, and we climbed the stairs to his apartment.

He looked terrible. He had lost a lot more weight. His once portly looks were now a mass of sagging skin. We didn't have to say anything. He could see it in our eyes.

"I know. I look like death warmed over. Well, the fact is, I'm close to it. I give myself another month at most."

"Have you seen a doctor?" I asked futilely.

"What for?" he answered. "There's nothing a doctor could do at this point. But forget me. Tell me about your trip. How did the two of you end up together?"

We gave him the details, taking turns telling him about the cave, the notebooks, Mitch Webster, Stan Hooper, my communication with Natalie—which I hadn't yet told Alan—and everything else.

"So Stan is still alive," Jim muttered, shaking his head. His eyes suddenly came alive. "Alan, you have to go after him."

"I can't."

"What do you mean you can't?"

"I'm done, Jim. This life has taken its toll on me. I can't do it anymore. I know I'm never going to find my way home, so I'm going to find a new place to live. I don't know where or what time period that will be yet. It can't be here. Those NSA guys will be all over me. But I'm done. No more reports, no more worrying about who's breaking the rules—like I'm a good one to talk. When I find a place to settle down, I'll destroy my Portal Finder. You won't have to worry about me."

"I won't worry about you anyway," answered Jim. "I'll be dead. But I am worried, Alan. Stan could do so much damage with his recklessness. I feel responsible. I feel that our whole program is responsible."

I had been sitting there slowly making up my mind. Oh, who was I kidding? I had already made up my mind.

"Jim," I began, "there's another option. I'd like to go back. It's obvious to us all that I need to help Natalie. Can I ever get her home? I don't know. Maybe you can give me the portal locations and time periods you guys have used to at least get us back here, in 2021. She will have lost a few years, but she'll be home close to the time she left. Meanwhile, I'll try to intercept Stan."

"What would you do if you found him?" asked Alan.

I looked him in the eyes.

"Whatever is necessary."

Jim and Alan each stared into space, processing my offer.

"What would you need from me?" asked Jim, his mind made up.

"Instructions on how to use the Portal Finder, and any notes you have on portals throughout the world—anything that would make our return journey a little easier, taking into account that I'll also be chasing Stan. With Beryl dead, the only two people who shouldn't be roaming through time are Natalie and Stan. If all goes well, Natalie will be with me. And if I can find Stan, I'll neutralize him as needed and time travel will once again be a secret."

"Do you trust Natalie?" asked Alan.

"I don't know her, but my gut feeling is yes."

"Then let's get you up to speed."

*****

Jim and Alan spent a couple of hours instructing me on the use of the Portal Finder—surprisingly easy to operate—and the ins and outs of time travel that I hadn't yet been told. Jim said he'd have the list of known portals for me the next day. Alan decided to spend the night at Jim's, and I sleepily made my way back to the hotel.

*****

The next morning, I headed over to see Hal.

Hal told everyone that he was not to be disturbed for any reason, and he hustled me into his office.

I handed him Beryl Dixon's manuscript.

"It'll be up to you to authenticate it," I said. "I don't know what you'll do though if someone determines that the paper and ink are from a time before she was born."

"I'll get around it. Don't worry about that," he said. "You're sure that this is Beryl's?"

"One hundred percent."

"Well, thank you. I don't know what else to say. Why didn't you keep it?"

One look and he knew.

"Oh."

"Hal, are you sure you want to know all this?"

"I do. And before you start, answer this: you're planning to travel, aren't you?"

"I am. And I'll explain why as we talk. Also, I don't have Stan's notebooks with me—I had to ditch them quickly—but I'll get them to you before I leave."

I spent the next several hours bringing him up to speed. When I was finished, he asked, "If it's so important to keep all this secret—and I agree with you there—why are you telling me?"

"Because if I'm going to travel through time, I need someone as a contact. If I make it back, this can be our secret. If I don't, you can use it as great fodder for a novel. The fact is, I trust you."

"When are you planning to do this?" asked Hal.

"Soon, I guess. I just really made up my mind to do it. I have a lot to do ... a lot to think about. Do I keep my house on the assumption that I'll be back? How do I handle my bills? I guess I could hire a firm to take care of all that. Now that I've made the decision, I don't want to wait."

Hal seemed to be deep in thought. He finally asked, "You said that there's a span of a few months that you could arrive after going through the portal. What happens if you arrive before all of this? Before Natalie arrives. Before Stan arrives, or before he puts the trunk in the cave? It seems to me that it would screw things up."

"Yeah, and I don't know the answer to that. I have to think that it would be natural for me to arrive after all that—that the way time works, it couldn't have me arrive before I was in touch with Natalie, or before I found the trunk, could it? Who really knows? Jim said that the Portal Finder registers the date when you arrive. If it looks like I've arrived before all this happens, I guess I'll just try to lay low while I'm there. But it just doesn't make sense to me that I would arrive before I found that stuff. How else would I remember it? They said that you keep all your memories throughout time, so I can't remember something that hasn't yet happened. Jim and Alan agreed that while there is no real evidence either way, most likely I would arrive after all this."

"But they don't know for sure," said Hal.

"No. And it's enough to make you dizzy."

I had been thinking about it even before Hal asked the question. What if I *did* arrive before all of this? Before Stan, before Natalie, before Herb, or Beryl, or Max? Or what if I arrived before them and because I did, it changed time and they never showed up at all?

What if I was alone and lost in time?

Chapter 46

The next three weeks were busy. I flew back home to Florida and arranged for a management company to take care of my place. I talked to my accountant. I just said I'd be away for an extended period. It sounded better than "I'll be time traveling and might never get back." He let me know that bill-paying was a service he offered, and I quickly took him up on it. I packed everything I'd need into a bag, which included my Glock 23 handgun. It didn't look like anything you'd see back in the 1870s, but it didn't matter. It was the gun I was familiar with. I was taking it.

I drove back to Boston by way of Oklahoma to pick up Stan's notebooks. I left the Portal Finder in the storage facility. I'd pick it up on my way west.

On the way back, I got a call from Alan to let me know that Jim died. That made me sad. He was a good man. A kind man. He had provided me with everything I would need for my trip, including maps and lists of all the known portals. Based on his information, I consulted with Hal and we chose a portal in England as our official communication point. Hal said he'd journey there at least three times a year to check it and leave messages for me. Once I determined its exact location, I'd find some way to get the information to him.

While in Oklahoma, I stopped at a "cowboy" store. That's not what it was called, but they had everything I would need, clothes-wise, to travel back to Hollow Rock, Arizona in 1870. They also sold a bag for my belongings that wouldn't look out of place there.

I arrived in Boston on a rainy day. The cloud cover was so low it almost looked like fog, and the humidity made me feel as if I was back in Florida.

I had already said my goodbyes to Alan weeks earlier, so there was no reason to meet up with him again. My only reason for coming to Boston was to make final arrangements with Hal and to give him Stan's notebooks. We met in a dark tavern. I had already visited Hal at his place of business twice. A third time would be pushing it. So far, there was no reason to believe that the NSA knew anything about Hal's relationship with me, and I wanted to keep it that way.

"I promised Jim that I would never share anything about the time travel project, so please keep these in a safe place."

"Having second thoughts about trusting me with all this information?" asked Hal.

"Not in the least," I answered. "Just trying to take my job seriously."

"You don't have to worry. After I read them, they will never see the light of day."

"When I leave you a message—assuming I can—I will number each message with the day that I've been gone: Day 42, Day 137, etc. That way, you'll know in what order I wrote them."

"And when I send you anything, I will label it with the date I sent it," said Hal.

After finalizing everything, we made some pleasant conversation for a while, but I was anxious to go. Frankly, I was nervous about my upcoming trip. Hal could sense it.

"Go, Ray. Get out of here. Your anticipation is oozing out of you."

As we were saying our goodbyes, my phone rang. It was my

prepaid phone. I had canceled my phone service and thrown away my other cell when I was in Florida. I had also disabled the Wi-Fi on my laptop and put it in a safe deposit box at the bank. There was no way Mitch and friends could follow me now.

"Hello?"

"Ray, it's Alan. I'm coming with you. I ran into Mitch and the bald guy. I should say, they found me. They told me to get out of town. They tried to call you, but your phone was out of service. Their division has been closed down. They're being reassigned and all of their documentation is being destroyed. Anyone featured prominently in their research is being contacted. Mitch thinks that means eliminated. They can have nothing remaining. He said that they're going to go after me, Herb, Max, Stan, and you. They'll never find the others, but I think you and I are going to have big targets on our back."

"They wouldn't kill us," I said. "They're the government." The ridiculousness of that statement hit me the moment I said it. Governments do that all the time.

"Never mind," I said. "Okay, where are you?"

"I'll be in Boston Common in about an hour. I have to grab a few things."

I knew that the few things included the Portal Finder.

"I'll look for you where Newbury Street hits the Common in one hour," said Alan. "Ray, be careful."

I hung up. Hal was giving me a questioning look.

I lowered my voice and Hal leaned in closer.

"Alan said that Mitch called him and told him to get lost. He tried to call me. He told him that they closed down the division they worked for. Mitch and his partner are being transferred to another department."

"And?" asked Hal.

"That's the weird part. He said they are purging everything—notes, documentation … everything. And people."

"You mean people like you?"

"According to Alan, yes. Why would they do that?"

"Someone talked," said Hal. "That's all I can think of."

"So?"

"This was all top secret, not to mention the fact that it was on the fringe, so to speak. My guess is that they were doing this without proper authorization. Government funds without the government's knowledge. This was one of those secret groups— someone's pet project. The pet project just got exposed and they have to make it disappear quickly so that if someone asks about it, they can deny that it ever existed. Either someone talked or an audit exposed some missing funds. Either way, someone is panicking."

"They've had this division for at least ten years," I said. "That's a long time to keep it a secret."

"Which might not have been a problem if they'd had any success," said Hal, "but how much success have they had? If I had to guess, this time travel lead was the most interesting project they had. But they've gotten nowhere on it. Practically everyone they've spoken to has disappeared. They can't possibly have anything concrete to show for all the money that was funneled their way."

"I don't think they know about you," I said.

"No. My only exposure to them was when they came into the office after Stan disappeared. They're not interested in bumping off people like me. It's the suspected travelers and people close to them like you."

"How about Stan's ex-girlfriend?"

"I doubt it," said Hal. "After all, how many people did they talk to over the years. They can't kill them all. That's why I think it's just the major players. Ray, be careful."

Funny, Alan had just said the same thing.

"Get out of town quickly," he added.

"You mean, get out of this time period," I answered.

"That too. Call me before you leave so that I know you made it."

We stood up and shook hands.

"I will, Hal. You be careful too."

A few minutes later, I was in my car, headed for Newbury Street. I made a few random turns—for two reasons: One: I was early and had to kill a few minutes; Two: Just in case there was someone on my tail, I'd be able to detect them. But a half-dozen turns later, I was convinced that I was alone.

Exactly an hour after Alan's call, I was in front of the Boston Common. There was no parking, so I was going extra slowly, much to the annoyance of other drivers.

Then I saw him. He was running across the grass. Was someone chasing him? Not that I could see. But he looked scared. He was ten feet from my SUV when he stumbled. I reached over and opened the passenger door. He was on his knees.

Oh my God, he'd been shot!

Who shot him? I didn't see anyone. And then I heard it. A drone. I looked up and saw it. It was a tiny thing, not like the big ones in the movies. This was no bigger than the kind you bought at Best Buy.

I heard a *pop* and saw Alan flinch. I heard a woman scream and point at him, then point at the drone. Alan was holding onto the passenger side of the frame of the SUV.

"Get in!" I yelled.

He threw a bag into the car. I knew what was in it—the Portal Finder.

"No, go," he said weakly. "I'm done. Go, get out of here. Take care of the bag."

Another *pop* and he dropped to the ground. I stepped on the gas, the motion closing the door. My back window shattered. I looked in the rearview mirror and saw the drone following. I made a few quick turns, but it was still on my tail.

And then the rain began. It had been getting darker and darker, and the cloud cover was getting lower and lower. As I drove, the fog I had experienced earlier was closing in again. It was now pouring, and I couldn't see twenty feet in front of me. If I couldn't see, then the drone couldn't see either. There were no more shots, and I could no longer see the drone behind me. I had caught a break.

I saw a parking garage on my right and turned in. I grabbed my ticket and drove up the ramp a couple of floors until I found a quiet corner spot. I backed in, so as not to show my broken back window.

I took a deep breath. My hands—hell, my whole body—was shaking. I sat there for a long time until I had regained my composure.

The rain had saved me this time.

But what about next time?

Chapter 47

I had to make two phone calls. One to Hal to let him know what happened, and the other to a car rental company that delivered.

The rental company told me it would be about a half-hour. That was okay. It would take my heart that long to start beating normally.

"It's already on the local news," Hal said in place of hello. "Was that you?"

"If you mean me speeding away in my car? Then yes, that was me. Hal, they killed Alan."

"Oh my God, I was hoping that wasn't him, but deep down, I knew it was. Are you okay?"

"I am. I'm in a hidden spot. I'm getting a rental delivered. I can't drive my car. The police will be looking for it and have probably alerted the glass repair companies to be on the lookout for an SUV with its back window blown out. I won't need my car where I'm going, so a rental makes the most sense."

"Leave your keys in the SUV and tell me where it is. I'll come and get it in a few days. I know someone in the towing business. He'll load it on a flatbed and cover it, no questions asked. I have a safe place to store it."

"Thanks, I appreciate it."

"Was it really a drone?"

"It was. The only thing that saved me was the rain. It started pouring. Hal, they knew it was me."

"They probably had your car in their system. When you opened your door for Alan—yeah, someone got it all on their cell phone, so the whole world has seen it—the NSA knew it was you. The police don't though. They didn't get your plate number, so they're just looking for a blue SUV with a broken back window, and I'm sure the NSA hasn't passed on any information to them. You sure you're okay? Is there anything I can do?"

"You've done enough, and I thank you. I'm fine."

"Was that the Portal Finder he threw in your car?"

"Good question. I haven't had time to check."

I opened the bag. Mixed in with some clothes, some old money for the trip to 1870, his gun, and a box of ammo, was the Portal Finder.

"Yes, it was. I guess I'll take it with me."

"Ray…"

"Yeah, I know," I interrupted, "be careful."

"Yes. And take care of yourself. Tell Natalie I love her movies."

"I will do that," I said with a chuckle. The fact that I was able to laugh must have meant I was feeling a little better.

While I waited for the rental, I checked Alan's bag to see if there was anything I had missed. Nothing. For some reason, that made me sad. Was this all he had, after all those years of time traveling? He had been a lonely, unhappy man. A sad end to a sad life.

I counted the money he was bringing to Hollow Rock. It totaled $25. From all I'd read, it could tide a man over for a little while. Add that to the $125 I had (that had cost me a small fortune at the coin store), and I had enough to do some traveling while I was there. Assuming Natalie was coming with me, she probably had some money saved up.

The rental arrived a few minutes later—a white Nissan Rogue. That was good. They were all over the place. The less conspicuous the better.

I moved my bag and Alan's bag to the new car. There was nothing else that needed to go. I looked at the two bags and suddenly realized that I wasn't all that different from Alan. Everything I was taking could fit into one bag as well.

I left the keys under the seat of my SUV. Would I ever see it again? Did I care?

When I left the parking garage, it was still pouring. Good. Every little bit of camouflage helped. I also made a decision. Now that I knew I was a target, I couldn't use my credit card for gas purchases or hotels. The days of being able to stay in a hotel without giving your credit card were long gone, so I should plan on sleeping in the car at rest areas. I stopped at a bank and took out $1000. Then I stopped at a sports store and picked up a sleeping bag and a pillow. I'd put the back seats down, which would give me enough space for sleeping.

It occurred to me that I had used a credit card and given my license for the rental. I really had no choice there. Maybe it wouldn't occur to the NSA goons right away to check with the rental agencies. Hopefully, they were still looking for my SUV. A lot of "hopefullys."

I didn't drive far that day. Much of the day was already gone and frankly, I was exhausted. I stopped at a busy rest area somewhere beyond Albany. I dined on rest area food, used the rest area bathroom, and slept in the back of my Rogue.

I was up before sunrise—stiff from my accommodations—and back on the road.

The next couple of days were uneventful. I stopped at the storage facility outside Tulsa and retrieved the Portal Finder. When I finally arrived in Flagstaff, it was early in the day. There was no reason to stay in a hotel that night. If I was going through the portal, the sooner the better. I dropped off the Rogue, then asked the people there if there was someone who would like to earn a hundred dollars to drive me out to Hollow Rock. I had a taker immediately.

Less than two hours later, I was standing outside the now-familiar cave. I hadn't yet tested the Portal Finder. This was a good place to test it, seeing as how I was right outside the portal. Sure enough, it listed several portals in the readout, this one being first on the list. I selected it and it told me exactly where the portal was. It told me that I was only feet away from the entrance. I turned it off, then checked the cave for vermin, and entered. There were no messages for me in the usual spot.

I was nervous—more nervous than I had ever been before. I hesitated for just a moment, then squeezed through the tight entrance to the room.

I was in the portal.

PART FOUR

Chapter 48

The first thing I noticed was how cold it was. Was this something to do with time travel? And then I looked at the Portal Finder in my hand, I saw the date illuminated: November 12, 1870. Of course it's cold. It's the beginning of winter.

And then I did a doubletake. November 1870. I did it! Not only did I make it back to 1870, but I also made it back late in the year. That meant I arrived after all the events in the notebooks. Most importantly, it looked as if I arrived after Natalie's video to me. But would she still be here?

I dug into my bag and put my coat on. Then I put on my Stetson. I was just hoping that I looked the part of a cowboy. After just a moment's hesitation, I attached my holster with the gun to my belt and pushed it around toward my back. No one could see it under the coat, but I'd have it, just in case.

Before packing my bag for the trip, I tried to decide whether or not to bring Alan's gun and ammo as well as my own, and after much deliberation decided to. If I did meet up with Natalie, it might be good if we both had guns for protection. I was breaking the rules by taking weapons from my time period, but I didn't care. It could be dangerous, and I wanted something I was familiar with.

I squeezed my way out of the room and headed for the cave

entrance. What greeted me was one of the most amazing sights I'd ever seen. Hollow Rock was spread out below me. It looked nothing like my image of it when I was walking down the dusty road. It was alive! I heard music and saw people—real people. Any nervousness I had going into this was gone. I had been to a lot of places in my life, but nothing like this. I wasn't just in a different place. I was in a different place at a different time.

The old adventurous spirit was emerging. I couldn't wait to get down there and see the town—and hopefully see Natalie.

I was sliding down the hill when it suddenly occurred to me: What would I say if someone asked how I got there? I guess I'd just tell them that my horse died, and I was forced to walk. That sounded reasonable.

I sauntered down to the road that led into Hollow Rock. Excitement was surging through my body. I passed the welcome sign that had been in Stan's picture, and into the bustling little town. I wasn't sure how much bustle it was supposed to have, but it seemed particularly loud.

"Where'd you come from?" I jumped. It was a kid, maybe twelve years old, who had suddenly appeared at my side. I was going to have to be a little more aware than that.

"Sorry, you scared me. Horse died a ways back. Had to walk."

"Well mister, this ain't a good time to be here. The marshal got murdered yestiday and thems that did it are in the saloon. Cowboys. Herd's a few miles outta town. They just got paid and came in to celebrate. Celebrated too hard and one of 'em shot the marshal."

"Not Marshal Hawkins, was it?"

"Nah. He up and left a few weeks ago. This was his depity, Depity Cy. He got the job as marshal.

"Are there any more deputies?"

"One, but he ain't in town today."

"And the cowboys are all at the saloon, you say?" Natalie worked in the saloon.

"Yup. Six of 'em. Feelin' their oats, too. Most cowboys that come through here are good people. Not this crew. I'd keep my distance if I was you. You ain't got a gun belt on."

"Thanks for the warning," I said.

My first hour in Hollow Rock and already I was going to run into trouble.

I meandered my way toward the saloon, looking at everything along the way. A few people were staring at me.

In general, I'd have to say that the movie studios did a pretty good job of recreating western towns. But there was one thing they didn't get right—the people. As I looked at the townsfolk, I realized just how different they were. I didn't see a lot of smiling. They all looked grim. I wouldn't go as far as to say sad, but there seemed to be very little humor in their faces. Maybe I was being unfair, making a judgment so quickly, but it's what struck me. I knew that they led a hard life and they probably had very little time for fun, but some of these people looked positively morose.

I reached the saloon and took a breath. I could already hear the cowboys inside whooping it up. Somehow it didn't seem like a happy sound. They sounded like an obnoxious crowd. I'd have to watch myself. It would be so easy for me to go in there with a superior air. After all, being from the enlightened 21st century, with a good education, a lifetime of traveling the world—particularly in dangerous places—it would be easy to assume that attitude. That's exactly what would get me in trouble. I needed to lay low and keep quiet.

I entered the saloon.

"Hey, who're you?"

So much for laying low. In a town of this size, any new face was immediately noticed. I looked around at the patrons. Some were just curious, but others—mostly from the wild group—were wary.

"Horse died," I replied. My mouth was suddenly dry. "Had to walk."

"How come yer clothes look like they come right off the rack?" asked one of the cowboys.

"I brushed the dust off."

Suddenly I saw her. Natalie was surrounded by four of the cowboys. One of them had her on his lap and was feeling her up. She had a disgusted look on her face. That look changed when she recognized me. She mouthed "Ray?" I gave her a quick nod.

"You look kinda like a tenderfoot," said one of the two cowboys who weren't surrounding Natalie. "We have fun with them."

"You don't want to find out," I answered. I set my bag down, and as I did, I reached under my coat, pulled out my gun, and pointed it at him.

"What the hell is that?" asked the cowboy.

"A Glock 23 semi-automatic handgun."

"A what?"

"It's a pistol that can put a hole in you. That's all you need to know."

"Hey, well put it down," said the cowboy. The others had gotten up and were standing near the first guy. The one with Natalie on his lap had pushed her off. "You got six bullets and there are six of us. You better be a crack shot."

All the other patrons scrambled up and got out of the way. I felt like I was in a movie.

"Actually, I can waste a few. This holds thirteen. I can put two bullets in each of you and still have one leftover."

"That's a damn lie. No pistol can do that."

I shrugged my shoulders. "Oh, by the way, I'm really good with this."

I was too. The places I had to visit in my early life required that I know this stuff.

"I hear one of you killed the marshal yesterday," I said. "Which one of you?"

"It was the one with the big mouth, Ray," said Natalie, leering at the cowboys. She approached me. "Nice to see you. I didn't know if you'd come."

"Nice to see you, Natalie," I said, my eyes still on the cowboys. "And I didn't know when I'd get here."

"Kind of strange, isn't it? Well, you came at just the right time."

People were looking at us with confused expressions, so I focused my attention back on the cowboys.

I said to them, "My suggestion to you is to drop your guns and vamoose out of town."

Did I really say vamoose?

"All except the one who shot the marshal. I'll take you over to the jail until the deputy gets back."

"Like hell!" he yelled. He pulled out his pistol and I shot him in the chest. The guy next to him was drawing as I shot the first guy, so I shot him too. The others held their hands off to the side, indicating that it was over. One thing I quickly learned: unlike the movies, most cowboys were slow at the draw. I wasn't facing the Sundance Kid.

"Okay," I said, the adrenaline rushing through me. "Drop your weapons and leave. I'll make sure you get them back." They dropped their guns to the floor and shuffled past me. As the one who was manhandling Natalie passed me, I switched the gun to my left hand and struck him in the ear with the edge of my right hand. He fell to the floor.

He sat up slowly and asked, "What did you do that for?"

"For putting your hands on Natalie. Apologize to her."

He slowly got to his feet and tipped his hat at Natalie. "I'm sorry, Ma'am."

She kicked him in the groin and he dropped to the ground with a scream. Then he threw up.

"That's to remember me by," she said.

I put my gun in its holster. People had been staring at it and the less they saw of it, the better.

The owner of the saloon came over and told me that he'd have the bodies of the two dead men taken care of.

"Nice shooting. Quite the gun."

"Thanks."

As I turned away, Natalie put her arms around me and kissed me hard on the lips.

"It's nice to meet you, Ray Burton. I'm glad you came."

Chapter 49

She still had her arms wrapped around me. The men in the saloon slowly returned to their seats and most were smiling as they watched us. They were the first smiles I had seen amongst the townspeople.

"Do you have a coat?" I asked.

"In the back. Also a change of clothes. Can I hope that you don't plan on sticking around and that maybe I'll be going with you?"

I smiled at her. I was holding the famous actress Natalie O'Brien ... in 1870. A little weird, but definitely nice.

"Yes, I think you can assume that."

We went into the back room, where she quickly changed behind a screen, then accompanied me out the door into the saloon.

"I need to do something first," I said.

"Are you okay?" Natalie asked with alarm. "You're shaking."

"I am shaking, but I am okay," I responded. When I had entered the saloon, I noticed Charles Martin tending bar. "There's someone I have to meet."

I walked over to where he was standing behind the bar.

"You deserve a drink on the house for slaying the dragon and winning the damsel's heart," he said. "What can I get you?"

I felt like a kid meeting Santa for the first time. I was still shaking, and my mouth had gone dry. I had a lump in my throat.

"I … I don't want anything, thanks. But I need to ask you a question. Are you Charles Martin?"

"I am. Have you read some of my stories?"

"I'm afraid I haven't, though I'd love to. This might not make any sense to you, but I have to say it anyway. You've been a big inspiration to me. I'm a journalist, and I'm a journalist because of you."

"You've never read my work, but I inspired you? Well, that's a new one."

"I know it sounds odd, and I really can't tell you more than that."

"Where are you from?" he asked.

"New York," I answered. Not a lie since I was born in Rochester.

"Then you must know my publisher, Beadles."

"I've heard of them," I said. "Look, I don't want to take you away from your work, but I was wondering: can I shake your hand? It would mean a lot to me."

"I'd be honored, friend."

And there I was, shaking hands with the picture on my wall. I felt a tear roll down my cheek and quickly brushed it away.

"My name is Ray. I'm not sure how long I'll be in town, but I'd love to stop in and talk to you."

"It would be my pleasure, Ray. And I'll bring in a few of my books. My gift to you."

"What was that?" asked Natalie, as we left the saloon. "How could you know about Charles?"

"I'll tell you the whole story in a little while. How are you doing?"

"I'm better now. It's been so lonely here. It wasn't much fun when the others were here, but now it's downright depressing.

I've never been totally accepted by the townspeople. They know I'm different somehow. I think I scare them a bit. Did you come for me or just for the adventure of it?"

"For you. I told them—the colleagues of Max and Herb, that is—that I'd also try to find Stan and figure out a way to shut him up. He's making a mess of things. But Stan isn't my focus. You are. You're the one I came for. If I find Stan in the process of getting you home, fine. But getting you home is my main priority. We might get there a few years after you disappeared, but if we get lucky, at least we'll be in the right century."

"I would be good with that. Max said it's hard to find a specific time that you're looking to travel to. Do you think we can make it?"

"I hope so. Nothing is guaranteed, but I have a list of portals throughout the world. If we can pick the right ones, we might just do it."

"I'm glad you can handle yourself. That may come in handy. Thank you for sending those articles. They gave me an idea of who might come for me. You've led an interesting life."

I laughed. "And it's getting more interesting."

"To put it mildly," said Natalie.

"I realize that in real-time for you, you've only been gone a few months," I said, "but do you miss your career? It certainly misses you."

"No. I was going to do one more movie, then I was going to retire at the ripe old age of thirty-one."

"Really?"

"Really. I was getting tired of the life. Everything was based on image. I'm not that kind of person. I wanted to escape to someplace quiet. It's because of that decision that I'm here."

I gave her a questioning look.

"Randy, my 'boyfriend'"—she made quotation marks in the air—"was the only one I had shared that information with. Big mistake! He wanted to talk some sense in me. That's why he suggested we go away for a few days."

"Let me guess," I said. "He was afraid he'd lose his meal ticket."

"Exactly. I was going to end it with him anyway, which makes telling him about my decision extra stupid. I let him convince me to have one last weekend together. Worst decision I ever made."

"Well, let's see if we can correct that. What's the best way to get to California?" I asked. "We need to go to San Francisco. That's where the closest portal is. It's also where Stan went, although I doubt that we'll find him there."

I told her the story of looking him up on Google.

"So is there a stage? A train? Or do we just ride?"

"The next stage will come through in a couple of days," she answered. "A couple of times I almost got on it and headed west, but after getting your message, I decided to stick it out a while longer. The stages have been held up a lot lately, but that might still be our best bet. I don't know where the country is with the building of the railroads. I haven't been here long enough to figure that out. Trying to ride out on our own might prove to be dangerous for a lot of reasons. The stage will take us to San Francisco."

"It sounds like you've already given this thought," I said.

"I've given it a lot of thought," she responded. "If I was going to leave here, I figured I'd head to San Francisco. I thought it might feel a little more normal than this place."

"That's what we do then," I said. "I'll get a room for a couple of nights, then we can head out. I think you can quit your job now."

"Gladly. And I have some money saved up. Not a lot, but enough."

"I have about $150 in current money," I said.

"Then that'll be plenty," she said. "And by the way, you don't have to take a room at the hotel. I moved into Herb's shack when he was killed. It's nothing much, but it's decent."

"I accept the offer."

"What'll we do for money when we get to the different time periods?" asked Natalie.

"We'll figure it out," I answered. "One portal at a time. San Francisco is next. It'll take us to the late 1960s. Figuring it would be our next stop, I made sure to bring some money for that period—nothing printed after about 1967. After that, we're just going to have to improvise."

We walked through the town to her house. A lot of people stared at me as we walked.

"I feel like I'm in a fishbowl," I said.

"They're very cautious about new people, especially a new person who just killed a couple of men. They're a little nervous, to say the least. They haven't had this many shootings here ... ever, as far as I know."

We walked into her house and I was immediately shocked at how bare it was. The house had been shoddily constructed. I could see gaps in the walls. The place was freezing.

"Not one for decorating, I see?"

Natalie laughed, then said, "As you can tell, I wasn't planning on staying." She opened the woodstove and added some kindling to the still-warm embers of an old fire. In a few minutes, she added a small log. In no time, she had a roaring fire going. She closed the door to the stove, then said, "I don't have much in the way of food. I usually eat at the saloon before and after work."

"Did I see a restaurant in town?" I asked.

"You did. I've been there a few times, mostly with Herb or Max. It's pretty good."

"Well then, that's where we're eating every meal until we leave."

"You sure you can afford it?" she asked, chuckling. "It'll probably cost us about fifty cents for the two of us."

"Just don't eat a lot."

An hour later we were sitting in a comfortable little restaurant, owned by a friendly Swedish couple. I was starving, so I ordered the largest steak they served. When we had walked over, the townspeople tipped their hats to Natalie and greeted me with a nod or a two-finger salute. One person even thanked me for "clearing out that bunch." I noticed though, that no one got too close to us. I saw men sneak peeks at my belt in the hopes of seeing my strange gun.

"Good thing I didn't bring a machine gun," I said as we ate.

"Tell me about the world after I left," Natalie said.

So I spent most of the meal talking about movies, disasters, deaths of famous people, politics, and anything else I could think of. But while I was talking, something was nagging at me.

When I finished the global update, I asked, "Do you think I changed history by shooting those two men? Was it a mistake to bring my gun? I brought one for you, by the way."

"I used to get into this discussion a lot with Herb and Max," she said. "Not so much Stan. He didn't seem to care. We never came to any substantial conclusions. Who's to say that the deaths of those men weren't preordained? Maybe you were the one who was supposed to kill them. I guess all we can do is leave as small a footprint as possible. Keeping your gun hidden as well would help. But really, us just being here is upsetting history. There's nothing we can do about that."

When we arrived back at her house, I offered to sleep on the floor. She laid some blankets on the floor in front of the woodstove for me. Before going to sleep, Natalie stoked the woodstove so it would last the night. I was exhausted from the day and fell asleep almost immediately.

Sometime during the night, I felt her slide in next to me under the blanket and put her head on my chest. I put my arm around her and pulled her close.

That's how we woke up the next morning.

Chapter 50

Over the next two days, I visited Charles several times. As promised, he provided me with some of his books. No wonder very few of the dime novels survived. They were cheaply made. I was somewhat disappointed—but not entirely surprised—to find that the books were not very well written. They were sensationalistic and unbelievable. It didn't matter. Just meeting Charles Martin had become one of the highlights of my life. We had some great conversations about writing and about his experiences in the Civil War. I related some of my experiences but changed the locales and details to fit the times. When the time came, I was truly sad to say goodbye to him.

When the stage arrived, some of the townspeople—all men— came to see Natalie off, telling her sincerely that they would miss her. My impression was that she had livened up the saloon—and their lives—just a little bit.

The driver was a grizzled old guy—a stereotype if I'd ever seen one. The man riding shotgun up top was a little sleazy looking. He was young, with wild hair almost to his shoulders and a wisp of a mustache. There was just something about him. And then it hit me. Natalie had said that the stages were getting robbed a lot. What were the odds that this guy was part of the gang? They knew that if they robbed this one, the guy wouldn't give them any fight. How many other stages had someone like him riding shotgun? Was my 21st century cynicism allowing me to see things people in this era couldn't? Or was I just imagining it?

The movies always made the seats on the stage look really uncomfortable. The movies weren't accurate enough. The seats were hell. I had never sat on something so uncomfortable in my life. The only other passenger—a portly man sitting across from us who seemed to be some kind of traveling salesman—didn't seem bothered by the seats. Maybe my 21st century butt was too pampered. I guess you just got used to it. Somehow, I didn't think I'd ever get used to it. It was going to be many days of agony.

Assuming we didn't hit any snowstorms, the trip would take about twelve days—twelve long days. I wasn't looking forward to it.

As expected, the trip was murder. The days were ten to twelve hours long. We would make stops at stage stations to change horses and get a bite to eat, but then we'd be on the road again. We would stop for the night at a home that would provide primitive lodging. A few of the nights, we slept on dirt floors. We kept our bags in the stage with us, not up top like in the movies. That was reserved for other cargo. Luckily, there were only three of us in the coach—which was unusual. Our traveling companion attributed it to the cold weather and chance of snowstorms.

The driver was a nice guy. Not very clean, but nice. He was always spitting tobacco juice, and it would often come in my window. I had to move closer to Natalie to avoid my left side turning brown. Neither of us minded it at all.

Natalie and I were becoming closer with each day. She was as genuine a person as I could have hoped for. Being around her made me understand why she had wanted to escape the movie world. But she also seemed to genuinely have feelings for me, even though I was almost twenty years older than her. Just as she had the first night, the second night back in the cabin she had slept with me on the floor. No sex, just companionship and the need to be close. There was something more, but we'd only known each other for a few days, so I guess I'd see where it led.

The traveling salesman's name was Hugo. In the movies, the traveling salesman in the stagecoach was always talkative. Not Hugo. He was a nice enough guy, but he was more into reading than talking. Right now, he was reading *Last of the Mohicans*. Great movie. I never read the book. I appreciated the fact that he was quiet. It gave me time to think. Natalie was leaning against me, asleep.

I'd had time to read Jim's portal chart. These were portals that the travelers had either used themselves or had discovered in their travels. From what I could tell, if Stan had gone to California first—which seemed the only logical choice—the England portal made sense as the next destination. Once we got to England and found the portal that would take us to the 40s—arriving during the war—there was another one that would take us to the late fifties. After that, it seemed like we had a lot of choices, none that would take us to 2021 or beyond, though. I already knew that once we hit the 21st century, it had to be after I left. It would create too many problems for me to arrive before that. Natalie too. Now that she knew me, she'd have to arrive after I left, as well. It would all be tricky, but one step at a time. Jim wasn't so sure the portal would even let us arrive before we left. Something technical about how time works. It kind of made sense to me—but there was very little about time travel that I totally understood.

The added advantage to England was that it was the location of the portal Hal and I were planning to use to communicate. It wasn't the same portal that we'd arrive through, but it was close by. It was one-way from 2021 (and surrounding years) to 1958ish, which was the year the portal we were coming in on would arrive. It was the reason I chose that location.

I was shaken out of my thoughts by the slowing down of the stage. I heard Charlie yell out, "Oh, shit." The man riding shotgun—funny, I was never told his name—leaned over from his perch up top so we could see him. His hair was hanging down. It was so dirty, I could almost smell it.

"We got us some stage robbers up ahead. Nothin' to worry about. They don't kill people or," he looked at Natalie, "molest women. They might relieve you of your money though."

He didn't seem at all concerned.

The stage stopped. Natalie squeezed my hand.

"Give me your gun," I whispered.

She slid it out of her bag and handed it to me down by my leg. I took it and put it in my belt, on the opposite side of my back from the other gun.

"They'll go through your bag. They'd find it there."

"What about your bag?" she whispered. "It's got the Portal Finders. What are you going to do?"

"Don't know yet. I guess I'll play it by ear."

I heard Charlie talking to the bandits. He was explaining that he only had three passengers and wasn't carrying any gold.

"I know you're carrying the payroll for all the stage stations along the way," answered a deep-voiced man. He sounded like the head honcho.

"C'mon men, you know that they need that money. We can't have them close down. We'd have nowhere to stop. We'd go out of business. Then who would you rob?"

Charlie had a point, but not one that the bandit accepted.

"You people in the coach," yelled the bandit. "C'mon out."

I got out first, followed by Natalie, then Hugo.

"I'm not carrying," I said, hoping I had used the correct terminology for the times. I pulled my coat back so they could see.

"Stupid man, not having a weapon," said the bandit.

There were four of them. One was holding the reins of the stage's lead horse. He had his gun out covering the driver and the dirty-haired guy riding shotgun, and one was already on the roof of the stage, throwing things down. Other than the one guy covering the driver, everyone had their guns holstered.

"What's in the stage," asked the leader.

"Nothing," I answered.

The guy up top dropped down and entered the stage.

"There's two bags pushed under the seat," he called out.

"You lied to me," said the bandit, looking directly at me. "There must be something good in the bags."

He turned his attention to the man in the stage, leaving only the guy holding the horses as the one pointing a gun. They were way too cocky. They must've known that people usually didn't resist.

"What the hell is this?" came a voice from beside the stage. "Hey, we got two of them."

The Portal Finders. It was time to act.

The guy holding the lead horse was craning his neck to see what was going on. I slid the Glock from my belt. I had slowly moved a little closer to the guy with the gun, hoping I could just disarm him. No such luck.

He looked up and I pointed my gun at him.

"What the hell is that?" he said in a voice the others next to the stage could hear. I had no choice now. I shot the guy in the chest. The leader turned and pulled out his gun in one movement, but I had my gun already trained on him.

"I wouldn't," I said threateningly.

He looked at my gun questioningly, but he already knew that I had shot one of his men. He dropped the gun.

"You, in the stage," I called out. "Throw your gun out first, then follow it."

He did as I said and stood next to the other bandit. I saw a movement out of the corner of my eye. At the same time, the bandit leader glanced up at the top of the stage. The greasy-haired guy was slowly raising his shotgun.

I moved my gun so that it was pointed directly at him.

"Why don't you throw down that shotgun and join us down here?"

"Whatcha doin'?" asked Charlie. "He's my shotgun."

"He's also working with this crew," I said. "He's backup in case things go bad."

"You don't say," answered Charlie. "Knew there was a reason I didn't like him." He pushed the greasy guy from the driver's box and the guy landed on his face.

"I ain't workin' with them," he said, spitting out dust.

"Well, we'll see," I said. I pointed my Glock at the leader. "In one second, you'll be known as Gimpy if you don't tell me the truth.

He could tell I wasn't joking.

"Yeah, he's one of us."

I had Natalie and Hugo collect their guns and put them in the stage. Charlie helped me tie the men up, then tie them to their horses. The greasy guy took the horse of the dead one. We tied them securely to the pommels of their saddles and tied the horses to the back of the stage. We'd be hitting a town later in the day. Charlie could deposit them there. Once it was all done, we got back in the stagecoach and were on our way.

Natalie looked at me with a smile, then kissed me deeply on the lips.

Hugo averted his eyes.

"Yes," Natalie said. "I'm glad you can take care of yourself."

Chapter 51

We arrived in San Francisco days later, sore and exhausted.

I had been to the city numerous times in my life, but it never looked like this. Most of the streets were dirt, the houses plain, and not a skyscraper in sight. It was only the hills the city was built on and the bay in the distance that told me where I was.

It certainly was a city, though, especially compared to all the small towns we had ridden through on our way here. It was bustling and it was crowded. On the way, Hugo, who lived in San Francisco, told us that the population was hovering around 150,000. The Comstock Lode in the mountains near Lake Tahoe was responsible for the city's rapid growth. And because of it, there was already a lot of wealth in San Francisco. The residents had no idea what they were building—simply because the city was growing so fast—and very few probably had any vision of what the city would someday look like. But they were building a life. Sadly, they also had no idea that the city would be destroyed by an earthquake in another thirty-six years.

Charlie dropped us off at his company's stage station. I knew we'd have enough money for the short time we would be in the city, so I gave him $20 as a tip. I thought he was going to hug me, but I thanked God that he didn't. I don't think stagecoach drivers were used to getting tips. He wished us well in our travels. If he only knew!

Hugo gave us directions to the nearest hotel. We shook hands and were on our way. It was strange that after all those days of traveling together, we hadn't formed any kind of bond. We felt closer to Charlie than we did to Hugo.

"I know we're anxious to be on our way to the next century, but I'd like to stay a couple of days if you're okay with it," said Natalie as we approached the hotel. "It's fascinating to be here."

"It is," I answered. "I'd be happy to stay. We're on this journey, so there's no reason why we can't appreciate the places we see."

She took my hand and didn't let go. We had found ourselves holding hands often during the long trip here. And the way she looked at me sent shivers down my spine.

We walked into the hotel and Natalie stopped short.

"Max!"

Sitting on a couch in the lobby was the man I had seen in so many of the pictures. He looked different somehow. He was tired. It showed in the bags under his eyes and in the painful way he rose when he saw Natalie. Is this how all the time travelers ended up? Jim and Alan were both at that stage shortly before their deaths. And my understanding was that Herb was in a similar way. Then there was the traveler they assumed committed suicide. It didn't bode well for the time travel industry.

"Natalie! Oh my God. How did you get here?"

He gave her a big hug and looked at me warily. I stuck out my hand.

"Ray Burton, from the year 2021. I came back to bring Natalie home, if possible, and to try to stop Stan Hooper from making a total mess of things."

"But how … why?"

"We need to find a quiet place to talk," I said. "There's a lot to fill you in on."

He asked Natalie, "You trust this guy?"

"With my life."

"Does this hotel have a good restaurant?" I asked. "We're starving."

It did. Once we were seated, I filled Max in on my adventures, from the moment I found Stan's trunk to accessing the portal myself. I had already told Natalie a good portion of it but managed to remember things I hadn't told her.

"So Jim and Alan are dead," he said sadly. "Good men."

"Even though you were trying to have Alan killed?" I asked.

He winced. "Who told you that?"

"My NSA friends."

He hung his head. "Not one of my shining moments."

"And you left Hollow Rock in pursuit of Stan?" I asked.

"I had to. He took my Portal Finder. I knew he was heading here. He knew about the San Francisco portal. I was hoping I'd catch him before he went through it, but I haven't seen any sign of him, so I'm afraid I missed him. I have no idea where the portal is, so I'm stuck here."

"Or not," I said. "I have Herb's Portal Finder…"

"That's right!" exclaimed Max, drawing looks from some of the other diners. "Would it be okay if I accompanied you?"

I looked at Natalie. I couldn't read her expression, but she gave a nod. I had the feeling based on things she had said that she didn't care much for Max. He was a friend by necessity. My feeling was that he could stick with us when we went to 1969 San Francisco, and maybe to England if we missed Stan in San Francisco. After that, I think Natalie and I wanted to continue without him. I said as much to him, trying to put it as nicely as possible.

"But I'd still be stuck somewhere," he said.

"No," I said. "I haven't told you about this part. I have two Portal Finders—Herb's and Alan's. You are welcome to one of them."

I thought he was going to kiss me.

"That totally changes my life. It allows me to find the place I can settle down for the rest of my life. I'm a loner by nature, and I just want to find somewhere quiet—and where I won't stand out."

"You're not going to try to make it home?" I asked.

"No. I have no interest in going home," he answered. He hesitated, then looked at both of us. "You know that the odds of you finding your way back to your own time period are slim, right?"

"We're aware of it, but all we can do is try."

We retired for the night. Max was staying at the hotel and we agreed to meet for breakfast. Natalie asked me if I'd mind sharing a room with her. She said she wasn't comfortable staying alone.

Being the chivalrous kind of guy that I was, I agreed.

We made love that night for the first time. It was tender and sincere. The feelings we had for each other were real, not caused by two people being thrown together in a tough situation. I thought back to when I would watch her on the screen and harbor my little crush. But I wasn't making love to a movie star. I was making love to a genuine, sensitive woman. I was making love to the woman I wanted to spend the rest of my life with—no matter how many centuries that encompassed.

*****

Natalie and I spent the next two days exploring San Francisco, but by the end of it, we were anxious to go. The city got old quickly. Yes, it was busy and bustling. Yes, there were areas showing off the wealth of its residents, but it wasn't what we needed to see. It wasn't our life. San Francisco in 1969 wasn't going to be our life either, but at least it would be more familiar.

We were also keeping our eyes out for Stan. Max joined us for breakfast each morning, then would go out on his own in search of Stan. I had to agree with him though. Stan was already gone. Maybe we'd catch him in 1969. If we were lucky, maybe we'd get there before him and head him off at the pass, so to speak.

Max had agreed to accompany us to 1969, and then maybe to England. From there, he'd go out on his own. We just hoped we could find Stan and put an end to that part of the journey.

When thinking about Stan, I often wondered—especially when I found out that he had made it out of Hollow Rock—why he had put in his note that he was going to die in 1870. I brought that up to Natalie and Max at dinner one of the nights.

"Stan was really sleazy," said Natalie. "He would say what he thought you wanted to hear and would ingratiate himself to you. I found him kind of interesting at first. But his true colors showed themselves pretty quickly," she added.

"He was a weasel," said Max. "He was there to take—by his own admission, I might add—which made him dangerous. He was so focused on the thought that he could gather items from that period and take them home, he ignored Herb when Herb told him that the portal was one-way. As for why he wrote that note? All I can assume is that when he wrote it, he was sure I was going to kill him. I had decided to do that in the interests of science. We couldn't have him running around through time as a loose cannon. It was the same reason I had to take care of Randy, Natalie's boyfriend."

"Ex-boyfriend," said Natalie. I could see a flash of anger in her eyes, quickly dissipating. "But yes, I have to agree with Max. I think Stan knew his life was in danger. He was obsessed with wanting to be remembered, so he left the trunk. It was probably right after that that he decided to sneak out."

We left on the fourth morning there. The Portal Finder led us to a thicket of trees far out from the city. When we zeroed in on the entrance, Max said, "Be careful. This is a hidden spot in 1870, but who knows what it will look like a hundred years from now. Portals tend to remain hidden. I'm not sure why. It might have something to do with the energy they produce. Still, we don't know what we're walking into."

We each took a breath to calm down, and we stepped through, Natalie and I holding hands. We emerged in a dark corner of an alley. The city had taken over the whole countryside. It was warm. Summer. I looked at the date: September 16th, 1969. That was lucky for Natalie. She just had her shorts, top, and sneakers from when she went through the Hollow Rock portal. We quickly changed out of our 1870 outfits. Our 21st-century clothes would fit in just fine here.

"You're not old enough to remember any of this, right?" asked Natalie.

"I'm old, but not that old," I responded. "Actually, I'm going to be born next year."

That hit our funny bones, and we had a much-needed laugh.

"Funny that we change centuries and can laugh again," said Max. "It was much too solemn back there."

"It was," agreed Natalie. "I'm glad we're gone. I almost feel like we're home again."

"How should we do this?" asked Max.

"Well, the bad news is that we've arrived after Stan. The *Chronicle* article I read was dated mid-August, so he was here at least a month ago. That doesn't mean he's not still here. Natalie and I are going to find the author of that article. Maybe you can check out hotels. My guess is that it would be a low-end establishment. From everything I've heard about Stan, he didn't have a lot of money. Maybe even a YMCA."

"What's that?" asked Max. So I explained.

"I don't know if anyone will pass on the information to you about Stan, but it's worth a try. I say we just give ourselves a couple of days. If we don't find him, we head to England and the portal there. Let's meet at Powell Street Station at 4:00. Then we can find a hotel for the night.

"I also have a favor to ask," I said. "We're going to have to fly to England and we have nowhere near enough money for the flight. We need to figure out a way to earn the money. It's 1969. I could place a bet on the Miracle Mets winning the World Series, but that's weeks away. Plus, we don't even have enough to place a decent bet."

"I'll get the money," said Max. There was no hesitation or question in his voice. I didn't want to ask.

*****

"Do you think Max will make any headway with the hotels?" Natalie asked once we had taken off on our own.

"Probably not, but I didn't particularly want him with us. I got the feeling you don't care much for Max."

"Taking it upon himself to kill Randy was wrong. I get it, Randy was acting irresponsibly and didn't show any inclination to stop. Something had to be done, and maybe eliminating him was going to be the answer. Randy was being stupid, but it didn't mean he had to die. And Max just took it upon himself to kill him. It just wasn't right. And last night you said that he tried to have Alan and Herb killed?"

"He did. I guess they both broke the time travel rules and he took it upon himself to eliminate them. The irony here is that he ended up blabbing to the NSA."

"I wonder if that was the first time," said Natalie. "I don't think so. He seems like a tortured soul, like someone consumed with guilt." She hesitated. There was something else she wanted to say. Finally, she added, "I slept with Max a few times in the beginning. I'm not proud of that. I never even really liked him. I was just so lonely."

I felt a pang of jealousy but kissed her and told her that I understood. And I did. But I still felt the pang of jealousy.

As we walked, it was hard not to laugh. Everyone looked like they had just returned from Woodstock. I had read a lot about the 60s, and even liked a lot of the bands from that era. I had seen the movie *Woodstock* and had watched a lot of documentaries of the time. But nothing could prepare me for seeing it all in person. I'm sure every era has things that are funny to someone observing it from afar, but this was special.

"Can you believe it?" I asked. "Richard Nixon is president. No one has heard of Watergate, or Woodward and Bernstein."

"I don't like time travel," started Natalie, "This isn't my era. I feel so out of place here."

"Yeah, I have to agree with you."

We found the *Chronicle* building and I asked to speak to James Robards, the author of the article on Stan. It took a while, but eventually, a young guy looking very much like a hippie stepped out of an elevator. He approached us with a questioning look. That morning, we had done some clothes shopping to blend in a little better, so I knew he wasn't questioning our taste in clothes.

The guy couldn't have been older than twenty-five, but he had already developed the reporter swagger.

He didn't offer to shake.

"James Robards. You were looking for me?"

"I'm Ray and this is Natalie," I said too quickly. Natalie gave me a questioning look. "We're looking for someone that you interviewed recently, and we were wondering if maybe you had a clue as to where he was headed from here."

"Well, I don't give out information on my sources, but who are you talking about?"

"Stan Hooper."

Robards rolled his eyes. "That wacko. Don't ever let me see that guy again. It wasn't my favorite article to write."

"How often do you get people saying they are from the future?" I asked.

"Please don't tell me you're from the future," he said.

"No, we're from the past. We're just catching up."

That got a good laugh out of him.

"Seriously though, he swindled a lot of money out of my parents with this time travel garbage, and I need to locate him."

"Are you going to beat him senseless?"

"I wish. No. Once I locate him, I will sic the cops on him."

"I wish I could help you," he said, "but I can't—and it has nothing to do with protecting my sources. As far as I'm concerned, he deserves to be behind bars. He dropped out of sight right after we talked. The only possible location I have for him might be England. At some point in the conversation, he said something about heading to England next."

"If you didn't like writing the article, why did you do it?" asked Natalie.

"Hey, I'm young. I still need to earn my stripes. The best way to do that is to keep writing. Yeah, the subject is crap, but my editor might eventually see that I know how to write, and he might give me a real assignment. Until then, I have to deal with the Stan Hoopers of the world."

"I appreciate your willingness to meet with us," I said.

"Happy to. And I hope you catch him. Do you know what he said to me as he was leaving? He said, 'Remember the name Stan Hooper in 2011. Then you'll know that everything I told you is true.' Hell, I probably won't even be alive in 2011. Take care."

As we were walking away, Natalie asked, "So, do you think he'll ever amount to anything as a reporter? And what was that in the beginning? You seemed almost uncomfortable."

"Are you ready for this?" I asked. "Yes, he becomes a hotshot reporter, then an editor at *Time* magazine. I didn't recognize the name right away—until I came face to face with him—because he later goes by the name James Henry Robards. That's the name he's famous for. And—get this—I actually met him back in the late 90s. My career was just taking off and I went to a writer's conference in Chicago. Robards was the guest speaker. At the cocktail portion of the event, I sought him out and introduced myself. You know what he said?"

Natalie shook her head.

"Haven't we met somewhere before?"

Chapter 52

"Seriously?" asked Natalie.

"Seriously. He probably recognized my first name, and something about my face probably registered with him. I look older now, but in the 1990s I probably looked similar enough to the way I look now. Put together, it was enough for me to seem vaguely familiar to him at that time. It kinda gives me goosebumps when I think of it."

"I can imagine. That's why I don't like time travel. It also makes me realize why people like Max and Herb—the only two of that group I know or knew—are or were burning out. We feel this way and it's only the second place we've been."

We met up with Max back at the hotel. We gave him a quick rundown of our meeting with Robards. Max hadn't had any luck finding Stan, but he was successful in the money department. He pulled a small bag from the closet and dumped it out on the bed. There were masses of twenty-dollar bills—a few hundred of them, at least.

"Where did you get this?" I asked incredulously.

"Don't ask."

"I *am* asking," I replied. "This can't be anything legal."

"It's not," he said, "but sometimes you just have to do what is necessary."

"Did you rob a bank?" asked Natalie.

When he didn't answer, she said, "Oh my God, Max. You can't do that. You can't do it for so many reasons. First, because someone might've gotten hurt. They didn't, did they?"

He shook his head.

"Second, it's illegal. Third, you might get us all arrested if we try to use it."

"We won't be. There's no way they can track it to us."

Natalie looked at him doubtfully, then said, "And fourth, it's against your own rules of time travel. You are not supposed to interfere. You are not supposed to change history."

"Who says I changed history? Maybe I'm the one who was supposed to rob the bank."

"Oh come on, Max," I said. "That's too convenient. If you're going to say that, then why have rules at all? You were ready to have people killed—no, never mind that, you killed someone who was breaking the rules. How does this make you better than any of them?"

"I never said I was better than any of them. In some ways, I'm worse. But here's a rule that obviously no one told you: if we find ourselves in desperate situations, we do whatever we have to do to get out of it. Protecting our identities and where we come from is first on the list. Killing someone to get out of a situation is the very last resort, but if we need the money and we don't have time to earn it, we go for the larger institutions first—a place that won't miss the loss. The rule is to impact as few people as possible. There were three people in the bank. No one was hurt, I stayed clear of any video systems, and I wore a disguise. I've done this before. I know what I'm doing."

"The more I learn about this time travel project," I said, "the more I'm realizing that it's like any other governmental or pseudo-governmental organization. It's full of arrogant, self-serving assholes, who feel that the rules apply to everyone else."

Max sat heavily in a chair. "You're exactly right. And it's why all of us in this program are just a little off-kilter. It all started—we all started—with the best of intentions, but like everything else, the best intentions don't mean much the minute you break the rules for the first time."

He had tears in his eyes and I felt sorry for him. I looked at Natalie. I think she was feeling the same way.

"Well," I said, "What's done is done. I guess I just don't understand very much about everything that's involved and the rationalizing that sometimes has to happen. But I appreciate your efforts to find us the means to get to England. I'd like to suggest that we buy the tickets as soon as possible. Tomorrow, Natalie and I can visit a few banks and change a lot of these twenties to hundreds. It'll be a little less suspicious at the airline counter."

"Don't we need passports to fly internationally?" asked Natalie.

"Already taken care of," said Max. "Remember, I've done this many times before. I found someone who can make up fake passports. If we see him now, he can have them ready tomorrow." At my raised eyebrows he said, "To be a time traveler, interacting with less desirable types is a necessity."

"How are we going to get the Portal Finders—or the guns, for that matter—through security?" asked Natalie.

"This is 1969," I said. "There is no security. I did an article on this once. There were a lot of hijackings around this time, so it's when they started to get serious about protecting the airlines. But nothing has happened yet regarding it. We'll be fine."

"Unless we get hijacked," said Max jokingly.

*****

The next day was busy. Max picked up the passports while Natalie and I changed a lot of the twenties into hundreds, then the three of us took a cab to the airport to buy tickets to London. We bought new carry-on bags to look a little more modern, stored our belongings in them, and took them with us to the airport, just in case there was a flight that day.

There was. We searched the flight boards when we arrived and saw that TWA had a flight leaving in a few hours. We went to the ticket counter and were told that the flight wasn't full. Natalie and I could sit together, but Max had to sit alone. I think he preferred it that way.

It was going to be a long flight. There would be a layover in New York for the plane to refuel, but we wouldn't have to change planes.

We were tired and it was a night flight, so we fell asleep almost immediately. Being able to sleep through the first leg of the trip made it seem a lot shorter. We were allowed to leave the plane for a few minutes in New York, but Natalie and I decided to stay on board and guard our bags. If the Portal Finders were ever stolen, we'd be up the creek.

We walked up and down the aisles of the plane for exercise. We were the only two who had remained. Even Max took the opportunity to stroll around the airport, knowing that we'd be watching his bag. As we were about to sit down, Natalie grabbed me and kissed me.

"I'm so glad you came into my life," she said.

"It doesn't bother you that I'm twenty years older?"

"I couldn't care less. Do you know how many dates I had with hot young actors? More than I care to remember. Do you know how many of them I was interested in dating a second time?" She held up her fingers shaped like a zero.

"And Randy?"

"A friend hooked us up and told me not to be so picky. So we dated for a couple of months. He was kind of fun in the beginning, but that wore off quickly. Age isn't important to me, Ray. Besides, you said you were born in 1970?"

"Yes."

"I was born in 1979, so you're only nine years older than me."

"Maybe technically," I said. "But for you, time stopped in 2009. You're only thirty. It continued for me. It's 2021 in my life."

"Ray, I don't care about any of that. For me, it's all about the man and who he is. You're kind, you're caring, you're capable, and I'm falling in love with you. Simple as that. You want to argue the point?"

"I think not," I said, taking her hand.

That certainly made the second leg of the journey better.

We arrived at Heathrow around mid-morning. It seemed like we had been traveling for days.

"There's no sense in us hanging around London," I said. "We can assume that Stan already went through the portal. We're either going to find him at the next stop or not at all."

At the airport, we exchanged some of the U.S. money for British money and went for a nice meal. We found a coin shop and bought as much pre-World War II money as we could. We didn't know how long we would be in that period and we didn't want to run out of cash. We also went to a vintage clothing store and asked for clothes that would have been worn in the 1940s. We told the owner that we were going to a 40s-themed costume party. The elderly owner clapped her hands and said, "Oh how fun!" in a stereotypical old lady English way.

Now to find the portal.

The direction screen on the Portal Finder was a cross between a GPS unit and a compass. It would take us exactly where we needed to go, without the detail of a GPS.

"I hope the portal isn't in Buckingham Palace," said Natalie.

"It's leading us to the Thames," said Max, ignoring the lightheartedness of her comment.

"Then I hope it isn't *in* the Thames," I said with all

seriousness. "We don't know how many centuries the portal has been there. The river might have risen in that time."

We caught a cab and took it to the docks. We had the driver pull over at a spot in the general location of the portal. It was a lonely area full of empty warehouses.

As he drove away, there was silence.

"Kind of spooky," said Natalie.

"It's the weekend," I said. "Probably very little business today. It also looks like an area that has suffered over the years. A lot of these look abandoned. That's good for us."

"This way," said Max, looking at the readout.

We walked down a line of warehouses for a few minutes, until Max told us to stop.

"It's in here. And it looks like we aren't the first," he said.

The window in the office door was broken. I tried the doorknob and the door swung open.

"Looks like Stan was here," I added.

Max led us down some stairs to a basement level.

"I can't believe a building so close to the river has a basement," I said.

The folly of a basement became clear to us when we reached the bottom of the stairs and found ourselves ankle-deep in water.

"Yuck," I said.

"This way," said Max.

He led us over to a far wall. Some of the concrete wall had been chipped away, revealing a hole just large enough to squeeze through.

"This is it," said Max. "The building must have been built over the portal. I think we can thank Stan for doing all the work of creating the hole in the concrete."

"I'll thank him later," I said. I opened my bag and took out my gun and put it on my belt, then I took out my own Portal Finder and held it. At Natalie's questioning look, I said, "Just in case the luggage goes astray in the process, I want to make sure I have the Portal Finder with me."

She nodded.

"Let's do it," said Max.

We let Max go first, then Natalie and I followed, hand in hand.

We took about thirty steps, and then everything changed. There was suddenly light, but it wasn't sunlight.

A loud explosion split the previous silence and more flashes of light appeared. Three more explosions, seconds apart. The building was shaking.

I looked at the other two, the fear I was seeing in their faces probably reflected in my own.

"We've arrived in the middle of an air raid!" I yelled.

Chapter 53

"Where do we go?" shouted Natalie.

I thought hard, then it came to me.

"Stay in the portal," I yelled. She looked at me questioningly. "It was still there in 1969, so it wasn't destroyed. It's probably the safest place for us."

Max hadn't heard me. I saw him running up some stairs—not the same ones we came down. He was almost to the top.

"Max!" I yelled.

A massive explosion blew me to the floor. Natalie went down next to me, a second before I lost consciousness.

*****

"Ray, wake up. Please wake up." Someone was shaking me.

I opened my eyes. Natalie was looking down at me, tears rolling down her cheeks making tracks in a layer of soot. I could also see blood on her forehead.

I was awake now. What had happened? A bomb. A bomb must have hit the building.

"Are you okay?" I asked. "You're bleeding."

"So are you," she answered. "I'm fine. And I don't think any of your cuts are bad. I think we'll live."

"And Max?" I already knew the answer.

She pointed in the direction Max had gone. There was nothing there. That whole half of the building was gone. There were pieces of the building in piles strewn all over the basement, but the bomb had blown most of it away. There was no sign of Max. He had been blown up.

We hugged for the longest time, feeling sad about the demise of Max. Neither of us had particularly liked Max, but he was one of us and now he was gone. When we had composed ourselves, I looked around for the Portal Finder. It was only a few feet away and the lights were still on. It seemed to be working.

"Max's Portal Finder must have been destroyed," I finally said, trying to get focused. "Let's find our luggage. Before we leave, we need to change into our 1940s clothes. Our luggage looks vanilla enough to blend in with this era. Luckily, I had most of the money in my bag."

"Our clothes are clean," said Natalie, pulling her outfit out of her bag. "That will seem strange for people just in an air raid."

I looked over at the basement that we were going to have to climb out of.

"They won't be for long."

It was now evening, and I could see the reflection of flames from nearby burning buildings. In the distance, a siren was sounding the all-clear signal and I could hear sirens from fire trucks and ambulances.

"We need to leave now," I said. "It's going to be hard to explain what we were doing here, not that anyone probably cares at this point. I guess if someone sees us, we'll just say we got lost and came in here to escape the bombs."

Once we had changed, we gathered our bags—my gun and the Portal Finder were now safely packed inside my bag—and tried to figure out a way to the surface. It took us almost an hour. I had to stack pieces of wood in strategic spots and we found footholds and handholds to assist in the climb. Our bags were hanging around our necks to give us full use of our hands.

At one point, I looked over and saw a hand missing three fingers lying on top of a piece of wood. I quickly threw another piece of wood on top of it. I think Natalie was aware of what I was doing, but she made a point of concentrating on her climb.

When we reached the top, I looked around at the devastation. London had been hit hard. It was going to be a long night for the residents.

We started walking toward the main part of the city. We didn't see many people at first, but then I realized that we hadn't walked through any residential areas yet. Where we had been was comprised of mostly empty warehouses.

When we arrived at a residential area, we found that it hadn't been hit hard, but we heard someone yelling for help. The voice was muffled, and it came from behind the house we were passing. As we hurried into the backyard, the voice became more distinct. Then we saw the reason. A tree had fallen across the trapdoor to a bomb shelter. The man doing the yelling had been able to raise the door several inches, but the tree prevented it from moving any higher than that.

"We'll get you," I called.

"Thanks, mate." The voice seemed calm, as if he was inviting us in for a cup of tea.

The tree wasn't particularly heavy, but they never would have been able to push their way out. Natalie and I picked up one end and moved it off the door. It immediately opened and a family of five climbed out.

"Ah, the house is still there. Splendid."

He held out his hand to shake.

"Thanks again, mate. We're lucky you came along. You're not from around here."

"No," I replied. "We were stuck down the road and we're

working our way back into the city."

"Yanks. Splendid. Nice to meet you. I'm Thomas Leech, and this is my wife, Mabel, and my daughters, Gwen, Alma, and Norma."

The three daughters looked to be in their teens. Thomas was a little man with a sharp nose. Mabel was a bit taller and a lot rounder than Thomas. In a wrestling match, he wouldn't stand a chance against her.

"Are you a flyer?" he asked.

"No, we're journalists. My name is Ray Bean, and this is Natalie Fox."

When I heard the accent, I immediately thought of the English character, Mr. Bean, and it was the only name that came to mind.

Thomas pointed to a crater.

"Bomb hit there. That's where this tree was."

I helped him move the tree back near the crater.

"You were lucky it didn't hit the house," I said.

"Aye, we've been fortunate," answered Thomas.

"Come in for some tea," said Mabel.

I looked at Natalie and she smiled.

"We'd love to," she said. "If it's no bother."

"Goodness," said Mabel, "it's no bother at all. If not for you, we'd have had to stay down there all night. The girls would've complained the whole time. And Thomas snores. You saved me from a fate worse than death."

"Which hotel are you staying in?" asked Thomas.

"We haven't checked into one yet," I said. "We were at Wendling with the 392nd Bomb Group. We took a train in today and were checking out the area." I picked that out of thin air. I had once done an article on the various bomb groups stationed in England and had visited the old Wendling site.

"Then you'll stay with us," said Mabel. "We have an extra room."

"Oh, we can't impose like that," said Natalie.

"Nonsense. You're staying. That's all there is to it."

"I wouldn't argue with her," said Thomas, laughing. "It never ends well."

We ended up having a comfortable night. We talked to the girls a bit. They asked all kinds of questions about America. We tried to put ourselves mentally into the 40s to accurately answer their questions. The oldest girl, Gwen, was dating an American flyer stationed at Wendling and asked if I knew him.

"I'm afraid we weren't there long enough to get to know any of the boys," I said, trying to think fast, "but we're heading back up there in a few days. Leave me his name. I'll see if I can look him up."

I was piling on the BS, but I had to make sure no one got suspicious.

We slept well that night and were treated to a porridge breakfast the next morning. By ten o'clock, we were on our way, a little sad to be leaving such a nice family.

"How are we going to find Stan?" asked Natalie.

"I honestly don't know," I replied, "and to be honest, I'm caring less and less. That was never my main reason for coming — not even close. I'm not responsible for him. I certainly don't want him to do anything that changes history, but if we don't run into him, I want us to continue with our plan."

"Which is?"

"Take the portal here in England that goes to the late 50s, and then we can figure it out from there."

"Or, we can hang around England for a while," she said, taking my hand.

"We could do that."

"I almost hope we don't run into Stan," said Natalie.

Someone wasn't listening to Natalie's wishes. We ran into Stan an hour later.

Chapter 54

I couldn't tell if the previous night's bombing had been particularly bad, or if what we were seeing was an accumulation of weeks of German bombing raids. As we walked into the city, buildings were down, and rubble littered the streets. We saw something interesting though. People were going about their business despite the devastation. I didn't see crying and I didn't feel a sense of hopelessness. Shops were open for business, and in some of the larger buildings, I could see men and women at their desks, working as if nothing had happened.

"Is it the time or the character of the people?" asked Natalie. "They are heavily under siege, and yet, life goes on for them."

"Probably a little of both," I said. "And I know that Churchill was a great inspiration to them. It's impressive."

We reached the hotel recommended to us by Thomas. It was a medium-sized building in the middle of a surprisingly unblemished block. We registered as Mr. and Mrs. Ray Bean and were assigned a room on the second floor.

As we turned to walk away, a thought struck me. I turned back.

"We were supposed to meet Stan Hooper here. Has he checked in yet?"

"Mr. Hooper did check-in but is out at the moment. Should I

let him know you're looking for him?"

"No, that's okay. We'll keep an eye out for him. We might be in and out ourselves."

As we walked away, Natalie said, "If I didn't know better, I'd say that sounded almost sexual in nature."

"Hmm, whatever gave you that idea?"

As we hurried up the stairs, Natalie said, "That was a great idea, asking about Stan."

"I wasn't sure how many hotels were left standing, so it seemed worth trying. At least we know he's still around."

We reached the room and I fumbled with the key. The anticipation of what was to come had me almost shaking. We finally entered the room, and I locked the door behind us. We were on the bed and out of our clothes in seconds. Almost getting blown up can do that to you, I guess.

*****

We lounged in bed for a couple of hours, then made our way to the bathroom. We were lucky. Many hotels of that era had communal bathrooms for each floor. The hotel room was small but had a homey touch. It would do the job for however long we were here.

"What are you thinking?" asked Natalie. We had finished in the bathroom and were sitting on the bed. I guess I was staring into space.

"I was thinking about Stan and what we'd do."

"Maybe we have to figure out what *he's* going to do," suggested Natalie.

"That makes sense…"

A knock at the door interrupted me.

I motioned for Natalie to grab her gun and wait in the

bathroom. I put my gun in my belt behind my back, then I opened the door.

I took one look at our visitor and once again began to wonder if Natalie and I were going to end up looking like that. It was Stan, but it wasn't the Stan of the pictures I had seen. He looked worse than Max, worse than Jim, and worse than Alan. Probably not worse than Herb, since Herb got his face shot off.

"You Ray Bean?"

"I am."

"The people downstairs said you were looking for me."

So much for not letting him know we were looking for him.

"Come in."

"Not until I know why you're looking for me."

"Hi, Stan." Natalie's voice came from behind me.

"Nat? What the hell are you doing here? And who's this?"

"Come in," I said.

He came in, but tentatively.

"Have a seat," I said, pointing to the one chair in the room. He sat, and Natalie and I sat on the bed.

"My name is really Ray Burton. I'm the one who found your trunk."

"Seriously? When?"

"In 2021."

"Wow, it made it. I can't believe it."

"You've had a lot of people pissed at you."

"So what?"

"Just thought I'd mention that."

"It's none of your business."

"It kinda is. You're going through history shooting your mouth off, totally disregarding the part about remaining anonymous."

"Doesn't matter," said Stan. "Nobody believes me anyway." His voice got louder. "Do you know that people actually laugh at me?"

"I'm shocked," I said. "Of course they laugh at you. You're upsetting the world they know. If someone said to you that they were from the future, would you believe them?"

"I already did."

"Right. Herb. I forgot. But not everyone is like you. Herb entered your life at a time when you were vulnerable … or susceptible to a story like his. You can't go around telling Winston Churchill things that haven't happened yet."

"How'd you hear about that?"

"The person you told recalled it in a 1965 interview."

"So I'm famous."

"No, the article never got any traction. If it'll make you feel better, the police in 2021 still haven't solved your disappearance in 2011. There was actually a ten-year follow-up article."

"I'm thrilled," he said, rolling his eyes. "So you must've come through the portal. Did you know it is only one-way?"

The guy was annoying me.

"Yes, Stan. Everyone knows that, except you from what I hear."

If he took offense, he didn't show it. "And that's how you met Nat?"

I decided to give him a short version of the story. When I was done, I asked, "Why did you put in the note about you dying in the year 1870?"

"Because I thought Max was going to kill me. I was convinced I was a dead man."

"What are your plans now?"

"I don't know."

I didn't believe him for a second. He had a plan. I could sense it.

"You look terrible," said Natalie, with a touch of softness.

"You don't know what it's like having people laugh at you."

"That's because we haven't been stupid enough to tell people where we're from," she said. The softness had been replaced by exasperation.

"I just wanted to come back and pick up a few things to bring home and sell," he said. "Now I'm stuck here. It's like I don't exist. But I do exist. They'll see."

Uh oh.

"What does that mean?" asked Natalie.

"Nothing. Look, I gotta go. Nat, it was good seeing you again."

He jumped off the chair and almost ran out of the room. Natalie looked at me with fear in her eyes.

"Yeah," I said. "Whatever he's planning, he's going to do it now. We have to stop him. I should have stopped him before he could leave."

"We don't know what room is his," said Natalie.

"C'mon," I said, jumping up. We ran down to the lobby.

"I need Stan Hooper's room number," I said. "Quick! We think he's going to hurt himself and we have to stop him."

"Oh dear," said the clerk. "I have his key. I'll go with you."

"Just hurry," said Natalie.

He was on the floor above us, at the end of the hall. We reached his door and knocked loudly.

"Stan, are you in there?" called Natalie.

No answer.

"Open it."

The clerk nervously put the key in the lock and turned it. I shoved him out of the way and opened the door.

The room was empty ... almost.

We quickly looked around. If he had a bag, it was now with him.

"We missed him," said Natalie. "Where would he have gone?"

"He was bitter," I said. "He was going to get back at someone."

"What's this?" asked the clerk. He was pointing to a box in the closet.

I opened the box and sank to my knees.

"Oh my God!"

Chapter 55

The box was half full of hand grenades.

"Oh my," said the clerk. "These are dangerous. They shouldn't be here."

"No," I replied. "The question is: how many did he take with him?"

"I should ring up the police," he said.

"That's a good idea. But answer this. How did Stan leave? Do you have a back entrance?"

"Yes, the door right next to his room is the stairwell to the back entrance."

"If he has the hand grenades," said Natalie, "he's going to use them. Where? Buckingham Palace?"

"He said 'they'd see' when he was talking about people laughing at him. Who would have done that?" I asked.

"Churchill's man?" asked Natalie. "You said he told the man what was going to happen in the future. The man recalled it years later, but what if he laughed at Stan when he told him?"

"He'd want to get back at him in a big way. He has hand grenades. What would be bigger than bombing 10 Downing Street."

"He can't do that," said the clerk.

"No, he can't," I said. "We have to go stop him. When you

call the police, let them know that there might be an attempt on Churchill's life. Which way is it from here?"

He gave quick directions, then as he hurried away, I asked Natalie, "Can you see anything that belongs to him? He can't leave any clues to his identity."

"No. He must have been living out of his bag. There's nothing here. He took it with him."

"Good, then we have to go. We have to stop him, but we also have to get that bag. No one can get their hands on the Portal Finder, and whatever else he has in there. I'm sure he's going to 10 Downing Street. God help me if I'm wrong."

"No, I think you're right. It makes sense. What will we do when we find him?"

"I don't know. I honestly don't know. Max would have killed him. I think Alan would have as well. Jim wouldn't have. I never met Herb, so I don't know about him."

"He indicated that he would, if necessary," said Natalie, "but I honestly don't think he would have been able to."

"It's easy to talk about, but not easy to do," I said.

She cocked her head and looked at me. "It sounds like you have experience in that area—before the three you killed in 1870, that is"

"Once. I had no choice. It was me or him. A really bad man. A story for another day. We need to go."

We left, taking the back way, and bringing our bags with us. Coming back to that hotel probably wasn't going to be a good idea. I didn't want to talk to the police. Luckily, our bags were fairly small, making them easy to carry as we hurried through the streets.

We reached the area around the prime minister's residence totally out of breath. There were all sorts of ornate government buildings in the area. We were standing on the corner of Whitehall and Downing. We could see the entrance to #10. There were guards out front and people walking by, but no sign of Stan.

"He'll have to work quickly if he's going to attack that building," said Natalie. "There's not a lot of room to work. They would probably catch him before he got too far. Are we still sure that this is his target?"

"It's the only one that makes sense. Then again, this is Stan we're talking about, so who knows?"

I was looking around as I talked. She was right about the lack of space. If he was going to throw a grenade, he'd probably only get one off before he was shot. He would want more than one chance at it. And then I looked up and I realized where the attack was going to come from.

"The building across the street," I said. "If he's on the roof, it's the perfect place to throw his grenades. He could probably throw a few of them before anyone would come after him."

"Do you think he'd be able to get away?" she asked.

"Seeing the condition he was in at the hotel, I'm not sure that *getting away* is part of the plan."

"Reaching the roof won't be easy," said Natalie.

I was impressed with her. Here was a woman who had led the comfortable life of a famous actress. The most stressful thing in her day was probably sitting while they applied the makeup. And here she was, trying to figure out how to reach the roof to take on a mad bomber.

I must have been looking at her, because she said, "You know, just because I'm an actress—or *was* an actress, it doesn't mean I led a soft life. I grew up in a bad part of Chicago and dabbled in some not-so-legal activities in my teens. Luckily, I got out of there. Even so, I've been skydiving, rock climbing, and have my SCUBA certification. I've also spent a lot of time on the gun range and am pretty good. I'm not helpless if that's what you were thinking."

"Actually, it was the opposite. I had no idea you had such a background, but I was thinking of how impressed I am with you. Now I know why you were able to hang in there in Hollow Rock, despite your desperation to get home."

"It wasn't easy, but I learned at an early age when to fight and when to wait."

"Well let's go fight," I said. "Let's follow this building around and see if there's a way to get to the top. And let's just hope that Stan holds off on his desire to be infamous just long enough for us to get up there."

We walked down Whitehall Street until we came to King Charles Street. We turned right. Halfway down the block was an entrance for cars that led to a parking area in the center of the rectangular building.

"Perfect," I said. "There has to be a quiet back entrance around here somewhere."

It took a few minutes, but when Natalie nudged me and pointed to a ratty-looking door, I knew we had found our way in. It was a kitchen—or more accurately, the filthy backroom to the kitchen. It was the room that boxes were stored in. It had quite a pungent aroma, almost like someone had thrown up.

"Yuck," I said.

"A common smell for the back room of a restaurant," said Natalie. "It brings me back to some harder financial times."

"Here are some stairs," I said. "It doesn't look like they are used much."

"Or at all," added Natalie.

They were dark and dusty and wooden. They'd been there a long time, and Natalie was right, it didn't look like they were ever used. They didn't creak, which probably meant they had been built back when things were built to last.

We climbed several floors. The doors to the stairs on each floor were closed and—like the stairs—hadn't been used for a long time. When we reached the top of the stairs, I listened at the door but heard nothing. I looked at Natalie for her thoughts.

She shrugged her shoulders and whispered, "Well, I suppose if we come out into a busy office, it'll be a little embarrassing."

I smiled and slowly turned the handle and pushed. The door stuck. There would be no unobtrusive entry, so I pushed harder. Finally, the door opened with a loud squeak.

The room was empty. It was an attic. The early evening light streamed in through filthy windows, illuminating a large number of rodents.

"Ugh," I said.

"Hmm, just like back home when I was a kid," said Natalie.

I guess we'd both had our share of rats—mine in some out-of-the-way places all over the globe, and Natalie back home in Chicago—so we carried on with our mission, looking for a door that might lead to the roof.

Again, it was Natalie who pointed it out. The door wasn't locked, but it opened stiffly. If Stan was on the roof, he'd found a different way to get there. There was a short set of stairs, and then another door. I retrieved the Glock from my bag. Natalie did the same with her gun. I pushed the door open and we stepped out onto the roof.

Everything was quiet, so Stan hadn't done whatever it was that he had planned. Once we'd gotten our bearings, we walked over to the Downing Street side of the building. I didn't see anything at first, making me suddenly doubt that I'd made the right assumption about Stan. There was more of a police presence than there was when we initially looked down the street, thanks to the hotel clerk calling them.

Then we saw him. He was sitting behind the wall overlooking 10 Downing Street. Natalie and I hid behind a rusty metal something-or-other that hadn't been used in a long time—just like everything else we'd run across in our journey through the building.

Every time we heard a car coming along Downing Street, Stan would peek over the top of the wall.

"What's he doing?" asked Natalie.

"I don't know. Scratch that. Yes, I do know. He's waiting for a car to come by to pick up Churchill. He doesn't just want to hit the residence, he wants to kill Churchill."

"Why?" asked Natalie. "What could he possibly gain by doing that?"

"Notoriety. Natalie, Stan has gone over the edge. I saw it to a lesser extent with Alan and with Max. They told me that they assumed that one of the other travelers had committed suicide. I'm realizing that the biggest mistake they made in this project was sending people out alone. You and I will make it because we're together. For those alone, it's just too much. In Stan's case, it came on much more quickly because he didn't have any of the training the others had. So for Stan, he knows the end is near and he wants to go down in history. It doesn't matter who or what his target is, just that it's something or someone big."

A car slowed down on the street below. Stan knelt and looked over the side. Something about that car was sparking his interest. It was now or never.

"Let's go."

We came around the corner of the metal structure. We were about thirty feet from Stan.

"Stan," I called out. "It's over."

He looked up with alarm and then reached for his bag.

At that moment, the low wail of a siren filled the air.

Air raid!

Chapter 56

I don't know what it is about the sound of an air raid siren, but it sends shivers down my spine. The sound affected me so much that I often wondered if I had lived in London during the war in a previous life. And here I was, in London during the war. How weird is that? The first time I ever heard that sound was watching (ironically enough) the original version of *The Time Machine*. It's when Rod Taylor stops his time machine in the middle of a war. It was a frightening sound.

Stan was looking at the sky, but there was nothing to see yet. I could hear the distant humming of planes though. They were getting close.

"Give it up, Stan," I said loudly over the whine of the sirens. "Even if you were able to kill Churchill or destroy part of the building, you wouldn't get the credit. The air raid would. You would still be invisible. Come with us. We'll find a way for you to make your mark on history some other way."

"Oh come on. Can't you see it?" He was crying. "This time travel shit will kill you. We're all dead. You and Nat just don't know it yet."

"Stan, we can still live our lives," said Natalie. "Ray and I are trying to find our way home. Come with us."

"You'll never make it home. Be real. None of us will. And

even if we did, I'd be going back to the same crappy life I left. I'm either a loser or I'm invisible. Which would you choose?"

The droning was getting louder. In a moment, the first bombs would fall. We needed to get off the roof.

"Come on, Stan. It's now or never. Think of the stories you can tell when we finally make it home."

"Screw you. You're no different from the rest of them. I'm unstable and you know it. Hell, *I* know it. The first chance you get, you'll kill me. I'm not stupid."

A series of explosions came from the other end of the city. The bombs were being dropped.

Stan was silent for a few seconds, then I saw something come over him. It was a look. I would never be able to explain it, but I felt it. As it turns out, Natalie did too. Stan's only out was to kill us. Then he could continue his self-destructive behavior until the time he chose to die. In his warped mind, now wasn't the time.

He raised his arm. He had a pistol in his hand. He squeezed the trigger and I felt something whiz by my head. The sound of the gun going off was almost lost in the explosions of the bombs that were coming dangerously close.

I brought my gun up, then I heard two shots from close behind me. I saw Stan double over and fall to his knees. He looked up at Natalie behind me.

"Nat?"

Another shot and he fell to the ground. I looked back at Natalie, but she was staring at Stan, a determined expression on her face and the gun now down by her side.

The bombs were too close now. I ran over to Stan and checked his pulse. He was dead. I grabbed his bag and was about to leave when a thought hit me. I couldn't let them discover Stan. He didn't have any ID on him, but there couldn't be any trace of him. He had to disappear.

I started to empty the hand grenades from his bag. There

were six of them.

"Go wait in the stairwell," I said to Natalie.

"Not until you do," she replied. "It's okay, Ray. I know what you're doing. It's what you have to do."

I hesitated. This wasn't going to be easy. The fact that Natalie understood what I had to do gave me some solace, but this might just be the hardest thing I'd ever had to do. But it had to be done fast. The bombs were chewing up a part of the city less than a mile from us. The noise was tremendous. Natalie said something to me, but I couldn't hear her.

I put four of the six hand grenades under Stan's body, and then I took the pins out of the final two, holding them so they wouldn't go off yet. I looked back at Natalie and she moved into the doorway. I put one of the grenades under Stan's head and the other under his chest. I took a deep breath and let go of the grenades. I ran back toward the doorway, but before I reached it, two almost simultaneous explosions rocked the roof.

I don't know if the force of the explosion knocked me over or if I tripped—my guess is the latter since Stan's body had absorbed most of the blast—but I landed on my face and felt the skin on my nose peel away from the coarseness of the roof. That would hurt later.

I took a quick look behind me to be sure that no one would ever be able to identify Stan's body. That one look was enough. They wouldn't. Meanwhile, the bombs were falling, but luckily, they seemed to be concentrated a few blocks over. I followed Natalie and we hurried down the stairs. When we emerged into the parking lot a few minutes later, the worst of the bombing was over, and we were feeling a little safer.

"We need a place to stay for the night," I said.

"On our way here, we passed a hotel a few blocks away. If it's still there, I think that'll be a good place."

The all-clear siren began to sound. We found the hotel a few minutes later and were able to secure a room for the night. We got up to the room, closed the door behind us, and collapsed on the bed. And then the tears came. I, who had been in dangerous situations for years, and Natalie, who had grown up on the streets of Chicago, had both reached the tipping point. We had seen enough and had done enough. We couldn't do anything more. We held each other and fell fast asleep, fully clothed.

*****

We woke up hours later, hungry and dirty. It was the middle of the night, so there was nothing we could do about the hunger, but luckily our room had a private bathroom. We shared a tub and soaked for over an hour, eventually making love in the tub. It was beautiful and somewhat cathartic. After the bath, we once again went to bed and slept.

We woke up around eight and got up and washed. Our clothes were a mess. We'd have to buy some more. They were serving breakfast downstairs in the hotel, so we cleaned our clothes as much as we could. Before going down, I looked in Stan's bag.

"Whoa!" I said.

"What?"

"Stan must have learned from the Max school of money-making. He has piles of money in here. This is good. The next portal will take us to the late 1950s—here in England. This money will still be good. We won't have the worry of figuring out how to acquire money."

"Is it enough to allow us to take a rest for a while?" asked Natalie, a hopeful expression on her face.

"Absolutely. We can rent a place and take as much time as we want to decide our next moves."

"Good," she said quietly. She was smiling.

"Here's his Portal Finder," I said. "Other than the money, everything else is clothes. We'll find a trash can and dispose of it all. I'll split the money into our bags—just in case we lose one of the bags."

The next portal was in a little town called Aldeburgh, up past Ipswich on the coast. I was pretty sure we could get there by train. We went down for breakfast. Some people gave us looks, so we explained that we had come into town without thinking of a change of clothes. People gave us directions to a half dozen clothing shops—it seems everyone had their favorite.

A few hours later, we were on the train to Aldeburgh.

Chapter 57

We arrived in Aldeburgh late that afternoon. It was a quaint little town. The England everyone always imagines. It hadn't seen any bombing, so it was hard to tell that there was a war on. But there were signs: houses with blackout curtains, civil defense wardens, and a "feel" in the air. You couldn't really get away from the war anywhere in England.

Aldeburgh had the portal we needed to travel to 1958 (or so). The town that held the portal from 2021—and the portal I could use to communicate with Hal—was in the nearby town of Saxmundham, a few miles inland. Saxmundham would probably be where we ended up living, for however long that would be.

We found a small bed and breakfast for the night. We'd look for the portal in the morning. We spent the late afternoon and early evening walking along the beach, soaking in the sea air, but we made it back to the bed and breakfast before it got dark. At that point, all the blackout curtains were put in place and the outside lights turned off. We were back in wartime mode.

The next morning, we went in search of the portal. It wasn't hard to find. It was in a deeply wooded area on the outskirts of town. The entrance to the portal was surrounded by heavy vines that we had to pick our way through.

"I find it interesting that the portals are all hard to access," said Natalie. "It's almost as if it creates it for its own protection."

"Yes, I think there is more to this than meets the eye," I said.

"Are we ready?" she asked when we had made our way through the vines. The Portal Finder told us that it was ten feet ahead of us.

"Have you got everything?" I asked. "Money, gun, extra Portal Finder? Do you need to pee before we go?"

"Funny," she said, smacking me on the arm.

We walked into the portal. It was no longer strange to do so. The nervousness we felt was minimal, although we still held hands. As long as it didn't accidentally deposit us in the land of the dinosaurs, we were becoming used to it.

We walked out of the portal, once again fighting the ivy, which seemed a little more overgrown than before, and walked to the road that led into the town center.

The Portal Finder read: May 30, 1958.

"Our clothes are about fifteen years out of date," I said. "Do you think it will matter?"

"We picked pretty bland clothes," Natalie responded. "They might be a little noticeable, but if we can find a clothes store pretty quickly, I think we'll be okay."

We managed to find one without too much difficulty. We had a few looks from people along the way, but it wasn't too annoying.

"How do we get to Saxmundham?" asked Natalie. "Taxi?"

"Let's look in the newspaper or find a bulletin board. Maybe we can find someone who's selling a cheap car. If we pay cash, they won't need any kind of identification. A car will give us a little flexibility."

It didn't take long. We found a little Ford with a beat-up body that seemed just large enough for us to squeeze into, leaving very little extra room. The owner asked us no questions, pointed out that we were American (good to know), and anxious to collect the cash. He assured us that the car "ran like a top." He was right. It was nothing to look at, but it ran beautifully. I had driven many times on the left side of the road, so it took very little getting used to.

Before trying to find a place to live, we followed the Portal Finder to see where the portal was. It led us to a rundown house on the outskirts of town. It desperately needed a few cans of paint, the windows were filthy, and the yard—including an overgrown garden—was a mess.

"Do you think it's in the house?" asked Natalie.

"I hope so," I answered. "Look."

I pointed to a small sign on a post from a local real estate firm advertising the house for rent.

"Could we be so lucky?" I asked.

We drove into town and quickly found the Realtor. She was a woman about my age, with a bubbly personality. When we told her which house we were interested in, she frowned.

"Yes, that one is available to let, but I have other ones that are a lot nicer."

"I'm sure," I said, "but there is just something about that one that appeals to us. We realize that it will take a lot of work to make it homey, but we are happy to do it."

"It might be for sale if you are interested," she said.

"We might," I said. "We can start by renting it and see."

She hesitated. I could tell that she'd been working up the courage to tell us something.

"I would be remiss in my duties not to tell you that this cottage has a strange history. Previous renters have moved out, saying that there is something odd about it. Sometimes things appear in the basement that hadn't been there before—cricket balls, toys, and various animals. They don't know how they got in there. They'd always show up in the basement. A dog appeared up one day with a tag that listed a phone number that doesn't exist and something under the phone number that didn't make sense."

My guess was an email address.

"They said that once a cat appeared while they were in the basement. Just suddenly arrived out of nowhere."

"That doesn't bother us," I said. "And I would definitely be interested in buying it."

We decided to rent it while she got the paperwork together for a possible sale.

"You know," I began, once we were again on our own, "this could turn out well. If we buy it under the names Ray and Natalie Bean, we could take control of this portal. We could set it up so that Hal can stay here when he comes to leave things for us in the portal. We can set up something with a local lawyer to pay all the bills on it when we finally leave, so that it is still in our name in 2021."

"That's a good idea," she responded. "But Ray? I don't want to leave anytime soon."

The place was a mess, and Natalie and I spent a few days getting it livable. Once we did, it was quite cute. After we'd been there a week, I decided it was time to leave a message for Hal.

Since Hal wouldn't know the exact location of the portal, I had done some homework before leaving and had found a law firm in Saxmundham that had been around since the fifties. I gave him their name and told him that I would leave an envelope with them for him, describing where the portal was located.

Once we had gotten the house in shape and had found the portal, I located the law firm and explained that I was leaving a package with them that wouldn't be picked up until 2021. Needless to say, they thought I was bonkers. I finally convinced them that I was serious—the large sum of money I was paying them helped seal the deal, of course—and they put the envelope in a file clearly labeled that it was not to be destroyed or put in storage. In the package were a note and a key. The note read:

Hal, we are well. It's 1958. Natalie and I will soon own this place (under the names Ray and Natalie Bean). Move-in. Stay as long as you want. This note permits you to come here whenever you want.

Next to the entrance to the portal, I put a table that would hold messages to Hal. I left him notes that I had made of our travels, as well as a letter to him. I wrote:

Hal, you'll find in the notes that both Stan and Max are dead. Natalie and I are living here. We haven't yet decided what we want to do next. We will still try to find our way home, but we need a rest and this is the perfect place for it. Looking forward to hearing from you. ~ Ray

A few days later, when I got my first package from Hal, I was like a kid at Christmas. He included articles about my disappearance, news articles about Alan's death, and he included a small camera, a couple of memory cards, and some spare batteries, in case I wanted to take some pictures. A camera was something I had chosen not to bring with me but had later regretted. He said that the law firm in Saxmundham celebrated the fact that he had finally picked up the package after sixty-three years. They had lots of questions that he made up answers to.

Natalie joined some groups in town and made a lot of friends. She even took a part-time job serving drinks at a local pub. Pretty soon, just about everyone in the sedate town of Saxmundham knew of sweet Natalie Bean and her rather reclusive husband. I wasn't really reclusive. I was just taking the suggestion of Hal and writing about all our experiences. Since there were no longer any Portal Finders for the NSA to locate in 2021, why not tell people about time travel from back in time? We hashed it around for a while and hadn't yet come to any conclusions, but I decided to write them anyway. We would have to change the names of all the others involved, so as not to conflict with the program in 2105 and could decide later whether to have Hal publish them.

Natalie and I were in bed one night, about six months after

arriving, when she suddenly said, "Ray, do you like it here?"

"I do. It's peaceful. I love driving to the sea and walking with you for hours. I love exploring with you. But most of all, I love living with you."

"How would you feel if we stayed here?"

"Is that what would make you happy?"

"It would, but only if it made you happy, as well."

"Then I guess we're staying here."

Epilogue

Ray, I found this in the August 2022 issue of *Time*. I'm trying to decide whether to contact Mr. Robards about you. Maybe it's time we start releasing your articles...Hal

THE CASE FOR TIME TRAVEL
James Henry Robards
Editor-in-Chief

Today, I am announcing my retirement from the publishing world. It's been an exciting and rewarding fifty-plus years that has slipped by far too quickly. It would be customary for me to use my final editorial to reflect on how the world has changed during that time. Instead, I am writing something more personal. It is a story I have held off writing for almost a year, to avoid dealing with the wrath of the skeptics and the laughter of my fellow journalists. Retirement, however, comes with benefits. It allows me the freedom to say what I want without worrying what others think.

The story I am about to relate is bizarre, to say the least. But it is all true. Some might think of it as the ramblings of an old man. But as my colleagues can attest, my mind is as sharp now as it was fifty years ago.

The story begins in 1969, when I was a young reporter for the *San Francisco Chronicle*. I was given the assignment of interviewing cult leaders, clairvoyants, mind readers, and the like for a series marking the end of the 60s. Some were weird, others sincere in their beliefs, and all of them turned out to be interesting to some degree. With one exception: a man named Stan Hooper. He claimed to be from the year 2011 and proceeded to inform me of all the technological advancements that would come about in the next forty years—most of them difficult to believe. At the end of this article is a link to my story from 1969. In short, I found the man obnoxious and arrogant, and I was happy to quickly forget about him … until a month later when I was approached by a man and a woman asking questions about Mr. Hooper. The man was in his late forties or early fifties and the woman looked to be around thirty. They introduced themselves as Ray and Natalie (no last names).

They explained that they were searching for Stan Hooper because he had swindled Ray's parents with a time travel scheme. The story seemed fabricated, but the two of them were sincere, and I immediately liked them. I explained that Mr. Hooper had talked of traveling to England where he would find a "portal" to transport him back in time to wartime England. Somehow, they didn't seem surprised. That was the last I ever saw of Ray and Natalie.

Or so I thought…

In the late 1990s, a young man approached me at a conference to introduce himself. He said his name was Ray Burton. He seemed familiar to me and I asked if we'd ever met. He assured me that we hadn't. It was one of those minor interactions that are easily forgotten, which is what happened in this case— until last year when Mr. Burton, who became a celebrated journalist throughout the early- to mid-2000s—disappeared without a trace. When I saw his face online, I knew him immediately as the "Ray" I had met back in 1969.

That got me thinking about the reason Ray had met with me. I looked up the name "Stan Hooper," only to find that someone with that name disappeared from Boston—again, without a trace—in the year 2011, the exact year Mr. Hooper said he was from. I saw a picture of him. It was the same Stan Hooper I had met. There was no doubt in my mind about that. If you read the article from 1969, it includes a picture of him. Look up his story, then you be the judge. In my research of Stan Hooper, I ran across an article from the mid-1960s by a man who once worked for Winston

Churchill. He told a strange story about a man named Stan Hooper who tried to meet Churchill to tell him about significant events that hadn't happened yet, like the Normandy Invasion and the date of Germany's surrender. As I previously mentioned, Mr. Hooper said he was heading to wartime England once he left San Francisco.

Anyone will tell you that I am a pragmatic man. If someone presents me with a theory, I demand proof. The idea of time travel has always been a laughable one to me. And yet, Stan Hooper was the man I met. The online picture of Ray Burton looked the same age as the man I met in 1969, which is also why he looked vaguely familiar when I met him in the 1990s when he was a younger man. I had met him, but in his world, he hadn't yet met me.

But it's not finished. The story gets stranger.

When I saw my first movie starring the actress Natalie O'Brien, I was convinced I had seen her before. I had never seen any of her other movies and had never seen her in the tabloids or on tabloid television, both of which I abhor. While it wasn't something that kept me up at nights, anytime I saw one of her movies the question popped into my head.

You can see where this is going.

When I was doing my research on Ray Burton, there was a reference to other famous people who had disappeared. When I saw the picture of Natalie O'Brien, an alarm went off in my head. Now I knew. The woman with Ray Burton back in 1969 was Natalie O'Brien, without question.

There's nothing I can do about any of this. The only proof I can provide is the original article with the Stan Hooper interview and picture. I can provide no proof at all to my claims about Ray Burton and Natalie O'Brien. Just know that these aren't the ravings of a man who's gone over the edge.

Then why do I even present this? Especially since it will only cause me to become the target of those who really *have* gone over the edge, as well as comedians and late-night talk show hosts?

I tell the story for one simple purpose—to get us thinking. Sometimes we need to step outside our comfort zones and question the "what-ifs".

Could time travel really exist? And if so, what were Stan Hooper, Natalie O'Brien, and Ray Burton doing in 1969? I looked it up: Mr. Hooper and Mr. Burton were both born in 1970, and Ms. O'Brien was born in 1979. And if they really are time traveling, is it of their own volition, or did they accidentally become trapped? More "what-ifs".

But to all of them, wherever they are, I hope they are well.

The End

ABOUT THE AUTHOR

Andrew Cunningham is the author of eleven novels, including the award-winning Amazon bestselling thriller **Wisdom Spring;** the *"Lies" Mystery Series*: **All Lies, Fatal Lies, Vegas Lies, Secrets & Lies,** and **Blood Lies;** the post-apocalyptic *Eden Rising Series*: **Eden Rising, Eden Lost**, and **Eden's Legacy;** the Cape Cod terrorist/disaster thriller **Deadly Shore**; and the time travel novel, **Yestertime.** As A.R. Cunningham, he has written a series of five children's mysteries in the *Arthur MacArthur* series. Born in England, Andrew was a long-time resident of Cape Cod. He and his wife now live in Florida. Please visit his website at *arcnovels.com*, or his Facebook page, *Author Andrew Cunningham.*

Made in the USA
Middletown, DE
19 April 2022

64463764R00169